新月王子：孟加拉民间故事集

FOLK-TALES OF BENGAL

[印] 戴博诃利 著

许地山 译

时代文艺出版社

图书在版编目（CIP）数据

新月王子：孟加拉民间故事集/(印)戴博诃利 著；许地山 译.
—长春：时代文艺出版社，2012.7（2021.5重印）

ISBN 978-7-5387-4084-4

I. ①新... Ⅱ. ①戴...②许... Ⅲ. ①民间故事-作品集-孟加拉国-古代Ⅳ. ①I354.73

中国版本图书馆CIP数据核字（2012）第143280号

出 品 人　陈　琛
责任编辑　付　娜
装帧设计　孙　俪
排版制作　隋淑凤

新月王子：孟加拉民间故事集

[印] 戴博诃利 著　许地山 译

出版发行/时代文艺出版社
地址/长春市福祉大路5788号　龙腾国际大厦A座15层　邮编/130118
总编办/0431-81629751　发行部/0431-81629755
官方微博/weibo.com/tlapress　天猫旗舰店/sdwycbsgf.tmall.com
印刷/保定市铭泰达印刷有限公司
开本/640×980毫米　1/20　字数/171千字　印张/15.5
版次/2012年9月第1版　印次/2021年5月第2次印刷　定价/49.80元

图书如有印装错误　请寄回印厂调换

出版说明

本书是印度作家戴博诃利1833年创作的东印度民间故事的集子"Folk-Tales of Bengal"，许地山翻译为《孟加拉民间故事》。原书为单册本，本次出版按照新的编排方式，拆分为两集。为了纪念许地山先生，本书仍然保留其《孟加拉民间故事》的译法，将第一集改为《吉祥子：孟加拉民间故事集》，第二集改为《新月王子：孟加拉民间故事集》。

许地山在宗教学、印度哲学、梵文、人类学、民俗学等方面的造诣颇深，而且他十分崇敬印度的"诗圣"泰戈尔，所以他对印度的宗教、哲学、民俗和文学也格外感兴趣，为此他还翻译了一大批印度文学著作，其中就包括这本具有"传播民俗学"价值的《孟加拉民间故事》。其实，许地山翻译这本书，不只是为了学术目的，更重要的是为了满足"爱读故事的芝子"。许地山和妻子周俟松（字芝子）的感情是令人羡慕的，周俟松爱看故事，许地山就专门为心爱的妻子翻译了此书。许地山曾对周俟松说："泰戈尔是我的知音长者，你是我知音的妻子，我是很幸福的，得一知音可以无恨矣。"两人的共同生活虽然只有12年，却胜似百年。

本书选择的是20世纪英国最杰出的插图画家之一——沃里克·戈布尔（Warwick Goble）的插图，他对东方绘画情有独钟，他的绘画技法也深受东方绘画的影响，所以他创作的东方民间故事插图更富有东方的异域特色，更能体现其民族风情，其唯美艳丽的画风与本书浪漫积极的基调也非常契合。

本书是1929年商务印书馆初版之后的首次简体中文彩图本出版，并且首次采用了中文和英语的双语版本，以满足读者的不同阅读口味，为读者尽心呈现绝美的阅读和视觉的盛宴。

译　序

　　戴博诃利（Lal Behari Day）的《孟加拉民间故事》（Folk-Tales of Bengal）出版于一八八三年，是东印度民间故事的小集子。著者的自序中说他在一个小村里，每夜听村里最擅于说故事的女人讲故事。人家叫她做三菩的母亲。著者从小时便听了许多，可是多半都忘记了。这集子是因为他朋友的请求而采集的。他从一个孟加拉女人那里听得了不少，这集子的大部分就是从她所说的记下来。集中还有两段是从一个老婆罗门人那里听来的；三段是从一个理发匠那里听来的；两段是从著者的仆人那里听来的；还有几段是另一位婆罗门人为他讲的。著者听了不少别的故事，他以为都是同一故事的另样讲法，所以没有采集进来。这集子只有二十二段故事，据著者说，很可以代表孟加拉村中的老婆子历来对孩子们所讲的故事。

正统的孟加拉讲故事的村婆子，到讲完一段故事以后，必要念一段小歌。歌词是：

我的故事说到这里算完了，

那提耶也枯萎了。

那提耶呵，你为什么枯萎呢？

你的牛为什么要我用草来喂它？

牛呵，你为什么要人喂？

你的牧者为什么不看护我？

牧者呵，你为什么不去看牛？

你的儿媳妇为什么不把米给我？

儿媳妇呵，你为什么不给米呢？

我的孩子为什么哭呢？

孩子呵，你为什么哭呢？

蚂蚁为什么要咬我呢？

蚂蚁呵，你为什么要咬人呢？

喀！喀！喀！

为什么每讲完一段必要念这一段，我们不知道，即如歌中词句的关系和意义也很难解释。著者以为这也许是说故事的在说完之后，故意念出这一段无意义的言词，为的是使听的孩子们感到一点兴趣。

这译本是依一九一二年麦美伦公司的本子译的。我并没有逐字逐句直译，只把各故事的意思率直地写出来。至于原文的词句，在译文中时有增减，因为翻译民间故事只求其内容明了就可以，不必如其余文章要逐字斟酌。我译述这二十二段故事的动机，一来是因为我对"民俗学"（Folk-Lore）的研究很有兴趣，觉得中国有许多民间故事是从印度辗转流入的，多译些印度的故事，对于研究中国民俗学必定很有帮助；二来是因为今年春间芝子问我要小说看，我自己许久没动笔了，一时也写不了许多，不如就用两三个月的工夫译述一二十段故事来给她看，更能使她满足。

民俗学者认为民间故事是重要的研究材料。凡未有文字，或有文字而不甚通行的民族，他们的理智的奋勉大体有四种是从嘴里说出来的。这四种便是故事、歌谣、格言（谚语）和谜语。这些都是人类对于民间故事的推理、记忆、想象等，最早的奋勉，所以不能把它们忽略掉。

故事是从往代传说下来的。一件事情，经十个人说过，在古时候就可以变成一段故事，所以说"十口为古"。故事便是"古"，讲故事便是"讲古"，故事的体例，最普遍的便是起首必要说，"从前有……（什么什么）"，或"古时……（怎样怎样）"。如果把古事分起类来，大体可以分为神话、传说、野乘三种。神话（Myths）是"解释的故事"，就是说无论故事的内容多么离奇难信，说的和听的人对于它们都没有深切的信仰，不过用来说明宇宙、生死等等现象，人兽、男女等等分别，礼仪、风俗等等源流而已。传说（Legends）是"叙述的故事"，它并不一定要解释一种事物的由来，只要叙述某种事物的经过。无论它的内容怎样，说的和听的对于它都信为实事，如关于一个民族的移植、某城的建设、某战争的情形，都是属于这一类。它与神话还有显然不同之处，就是前者的主人多半不是人类，后者每为历史的人物。自然，传说中的历史的人物，不必是真正历史，所说某时代有某人，也许在那个时代并没有那人，或者那人的生时，远在所说时代的前后也可以附会上去。凡传说都是说明某个大人物或英雄曾经做过的事迹，我们可以约略分它为两类，一类是英雄故事（Hero-Tales），一类是英雄行传（Sagas）。英雄故事只说某时代有一个英雄怎样出世，对于他或她所做的事并无详细的记载。英雄行传就不然，它的内容是细述一个英雄一生的事业和品性。那位英雄或者是一个历史上的人物，说的人将许多功绩和伟业加在他身上。学者虽然这样分，但英雄故事和英雄行传的分别到底是不甚明了的。术语上的"野乘"是用德文的"Märchen"："它包括童话（Nursery-Tales）、神仙故事（Fairy-Tales）及民间故事或野语（Folk-Tales）三种。"它与英雄故事及英雄行传不同之处在于，第一点，它不像传说那么认真，故事的主人常是没有名字的，说者只说"从前有一个人……（怎样怎样）"或"往时有一个王……（如此如彼）"，对于那个人、那个王的名字可以不必提起；第二点，它是不记故事发生的时间与空间的；第三点，它的内容是有一定的格式和计划的，人一听了头一两段，几乎就可以知道结局是怎样的。传说中的故事，必有人名、时间、地点，并且没有一定的体例，事情到什么光景就说到什么光景。

从古代遗留下来的故事，学者分它们为认真说与游戏说两大类，神话和传说属于前一类，野语是属于后一类的。在下级文化的民族中，就不这样看，他们以神话和传说为神圣，为一族生活的历史源流，有时禁止说故事的人随意叙说。所以在他们当中，凡认真说的故事都是神圣的故事，甚至有时只在冠礼时长老为成年人述说，外人或常人是不容听见的。至于他们在打猎或耕作以后在村中对妇孺说的故事只为娱乐，不必视为神圣，所以相对于神圣的故事而言，我们可以名它做庸俗的故事。

庸俗的故事，即是野语，在文化的各时期都可以产生出来。它虽然是为娱乐而说，可是那率直的内容很有历史的价值存在。我们从它可以看出一个时代的社会风尚、思想和习惯。它是一段一段的人间社会史。研究民间故事的分布和类别，在社会人类学中是一门很重要的学问。因为那些故事的内容与体例不但是受过环境的陶冶，并且带着很浓厚的民族色彩。在各民族中，有些专会说解释的故事，有些专会说训诫或道德的故事，有些专会说神异的故事，彼此一经接触，便很容易互相传说，互相采用，用各族的环境和情形来修改那些外来的故事，使成为己有。民族间的接触不必尽采用彼此的风俗习惯，可是彼此的野乘很容易受同化。野乘常比神话和传说短，并且注重道德的教训，常寓一种训诫，所以这类故事常缩短为寓言（Fables）。寓言常以兽类的品性抽象地说明人类的道德关系，其中每含有滑稽成分，使听者发噱。为方便起见，学者另分野乘为禽语（Beast-Tales）、谐语（Drolls）、集语（Cumulative Tales）及喻言（Apologues）四种。在禽语中的主人是会说人话的禽兽。这种故事多见于初期的文化民族中。在各民族的禽兽中，所选的主人、禽兽各有不同，大抵是与当地当时的生活环境多有接触的动物。初人并没有觉得动物种类的不同，所以在故事中，象也可以同家鼠说话，公鸡可以请狐狸来做宾客，诸如此类，都可以看出他们的识别力还不很强。可是从另一方面说这种禽语很可以看出初民理智活动的表现方法。谐语是以诙谐为主的。故事的内容每以愚人为主人，述说他们的可笑行为。集语的内容和别的故事一样，不同的只在体例。它常在叙述一段故事将达到极盛点的时候，必要复述全段的故事一遍再往下说。喻言都是道德的故事，借譬喻来说明一条道理的，所以它与格言很相近。喻言与寓言有点不同。前者多注重道德的教训，后者多注重真理的发明。在低级文化的民族中常引这种喻言为法律上的事例，在法庭上可以引来判断案件。野乘的种类大体是如此，今为明了起见，特把前此所述的列出一个表来。

我们有了这个表，便知道这本书所载的故事是属于哪一类的。禽语的例如《豺媒》，谐语如《二窃贼》，喻言如《三王子》、《阿芙蓉》等是。

孟加拉民间故事的体例，在这本书中也可以看出它们有禽语、谐语、集语、喻言四种成分，不过很不单纯，不容易类别出来。故事的主人多半是王、王子和婆罗门人。从内容方面说，每是王、王子，或婆罗门人遇见罗刹或其他鬼灵，或在罗刹国把一个王女救出来，多半是因结婚关系而生种种悲欢离合的事。做坏事的人常要被活埋掉。在这二十二段故事中，除了《二窃贼》及《阿芙蓉》以外，多半的结局是团圆的，美满的。

在这本故事里有许多段是讲罗刹的。罗刹与药叉或夜叉有点不同。夜叉（Yaksa)是一种半神的灵体，住在空中，不常伤害人畜。罗刹（Rakshasa）男声作罗刹婆，女声作罗叉私（Rakshasi）。"罗刹"此言"暴恶"，"可畏"，"伤害者"，"能瞰鬼"等。佛教的译家将这名字与夜叉相混，但在印度文学中这两种鬼怪的性质显有不同的地方。罗刹本是古代印度的土人，有些书籍载他们是，黑身，赤发，绿眼的种族。在印度亚利安人初入印度的时候，这种人盘踞着南方的森林使北印度与德干（Deccan）隔绝。他们是印度亚利安人的劲敌，所以在《吠陀》里说他们是地行鬼，是人类的仇家。《摩诃婆罗多》书中说他们的性质是凶恶的，他们的身体呈黄褐色，具有坚利的牙齿，常染血污。他们的头发是一团一团组起来的。他们的腿很长，有五只脚。他们的指头都是向后长的。他们的咽喉作蓝色，腹部很大，声音凶恶，容易发怒，喜欢挂铃铛在身上。他们最注重的事情便是求食。平常他们所吃的东西是人家打过喷嚏不能再吃的食物，有虫或虫咬过的东西，人所遗下来的东西，和被眼泪渗染过的东西。他们一受胎，当天就可以生产。他们可以随意改变他们的形状。他们在早晨最有力量，在破晓及黄昏时最能施行他们的欺骗伎俩。

在民间故事中，罗刹常变形为人类及其他生物。他们的呼吸如风。身手可以伸长到十由旬（约八十英里，参看本书《骨原》）。他们从嗅觉知道一个地方有没有人类。平常的人不能杀他们，如果把他们的头砍掉，从脖子上立刻可以再长一个出来。他们的国土常是很丰裕的，地点常在海洋的对岸。这大概是因为锡兰岛往时也被看为罗刹所住的缘故。罗刹女也和罗刹男一样喜欢吃人。她常化成美丽的少女在路边迷惑人，有时占据城市强迫官民献人畜为她的食品。她们有时与人类结婚，生子和人一样。

今日的印度人，信罗刹是住在树上的，如果人在夜间经过树下冲犯了他们就要得呕吐及不消化的病。他们最贪食，常迷惑行人。如果人在吃东西的时候，灯火忽然灭了，这时的食物每为罗刹抢去，所以得赶快用手把吃的遮住。人如遇见他们，时常被他们吃掉，幸亏他们是很愚拙的，如尊称他们为"叔叔"或"姑母"等，他们就很喜欢，现出亲切的行为，不加伤害。印度现在还有些人信恶性的异教徒死后会变罗刹。在孟加拉地方，这类的罗刹名叫"曼多"（Māmdo），大概是从阿拉伯语"曼督"（Mamdūh），意为"崇敬""超越"，而来。

这本故事常说到天马（Pakshiraj），依原文当译为"鸟王"。这种马是有翅膀能够在空中飞行的。它在地上走得非常快，一日之中可以跑几万里。

印度的民间故事常说到王和婆罗门人。但他们的"王"并不都是统治者，凡拥有土地的富户也可以被称为王或罗阇，所以《豻媒》里的织匠也可以因富有而自称为王。王所领的地段只限于他所属所知道的，因此，印度古代许多王都不是真正的国王，"王"不过是一个徽号而已。

此外还有许多事实从野乘学的观点看来是很有趣味的。所以这书的译述多偏重于学术方面，至于译语的增减和文辞修饰只求达意，工拙在所不计。

许地山

十七年六月六日 海甸朗润园

赠与爱读故事的芝子

目　录
CONTENTS

一三王子

从前有一位国王生了三个王子。他的百姓在某一天都到殿前启奏说："公义的化身，我们的大王啊！这国里被盗贼充满了，我们的财产很难保持得住。我们求陛下派人去把那班贼拿来，刑罚他们。"王于是对他的三个儿子说："我的儿呀，我已经年老了，你们却正在壮年时代，你们怎么能够忍见着全国的盗贼放肆呢？我现在希望你们出去为民众拿贼。"于是三位王子每夜一同出宫去巡逻。因为这事，他们在郊外建筑了一间休息所和一间马厩。在初夜时，第一个王子骑马出去巡查，却没看见半个贼。他回到郊外的休息所去。到了中夜，轮到第二个王子巡城，但他也没看见有什么动静，城中一个贼人也没有。他也回到郊外的休息所去。后夜到了，第三个王子骑着马到四城去巡逻。他走近父王所住的宫门，看见一个绝世的美人从宫里出来。王子心疑她在那个时候出来，便前去问她是谁，要到哪里去。女人回答说："我是罗阇乐斯弥，是守护这个宫廷的神灵。因为王今晚一定要被杀害，所以毋须我再留此地守护着，我要离开此地往别处去。"王子对于这个消息不晓得要怎么办。停了一会儿，他忽然想起来，问女神说："假使大王今夜不被杀害，你还能够回到宫里守护么？"女神回答说："自然我不拒绝。"王子于是请求女神进宫里去，应许她，他要尽力使王免于危险。女神听他的请求，再进宫去。王子随着她，可是一瞬间她便不见了。

他看见一个绝世的美人从宫里出来

王子一直走到王的寝宫，他看见他父亲躺在床上熟睡。他的年轻的第二王后，王子的后母，也躺在另一张床睡着。灯火虽还点着，可是很幽暗。王子发现了父王床上缠着一条非常粗大的毒蛇，他立刻抽出刀来砍死它。他把蛇砍死之后，还将它切成百十小段放在房中的槟榔盘里。当王子斩蛇的时候，不提防把血点溅在王后胸前。王子心里非常忧惧，因为蛇血也是很毒的。他自己说："我把父亲救活，却把母亲害死了！"不过，用什么方法把她胸前的血点拭掉呢？他想了一会儿，就用一条布在舌上绕了七重，俯着身体去把血舐掉。他正在舐着，王后便醒了。她睁开眼睛，看见是第三个王子。王子见王后醒了，不好意思再留在屋里，赶紧跑出去。王后心里想害王子，就把国王叫醒说："我的夫主，我的夫主！你醒着么？你醒着么？起来吧，我这里发生事故了。"王被她唤醒，便问她什么事。她说："我的夫主，你的尊贵的第三个儿子，是你平日最看得起的，他方才在这里咧。他跑到我床边摩触我的乳房，被我发觉了。他一定是怀着恶意进来的吧，他却是你的宝贵儿子！"王听了这话，自然非常生气，他对王后说暂且把事情搁下，到明天再来办理。第三个王子骑马跑回休息所，见着二位哥哥也没有对他们说什么。

　　天明了，王在早晨便命人把第一个王子招来，问他："如果有一个人向来是被我所信托的，现在我发现了他不忠不诚，你想我应当怎样刑罚他？"王的长子回答说："若有这样的人，他的头自当被割下来，不过在你没杀他以前，你须考究他是不是真正不忠诚。"王问他："这是什么意思？"王长子说："容我说一个故事给父王听吧。"他开始讲述下面的故事：

从前一个金匠和他成年的儿子同住，他的儿子娶了一个妻子，具有了解禽兽言语的能力。她丈夫和所有的人都不晓得她有这样的才能。有一天晚上，她躺在丈夫身边，听见一只豺叫着说："在河里流着一具尸体，谁去把它捞上来，使我能够吃肉，它可以得他指上的金刚钻呢！"女人懂得豺所说的话，又因为她的房子正靠近河边，所以她私自出去把尸体捞起。她丈夫并没睡熟，也起来远远地跟着她，看她在深夜里到河边去干什么。女人到河边，捞起尸体，果然看见指上戴着一颗很大的金刚钻。她没气力把那宝贝从尸体的硬指脱下来，便用口去咬，将她的身体伏在地上。她得着宝石，就私下回来，躺在床上睡着了。她丈夫远远看见她的行为，就很害怕，在她没回家之前就赶快跑回来。他想他妻子一定不是人类，一定是个罗刹。不然怎么会半夜里跑到河边去吃死尸？那一夜他一直在床上哆嗦，没曾睡着。

第二天一早他就跑到他父亲那里，说："父亲，你为我选择的那个妻子并不是真女人，乃是一个罗刹。昨晚我躺在床上的时候，听见河边一只豺在那里狂吠，她以为我睡着了，就起来，私自把门开了，一直到河边去。因为她在深夜独自一人跑出去，使我觉得很奇怪。我于是蹑着脚步，远远地随从她，她也没看见我，你想她在那里干什么呢？可怕呀，可怕！她走到河边，把一具尸体捞上来，一口一口咬着吃！这是我亲眼看见的。我在她正吃得有滋有味的时候，就赶快回到屋里，跳上床去装睡。没过一会儿，她又回来了。她把门关好，就睡在我身边。父亲呀，我怎能和一个罗刹女同住呢？她将来必定会在一个夜间把我吃掉的。"

老金匠听了，也觉得他儿子的性命非常危险，但他并不露出惊惶的样子。他们商量着要把女人送到密林中去，或者在那里可以使野兽把她吃掉。金匠的儿子于是来到妻子面前，对她说："我的爱妻，你早晨不必多煮饭了，你只熬一点粥和烙一块饼就够了。我要带你回家去看你父母，因为有人来报信说他们急着要看你。"女人听见丈夫要送她回娘家，就非常喜悦。她快快把早饭预备出来，夫妇俩匆忙吃完早饭就启程了。

他们要经过一个稠密的树林。丈夫想着到那里的时候便把妻子留下，容野兽来把她吃掉。可是当他们到林中的时候，妻子听见一条蛇在树边发出嘘声。她懂得蛇的意思是说："过路的人，你如果能把那边小洞里一只叫着的青蛙捉来给我吃，我便很感谢你。在那洞里满藏着许多珠宝，你可以拿去。你得珠宝，我吃青蛙。"妇人听见，立即进前去把青蛙拖出来，拿小树枝来掏那小洞。她丈夫在一边看见她忽然跑到树下那边，心里想着他的罗刹妻子要伤害他，他现出很惊惶的状态。妇人回头对他说："丈夫呀，来吧。你把这些珠宝拿起来，带回家去吧。"丈夫听见她的话，心里还在怀疑，不晓得要怎样对付。他颤抖着进前去，果然很惊讶地看见一大堆的珠宝。他们把宝贝捡起来，可是总捡不完，只能尽量将它们放在口袋里。

丈夫到那时，心里很诧异他妻子有特别的聪明，就问她用什么方法知道那里有珠宝。她说她自小就懂得一切禽兽所说的话，她昨晚上听见豺的话，到河边去，得着一颗很大的金刚钻。方才所得，乃是蛇告诉的。丈夫这才明白他妻子是个好人，于他将来的幸福，增益很多，于是把舍弃她的念头打消了。他看时光已经不早，就对妻子说："我的爱妻，时候已经不早了，我们不能在黄昏前赶得到你娘家，如果我们不赶紧走，恐怕就要被野兽吃掉了。我想我们还是赶回家去吧。"

他们二人因为背负着一大口袋的珠宝，所以走得很慢。到很晚，他们才走近家门。丈夫对妻子说："我的爱妻，你从后门进去吧，我把这些珠宝拿到前门去给父亲看。"她于是从后门进去。她一进门，可巧她公公跑到里边来找东西，手里还拿着一把斧子。他

妇人回头对她丈夫说："丈夫呀，来吧。你把这些珠宝拿起来，带回家去吧。"

一看见那罗刹媳妇独自一个人回来，心里断定他儿子必定是被她吃掉了。心急起来，他就把斧子往媳妇头上一劈，立刻把她劈死了。他做完这事不久，儿子已从前门进来，可惜太迟了。

第一个王子说到这里，便对他父亲说："这段故事就是要说明我方才对你说的，在没把那人的头割下来之前，须要考究他是不是真正犯罪。"

王又召第二个王子来，问他："如果有一个人向来是被我所信托的，现在我发现了他不忠不诚，你想我应当怎样刑罚他？"第二个王子回答他说："若有这样的人，他的头自当被割下来，不过在你没杀他以前，你须考察他是不是真正不忠诚。"王问他："这是什么意思？"第二个王子说："容我说一个故事给父王听吧。"他于是讲述了下面的故事：

从前有一个国王时常出去打猎，有一次，他又出去打猎，他的马送他到密林去，致他远离他的侍从们。他一直地骑，到了一个没有城市，没有人烟的地方。他走得渴起来了，可是附近没有水池，也没有流泉。后来他发现有些水点从树上滴下来。他以为是叶上的积雨，于是从身边取出一个小杯来，一滴一滴地接着，到快要满的时候，那些水点原来不是叶上的积雨。树上有一条很大的蛇缠在那里向着树叶吐它的毒液，毒液掉得像雨点一样。王以为是雨点，但他的马知道那是蛇的毒液。毒液已充满了小杯，王正要送到嘴边的时候，他的马忽然跳跃起来，把一杯毒液全洒在地上。王不明白马的意思，对它发怒，立刻拔出剑来把它砍死。

第二王子说到这里，便对他父亲说："这段故事，就是要说明我方才对你说的，在没把那人的头割下来之前，须要考究他是不是真正犯罪。"

王于是召第三个王子来，问他："如果有一个人向来是被我所信托的，现在我发现了他不忠不诚，你想我应当怎样刑罚他？"第三个王子回答说："若有这样的人，他的头自当被割下来，不过在你没杀他以前，你须考究他是不是真正不忠诚。"王问他："这是什么意思？"第三个王子说："容我说一个故事给父王听吧。"他于是讲述了下面的故事：

从前有一个国王，在宫中养了一只很可人的苏迦鸟。有一天，苏迦鸟飞出去呼吸新鲜的空气，遇见它的父母。那双老鸟叫它们的儿子回家去住几天。它们的巢离王宫是很远的。苏迦鸟对它父母说它很愿意回去，不过它得回王宫去先向国王请假，如得允许，第二天一早，就与它们一同启程。苏迦回来求王赏假，王因为爱它的缘故也就应许了。

第二天早晨，苏迦到约定的地方会它的父母，一同飞到很远很远的地方一棵高树上。那里便是它父母的巢。三只鸟同住着，彼此都觉得非常愉快，忽忽地已过了十四五天。苏迦对它父母说："父亲和母亲哪，国王只许我十四五天的假，现在已经满期了，明天我当要回到王宫去。"它父母以它所说为是，商量着要送些礼物给国王。它们想来想去，都觉得最好是送国王一个长生果。人一吃了长生果，是永不会老死的。

晚上它还与它父母一同安歇。第二早晨，它仔细地叼着长生果就向王城飞去。因为果子很重，它一天不能飞到王城，在道上过了一夜。它歇在一棵树上，想着要用什么方法才能收藏那果子。若是老叼着呢，它知道它一睡去，果子便要掉下来。幸好它看见树干上有一个洞，就叼着果子飞进去住宿。

那洞原来有一条蛇在里面住，蛇把它的毒液都滴在果子上头。在晨鸦未啼之前，苏迦便叼着长生果向王城飞去。它飞到时，国王正和大臣同坐。王很喜欢再见他的小鸟回来，还叼着一个很好看的果子放在他面前。长生果的形色是世间一切的果子所不能比较的。王将要拿来放在嘴里吃的时候，他的侍从急急地阻止他说，或者那是一个有毒的果子。于是他把长生果扔到墙边去。正巧在那里被一只牛吃了。不久，牛就躺在地上死掉。国王以为苏迦立意要毒杀他，就命人把它治死。他又叫人把那果子的核拿到城外的御苑种去。

长生果的种子这时已经长成树了，它开了一树花，后来又结得累累的果子。果子的形色非常美丽。国王命人用篱笆把树围起来，因为怕他的人民误吃而导致死亡。

王城里有一个老婆罗门人，他是以受人布施为生的，穷得很。有一天，他想着他的晚景难过，就对他的老妻说，与其沦为乞丐，不如到王的花园里去吃毒果而死。他妻子也没法阻止他，到晚上，他果然到御苑里去。他妻子在远地里跟随着他，也想着若是她丈夫真要吃那毒果，她也跟着吃，一同死掉倒还干净。夜深了，守园的人都睡着了。婆罗门人偷偷地走进去，走到长生果树底下。他妻子也到了。他摘了一个果子下来吃。他妻子对他说："如果你死，剩下我活着有什么用处呢？我也吃一个得啦。"她说完，自己也摘下一个来吃。他们吃完，一同回家，等候毒发。他们一同躺在床上等死。第二天早晨，他们不但没死，并且容貌也改变得像二三十岁人的样子，满身都是肌肉，很强健，很活泼。他们自己也很惊疑，因为他们的邻人都不敢认他们。

老婆罗门人变成了年轻的人，白发也变黑了，脸上的皱纹也没有了。他的老妻也变成一个俊美的少女，恢复她几十年前的模样。她的模样直赛过王宫里的美人。国王听见了这回事，于是命人把婆罗门人招来，问他。他对国王述说一切的经过。国王到那时才觉得苏迦原是好意，可惜早把它杀了。他很悔恨当时没有考究，就轻易地杀死苏迦。

第三个王子说到这里，便对他父亲说："这段故事，就是要说明我方才对你说的，在没把那人的头割下来之前，须要考究他是不是真正犯罪。我知道父王以为我昨晚擅自进宫，带着恶意跑到父王的寝室里。我要请你先听我的禀告，然后动怒，昨晚上轮到我守夜的时候，我看见一个女人从宫中出来。我问她是谁，她说是护宫神罗阁乐斯弥。她要离宫，因为王在夜间要被害。我请求她与我一同进宫，我誓要救王出险。我一直跑到寝室里，看见一条大蛇盘在父王的床上。我急用刀一挥，把它砍断了，再切成百余段放在槟榔盘里。当我斩蛇的时候，血花偶尔溅着我母亲的胸膛。我想若不快把它去掉，我就会害了她的性命，于是我用布缠在舌上去舐她胸前的蛇血。不幸她醒过来，看见我伏在她身上，就怀疑我有什么恶意。父王，这就是我昨晚所做的事。你现在听了，可以随你意把我拿去杀掉。"

王听了他儿子的话，非常喜欢，知道他儿子真是忠心，并无恶意。从那时候，他比从前越发爱第三个王子。

我的故事说到这里算完了，

那提耶棘也枯萎了。

那提耶呵，你为什么枯萎呢？

你的牛为什么要我用草来喂它？

牛呵，你为什么要人喂？

你的牧者为什么不看护我？

牧者呵，你为什么不去看牛？

你的儿媳妇为什么不把米给我？

儿媳妇呵，你为什么不给米呢？

我的孩子为什么哭呢？

孩子呵，你为什么哭呢？

蚂蚁为什么要咬我呢？

蚂蚁呵，你为什么要咬人呢？

喀！喀！喀！

二二 窃贼

（上）

　　从前在一个村里有两个人结拜为义兄弟，专以偷人家的货财为生，因为他们是出名的小偷，所以凡村里的人一丢了东西，不论是不是他们偷的，都归罪于他们。他们不能在本村居住，就离开那里，两个人商量要诚实地去做工。邻村有一个富人，不知道他们的来历，就雇了他们在家里当长工。他们的职务，一个是看牛，一个是浇园里的瞻婆迦花。贼兄一早就汲水去浇花，主人吩咐他得要将花的周围浇透了，留着几分深的水，他才可以去休息。他想着这是很容易的事，只要汲三两戽水就够了。他汲了一戽浇在树根周围，不一会儿就干了。他连汲了好些水都不够干土的吸收。一直到下午，他汲得非常疲乏，水还没满半分，他躺在地上睡着了。贼弟所管的事情也不见得比他义兄的强。他所管的牛是全村最强悍的牲口。当贼弟放它到草原去的时候，它伸直尾巴，不听约束，一直跑到很远的地方。它不吃草，只跑到别人的稻田去，把田上的稻子随意嚼食，还在那上头来回地蹂躏它。蹂躏了稻田，又跑到隔邻的甘蔗园里去，把人家的甘蔗也毁了许多。因此，稻田主与甘蔗园主都不答应这看牛的人。他紧紧追着那牛，从一个池子涉过一个池子；

从这块田追到那块田，经过的地方，都被人骂得很难听。他被人侮辱，连他的祖宗也被人叫出来侮辱，自己只好低着头不作声，由人骂去。他那一天真是难过！到太阳快西坠的时候，他才把那野性的牛牵住，慢慢地踱回主人家里去。

"好兄弟，你为什么这么晚才从田里回来呢？"贼兄这样问贼弟。

贼弟回答说："我的哥，我有什么可说的呢？我把牛牵出去，到草原就把它放了。草原那边有一个池子，池边还有一棵大树。我放了牛，由它自己去吃草。它一点也不搅扰我，所以我就把我的浴巾铺在树下的草上，躺下去享受那慢慢送来的轻风。我在不知不觉中就睡着了，一直睡到太阳下山才醒过来。醒时，我见牛已经站在离我身边不远的地方，等着我牵它回来。我的哥哥，你今天做的都是什么呢？"

贼兄说："我么？我也很享乐了一天。我只汲了一庰水去浇那瞻波迦花，不费力就把树根周围都润湿了。我做完这事，别的一点事也没有，一天的工夫都是我自己的。我于是躺在地上，逍遥自在地享受我这愉快的新生活。我一会儿啸，一会儿唱，最后就睡着了。我刚从梦里醒过来咧。"

他们两个谈完，彼此都相信各人的事业比自己的舒服。贼兄以为看牛一定比浇花舒服，贼弟却以为浇花比看牛省事。他们二人各自想着把工作对换来做。

贼兄说："我的弟弟，我倒想去看牛。我明天去做你的工，你来做我的，好不好？你愿意不愿意呢？"

贼弟："我的哥哥，我没有一点不愿意。我很愿意与你对换工作，你明天就去放牛吧。不过，我要告诉你一件事。我觉得整天睡在草地上很不舒服，如果你能带一张绳床去，你必定能享受得更愉快。"

第二天一早，贼兄真个去放牛。他带着一张绳床，试要去过他理想中的愉快生活。贼弟到园里汲水浇那棵瞻波迦花。他也想着只汲一两戽来浇就够了。可是一戽浇下去，再浇一戽，都不见根的四围现出润湿的样子。他汲得非常累。太阳已快下山了。他的工作还没有做完！最后他见天气已晚，就不再浇了。

贼兄在草原上也吃了一天的亏。他照着贼弟的话把牛牵到池边放掉，自己逍遥地放下绳床就要躺下。当他还没躺好的时候，那牛就在别人的田原上乱跑乱嚼。人家一骂，他就不能安然地躺着享受那漫游的轻风。那牛把人家的稻田和蔗园都毁了。他一面追，一面听着侮辱他的语言，还要扛着那绳床走。他把绳床扛起来，双脚飞跑追着那牛。这样的事情真是苦恼，如果他把绳床放下，又怕人家把它拿去，扛着吧，又很累赘。他舍不得丢了绳床，终于还是扛着它去追牛。牧童们看见他扛着一张那么笨的东西满处追牛，都拍手笑他，向他喝倒彩。贼兄又气，又饿，又渴，很后悔他不该把他的工作来和他义弟对换。经过一场辛苦，他接受了别的牧童的帮助，好容易才把牛牵回来。到家，已经是掌灯的时候了。

两个小贼在主人家里相会的时候，各人只对各人微笑，一声也不响，因为他们彼此都吃彼此的亏。各人心里自己明白。他们同住在一间屋里，到晚饭后，彼此又闲谈起来。

贼弟说："义兄，今天你的生活好过么？"

贼兄说："就像你昨天所享受的，不过我所享受的比你略为好些。"

贼弟说："人都叫这种事情为正当的工作，但我总以为我们从前的职业，窃盗，是最可羡的，偷东西比浇花放牛舒服得多咧。"

贼兄说："自然偷东西比一切的事情舒服。那还用怀疑么？我对诸天发誓，我实在不曾见过一只野性的牛像我们所看的那畜生一样，世间真是没有第二只恶牛比得上它。"

贼弟说："恶牛并不少见，我倒见过许多，我可没见过一棵瞻波迦树像园里那棵这么会吸水。你曾见过与它一样能吸水的花木不曾？我很怀疑浇下去的水都到了哪里去，莫不是树根底下有一个大池子？"

贼兄说："我想把那树的下面掘开看看底下到底是什么。"

贼弟说："等主人和主妇睡着的时候，我们一同去发掘吧。"

到了半夜，两个小窃贼携着铲子和铁锹到树下去。他们掘了很深，把土挖上来，贼弟忽然摸着些很硬很重的东西。他的锹也掘不下去了，两个人的好奇心被激发起来，使他们使劲地把土刨开。贼弟摸着一个大土罐，把手伸进去觉得里头装满了金币。他不愿意贼兄知道，就对他说："呵，原来是一块大石头，没有什么。"贼兄自然思疑他义弟一定摸着什么，也不作声，装作不理会的样子。他们两人各存独得的心，商量好不再往下发掘，都说没有什么，回到屋里睡去。过一两小时以后，贼兄见贼弟睡着了，就蹑着脚走出去，到树下把土再刨开。他发现了那是一大罐的金币。他喜极了，再往下掘，又得着一罐。他把两罐金子扛到池边，埋在淤泥里，又蹑着脚回到屋里。他轻轻地躺在贼弟身边，因为过累，不一会儿就睡熟了。

贼弟惦念着他方才所发现的金子，也没有睡足就醒了。他怕贼兄醒过来，也蹑着脚出去，到树底下，已不见了那罐金子。他想一定他的义兄把它搬走了，藏在一个隐秘的地方。他回到屋里，观察那睡着的义兄，试要从他身上发现那罐金子的踪迹。他发现了贼兄的脚沾了很厚的淤泥，从脚板一直到脚眼，于是断定他必是把金子藏在池边的淤泥里头。可是藏在池的哪一边呢？他慢慢地走出来，一直来到池边，绕了一周。他绕着池子走的时候，很注意他的脚步所经过的地方。那池子是方的。他觉得他走过四面，只有一面没有青蛙在他经过的时候跳进水里去，其余三面都有。他断定这必是方才有人在那一面工作了许久，所以把青蛙们吓跑了。这事使他断定金子埋在了哪里。他找来找去，至终把两罐金子找了出来。他把金子扛到牛圈里，把那只恶牛牵出来，把金子放在它背上叫它驮着走。他连夜离开那里一直往自己的村庄去。他偷了牛，还得了两罐金子！

贼兄一直睡到天明，到晨鸦乱啼的时候才起来。他睁眼一看，义弟已不在了。他赶快跑到池边，金子也被人拿走了。他断定这必定是他义弟办的事。然而他到哪里去了呢？他见恶牛也不在圈里，断定贼弟一定是骑牛回到本村去。想定之后，他就立意要去追他。但用什么方法可以再把那金子夺回来呢？他走到一个小城市用他所有的钱去买一双绣金的鞋子，又从小道一直跑到贼弟的前头。贼弟是从大道走的，所以慢一点，又加上一只恶牛驮着很重的金子，更是要慢了。这个贼兄早已想到，所以他想从小道去追他，一定追得上。他上了大道，把绣金鞋扔一只在道边，走了约一百尺，又扔下第二只。第二只鞋所在地方的旁边正有一棵大树，贼兄就爬上去，蹲着静静地等候他义弟经过。他蹲在密叶里，底下的人一点也看不见。

贼弟牵着恶牛蹒跚地来了。牛很不驯，在道上常与他闹脾气。他看见第一只美丽的绣金鞋扔在道旁，自己说着："真是好看的鞋，是用金线绣的呀！我现在是富人了，捡起来穿正合适。可惜只有一只，还有一只在哪里呢？"他没捡，一直地走。不到一会儿，来到放第二只鞋的地方，他说，"这可不是与方才那只是成对的！我真笨，为什么不把那只捡起来？现在回去捡也不迟，道上还没有人走咧。我把牛牵在树下再捡那一只鞋去。"说着，便把牛牵在树下跑去捡那一只鞋。他去捡鞋的时候，贼兄从树上爬下来，牵着牛，从密林的小道往他本村里去。贼弟回来不见了牛，他断定是中了他义兄的计，那牛和金子一定是他抢走的。他于是使劲地跑回本村。到的时候，他义兄还没曾到，他藏在义兄家的门边。不久贼兄牵着牛来到了。贼弟突然跑出来，对他说："哥哥，你平安回来了！我们把金子均分了吧。"金子本来不是贼兄发现的，他听见贼弟这样提议，有便宜，自然同意。

他们把牛背上的两个土罐卸下来运到小院里，再搬到房里。金币一个一个分置两堆，末了，只剩一个。他们彼此都不让，大家商议把它均分了。可是他们当中一个人得把那金子拿出去换钱才可以。现在的问题是谁该存着那金子等到明天早上到市上换钱去？他们争来争去，至终由贼兄保留着那剩下的一个金子。他们约定明天早晨再来均分换得的钱。

那一晚上，贼兄对他的妻子和同住的女人们说："你们都听着，明天义弟要来分金子的时候，你们可要帮我的忙，我不愿意分给他。他未来的时候，你们把一块布摊在院子里，我躺下装死。你们可以告诉人说我得了暴病而死，把一棵紫苏放近我头上。你们看见他来就放声哭。他看见这样光景，必定要走的。他一走，我就不用再给他一半金子了。"第二天早晨，贼弟果然要来分钱，在远处，他便听见女人的哭声。走到屋里的院子，他看见他义兄躺在那里，用布裹着，头边还放着一棵紫苏。妇人们啼哭着，说他昨晚得暴病死了。妇人们还埋怨他说："你们昨天到哪里去了？你们拿了什么回来呢？你在他身上做了些什么呢？你看，他死了！"她们说完又大哭起来。

贼弟早就看出这是他义兄装假，要赖他的钱，也不作声，他对妇人们说："我对于我义兄的死非常悲伤，我现在当为他预备丧事。你们都是女人，离开这里吧，一切的事都由我去办，好啦。"他拿了一大堆的稻草，把它们绞成绳子，将死人的腿扎得紧紧的。

他把义兄拖着走，说要送那尸身到火葬场去。贼兄被他从一条街道拖过另一条街道，把身体都擦伤了。他还是忍着痛，静默着，因为他一出声，就得把金子分给他义弟。贼弟把尸身拖到火葬场，太阳已经下山了。他捡了些干柴，一根一根地堆起来，忽然想起他没有带火种。他想着，如果他去取火，他的义兄必定要逃跑，怎么办呢？他想把稻草绳子结在树上，也不合适，不如把他挂起来吧。他把尸首牢牢地挂在树下，自己就到村里乞火去了。

正当贼弟去借火的时候，一群盗贼从那里经过。他们都看见那尸身挂在树上。贼头目对群贼说："我们这次出来打劫，一定可以得着胜利。婆罗门人和梵学家常说行人初出门一见尸首，诸事大吉利，所以这是一个好兆头。我们现在看见这尸首，今晚一定可以多得着财宝。我说，如果我们抢得了东西，就回到这里来均分，再把那尸身烧掉，然后分散，各自回家去。"群贼都赞成贼头目的提议。他们呼啸着蜂拥入村里去，把村里富人的宝货都抢了来。村里连一只小家鼠也不敢出来挡他们的道，他们又把富人杀了，再搬运他们的家财。这回所得很多，他们实在想不到。他们商量着回到方才遇着尸首的地方去分赃。

他们到的时候，贼兄还挂在树上，一声也不响，因为他恐怕一出声，就得将那一半金子给他义弟。群贼挖地成为一个小穴，把

他们都惊恐地飞跑着离开那里，把抢得的金银财宝都留在地上，一点也来不及带走

柴堆在那里，把尸首取下来放在柴上。他们正要举火，贼兄从柴上囔起来。他站起来，瞪着眼看那群贼人，嘴里发出一种怪声。群贼都吓得面面相觑，他们以为是恶鬼附着尸体作祟，个个都吓跑了。正在这个时候，贼弟又从树上跳下来，他们回头一看，觉得又来了一个鬼灵，更飞跑着离开那里，把抢得的赃物都留在地上，一点也没带走。两个贼兄弟这时才相对着各自大笑，把地上的赃物收拾起来，回家均分。他们因此过了些愉快的日子。

（下）

　　贼兄与贼弟各生了一个儿子，因为他们觉得做贼的生活比什么生活都舒服，就立意要训练他们两个儿子去做窃盗。在村里有一个专门教人偷窃的教师，开馆授课，时时发出难题去给他们的徒弟解决。因为他很有名，所以贼兄和贼弟都送儿子去给他教导。两个孩子将偷窃的知识和手段都学得很高明，不在他们父亲之下。教师要试他们的本领就出一个难题给他们解决。

　　离偷盗教师的住处不远有一间草屋，里面住着一对穷夫妇。那屋顶攀满了瓜藤。屋脊最高的地方长了一个很大的葫芦。穷夫妇日夜守着它，希望它长足了，可以摘下来换一点钱。他们晚上自然是要睡的，不过他们睡的时候也很关心屋顶的葫芦，很怕被人偷去。有时候小家鼠在屋顶咬稻草，把干泥踏掉了，他们也醒来，出去看看屋顶的葫芦还在不在。这样的光景，使偷儿很难下手，因为屋顶一点动静，睡在底下的两位主人必要注意。教师就把这个举来做难题。他对他的学生们说，如果有人能够把那屋顶的葫芦偷来，他就是冠绝全班的好徒弟。许多徒弟都不敢去偷那葫芦，唯有贼兄的儿子说他可以去。他对教师说如果许他用三样东西，他就可以把那葫芦偷来。三样东西，就是一条绳子、一把小刀和一只猫。教师说他可以用，他在那夜就准备去偷那葫芦。

贼兄的儿子在中夜便到那穷人的草屋，伏在檐下静听屋里夫妇俩谈话。一会儿，话声止住了，他知道他们已经睡着。再等一会儿，他就悄悄地爬上房顶。草屋受不起他的重量，自然要掉稻草和干泥下来。稻草和泥土掉下很多在穷人的妻子身上，就把她惊醒了。她摇着丈夫，对他说："出去看看吧，有人在上头偷我们的葫芦咧！"孩子在屋顶听见底下的人醒了，就使劲地捏着猫的喉咙。猫于是发出"喵，喵，喵"的声音。丈夫听见猫叫，便对妻子说："你没听见么？上头猫叫着咧。我想屋顶只有一只猫，并没有贼。"他们没出来，又睡去了。孩子于是轻轻地把葫芦割下来，用绳子把它结好，缒到地上。可是他用什么方法下来呢？屋里的人已经是在半醒半提防的状态中，他一动，人家必要发觉。他慢慢地爬，可是稻草和干泥直从房顶掉到屋里。妻子心疑一定是有人在上头偷葫芦，又对丈夫说一定不是猫，一定是有人在上头。男子不愿意出来，也是因为他听见猫叫，所以硬说是猫在那里。他们正在纷议不决的时候，孩子索性把猫捏得狂叫起来，还把它扔到地上，他也随着响声跳下来。丈夫对妻子说："那不是一只猫么？它已经跳下来了，我们可以安静睡着了。"

第二天早晨，孩子把葫芦拿到教师面前放下，且述说他所用的手段。教师赞美他，说他可以出去做窃盗了。教师给了孩子奖赏，还对他说："聪明的父亲生聪明的儿子，你真不愧为你父亲的儿子。"孩子回家把昨晚上的事和早晨教师的奖励告诉了父亲。贼兄对于他儿子的手段以为还够不上出去偷人家的东西。他要他儿子更显些本领，然后许他入社会去谋生活。他对儿子说："我的儿，你如果能够做我叫你去做的事，我就许你到人世里去谋生活。如果你能把这国的王后脖上那条金项串偷来给我，我就许你够得上出去谋生。"他儿子不迟疑地就应许了他。

孩子先到宫外去打听王和王后的住处，认熟了四个宫门和里面的墙垣门户。他对于宫中生活一切的习惯，王和王后的脾气，都打听得很清楚。他最注意的便是宫中的侍卫。至终，他选定一个晚上着手去偷王后的项串。他穿的是暗色衣服，身上只带一把剑，一把斧子，和许多大钉。宫中最外一扇门是狮子门，进了狮子门还得经过三扇门才能到王后的寝宫，每扇门都有十六个卫兵守住，他知道卫兵一定要换班的。王有许多卫兵，所以在各门值班守卫的每小时都要更替一次。这样。每扇门在一小时间必有三十六个卫兵同时在那里，孩子就在两班交替，人多的时候混进去。他从狮子门一直跟

029

着三十六个人混进去，藏在第二扇门外一个幽暗的地方。因为他的衣服在夜间不容易识别，所以没有人发现他。每一个小时，兵士换班的时候，他必随着大众混进去，一直进到宫里。他走到王后的寝宫外头，从窗门向里面望，看见有一点微光，还有一种断续的声音从楼上发出来。他认得那是女人的声音，断定是宫中说故事的女官正在伺候王和王后睡觉，在那里说故事咧。他知道王和王后在睡前必定有人在他们面前说几段故事给他们听。原来寝宫是一座三层的楼房，王和王后的寝室是在第三层楼上。他看见楼下的门都关了，院外四围都是卫兵，不好轻易动手。他本是想用钉子钉在墙上攀着上去的，可是他一钉便有声，纵然不会惊动卫兵和王，那说故事的女官一定也能听见，若是他嚷起来，他的性命可是危险。他早料到这个难处，便伏在一边，等待机会。

在寝宫外有一座铜漏，每小时要报时刻。那铜漏旁边悬着一面从支那来的大锣，铜漏一满，锣便按时打点。锣声很宏大，一打满宫都听得见，不但是满宫听得见，连城中附近的居民都能听见。那锣，每打一下就要延很长的时间，因为它的声音很能延长。孩子选定锣响的时间来钉钉子。锣响一下，他便钉一口钉在墙上。十点时分，他已钉上十口钉子。锣停的时候，他也不钉，静静地候着。十一点，他又钉了十一口钉子。这时他已到了第二层楼。到十二点，他钉了十二口钉子，一直达到第三层楼，王和王后的寝室里。他看见说故事的女官在床边没精打采地在那里说故事，王和王后早已睡着了。他蹑脚来到女官身边，悄悄地坐下。王后就睡在王身边一张很华丽的床上。从烛光中，他看见她脖上挂着一条宝光灿烂的项串。他仔细听那说故事的女官所说的是什么。她已经很疲乏了，王和王后早已睡去，哪里还听她所说的，不过她也得挨到了时候才能出去。她说着，停一会儿，打一个盹，微睁眼睛，又瞎说了一会儿，又打一个盹。孩子看见她如此，知道每夜说故事的女官到王和王后睡着后，都是敷衍了事。他不慌不忙，把女官的头割下来，自己穿上她的衣服，仍然坐在那里装作说故事的样子。王和王后只听见身边有人说故事，也不理会故事的内容，早就睡熟了。他把自己的衣服藏在身边，蹑着脚走近王后的床边，轻轻地把她脖上那条项串取下来。说故事的女官总要出去的，所以他又轻轻地开了门，一直来到楼下。他对卫兵说王后命她出宫办一点事。卫兵见是说故事的女官，没盘问他就放他过去。他用这个方法，一直出狮子门去。他乘夜回到自己的家，到时，已经快天亮了。他把项串交给他父亲，说是方才从宫里取出来的。他父亲见儿子这么有本领，双眼直看着他，好像不信是真的，以为是在梦境之中。他欢喜极了，对他儿子说："你所做的很成功。你不但像我一样聪明，并且手段比我还强。我的儿子，诸天必定保佑你，赐你长寿。你可以出去谋生活了。"

第二天早晨，王和王后醒来，看见满地是血，女官的头也被砍断了，赤着身亩溜溜地躺在地上。王后也发现她的项串丢了。他们想不出贼人是用什么方法进来的。难道宫中那么些卫兵都是死的么？王自然很生气，他想不出贼人怎么能够进来并安稳地逃走。卫兵们都对王说昨晚天快亮的时分只有一位女官说奉王后的命令要出宫办事，其余没有什么人出去，也没人进来。王命人到处追贼，都没有下落。最后他出了一个赏格，通告四城的居民说，如能把那凶犯拿到，必得重赏。可是赏格发出去了，还没有人来报信，王很生气，就命人拉一只骆驼来，叫它驮上两大口袋的金币，到四城去游行。王发出通告说："那凶贼既然敢偷王后的项串，我要看看他还有什么本领可以把骆驼背上两大口袋的金币偷去。"骆驼在城中游行了两天两夜，也没遇见什么。

第三天晚上骆驼去到一条街上，驼夫偶然站在街边和一个修道士对谈起来。那修道士坐在街边，在他的虎皮座前有一堆火。火边放着一把很大的火钳。修道士对驼夫说："好兄弟，你为什么天天拉着骆驼满城里乱跑？谁敢从王的骆驼背上偷那两大口袋的金币呢？下来吧，好朋友，下来同我抽一口烟再走吧。"驼夫看见他那么虔意，就从驼背上下来，把骆驼拴在就近一棵树上，走来与修道士一同吸烟闲谈。原来修道士便是贼兄的儿子假装的。他不但用烟给驼夫吸，并且加上很重的迷药，驼夫醉倒，睡在街边，孩子便把骆驼和两大口袋的金币驮回家去。夜间没人看见，所以不曾被发觉，他又是从小道走的。一到家，他便把骆驼宰了，把骨肉都埋在屋里的院子，外面一点痕迹也露不出来。

王那里一早就有人来报告说驼夫晕倒在一条偏僻的街边，骆驼和金币都不见了。他更是生气，果然觉得那凶贼是有点本领。他于是再出赏格说，如果有人能够把贼人拿到，就要赏他十万个卢比。贼弟的儿子听见有这番重赏，他也明知所有的事都是贼兄的儿子干的。在学堂里，他的手段总不如贼兄的儿子，所以他不很出名。这回他想他可以把凶贼拿到，就走到王跟前承揽这事。

贼弟的儿子化装成女人一直来到贼兄的家里，挨门挨户地哭，说，"施主善士呀，你们有骆驼肉，请给我一点吧。我的儿子快要死了，医生说要骆驼肉才能治得好。请救我儿的命，赐给我一点骆驼肉吧。"他一直乞到贼兄的家门，正好贼兄和他儿子都不在家，妇人们心软，想着把院子里埋着的骆驼肉挖出一块来给他。这事，若是贼兄和他儿子在家，一定是不能给的。可是女人虽然是贼眷属，也有几分慈心，就对他说："等一等吧，我

驼夫从骆驼背上下来，准备把骆驼拴在树上，好与修道士一同吸烟闲谈

进去拿一点骆驼肉来给你治你儿子的病。"她说着，真个进去取出一大块骆驼肉来。贼弟的儿子喜极了，他一直跑到王宫报告这事，王于是立刻派大队人马去把贼兄和他的儿子拿来，所有的赃物都被取出来了。

第二天早晨，王亲自审问他们。贼兄的儿子承认王后的项串是他偷的。他又把怎样杀了女官，怎样偷了两大口袋的金币述说一遍。他又说告发他的人和他父亲也是贼，也曾杀了许多人。他把报告人所犯一桩一桩的案件都诉说出来。王照他的允许把十万个卢比放在贼弟的儿子面前，说他应当受重赏。不一会儿，他又宣告说贼弟和他的儿子也有罪，命人把他们都活埋了。这就是贼兄弟父子的末路。

　　我的故事说到这里算完了，

　　那提耶棘也枯萎了。

　　那提耶呵，你为什么枯萎呢？

　　你的牛为什么要我用草来喂它？

　　牛呵，你为什么要人喂？

　　你的牧者，为什么不看护我？

　　牧者呵，你为什么不去看牛？

你的儿媳妇为什么不把米给我？

儿媳妇呵，你为什么不给米呢？

我的孩子为什么哭呢？

孩子呵，你为什么哭呢？

蚂蚁为什么要咬我呢？

蚂蚁呵，你为什么要咬人呢？

喀！喀！喀！

三　鬼夫

从前有一个不属于古林种姓的穷婆罗门人没有钱财，娶不起妻子。他认为，结婚是世间最困难的一桩事体。他到富人那里去求乞钱财，为的是要完成他的婚事。他需要很多钱财，并不是为婚礼的用处，乃是用来做聘金送给新娘父母的。他挨广地乞求，对富人们说了许多谄媚话和祝颂的语言，然后收集得仅仅够用。在相当的时间，他就与一个女子结婚了。不久，他把妻子领到他母亲那里说："母亲哪，我并没有什么能够供养我的妻子，所以无论如何，我当到远国去赚一点钱回来。我也许要出外好些年，若不得着相当的财产，我决不回来。现在我把我所有的都交给你，你可以好好地用。我的妻子也求你照顾她。"他母亲给他祝福，他就动身了。

　　婆罗门人出门的那一晚上，一个鬼灵化作他的模样来到他母亲家里。新婚的妻子以为是她丈夫中途折回来，就对他说："丈夫，你为什么这么快回来？你不是说要过几年才回来么？你改变了你的意思么？"鬼灵说："今天不是一个吉日，不宜出门，我蓦然想起来，所以赶回来，其实我也得着了些金钱哪。"母亲也没怀疑他不是她的儿子。鬼灵于是住在那屋里，认女人为妻，认老婆子为母。鬼灵和婆罗门人的言语、行动、习惯等都一样，好像两粒大小相同的青豆，虽是精明的人也难分辨。邻居的人都没怀疑他是个假的。

　　过了几年，真婆罗门人回家了。他一到家的时候，看见一个与

新婚的妻子以为是她丈夫中途折回来，就对他说："丈夫，你为什么这么快回来？"

他模样相同的人在屋里，他的言语行动全与婆罗门人没有区别。他对婆罗门人说："你是谁？你来此地干什么？"婆罗门人回答说："我是谁？我且问你是谁吧？这是我的家，那位是我的母亲，这位是我的妻子。"鬼灵说："这就奇怪了！谁不晓得这是我的房子，那位是我母亲，这位是我妻子？我住在此地多年，谁不认得我呢？你是从哪里来的流氓，敢说这是你的房子，她是你的母亲，她是你妻子。婆罗门人，我想你一定是认错了。"鬼灵说完这话就把婆罗门人逐出门外。婆罗门人心里自然不服，可是他不晓得要怎样办才好。后来，他把这件事提到王面前去告状。王把两个人叫来，他实在辨不出谁真谁假，所以不能判定曲直。一天一天过去了，王总想不出一个好方法来判决这案。婆罗门人每天到王面前，求王使他能够回到他自己的家，认他的母亲和妻子。王每次都对他说："你明天来吧，我明天给你判决就是了。"婆罗门人每次出宫，必流泪，捶胸顿地，说："这是何等恶劣的世界呢？我从自己的家被逐出来，我的母亲和妻子被人占了，也没人能出来主持公道！那是什么王呢！他连这样的公道人也不能做！他真是不公！"

婆罗门人每日从宫中出来都要说埋怨的话。他从城里出来，每天必要经过一个大草原，常有许多牧童在那里玩。牛群在草原上吃草的时候，牧童们都集聚在树荫下游戏。他们常假装做王和他的臣子玩。他们当中举出一个王，一个宰相，一个巡查官，还有许多侍从和卫士。他们在树下玩耍的时候，每次都见婆罗门人哭着走过去。有一天，牧童王问他的宰相那婆罗门人为什么哭。宰相不能回答，王就命他领着些卫士把婆罗门人叫来。一个装卫士的牧童说："王命你立刻去。"婆罗门人说："为什么？我刚从王那里出来，他叫我明天再去。为什么他现在又要我去呢？"卫士说："是我们的王召你。我们的牧王召你。"婆罗门人问："谁是牧王？"卫士说："你跟我来看看吧。"他于是随孩子们到树荫底下去。

牧王问他哭泣的事由，他就把一切都述说出来。牧王说："我明白你的事情了，我要把你从前丢了一切的权利都收回来给你。你只要到王面前，求他应许将这事交给我办就可以。"婆罗门人于是回到王宫，求王许那牧王判断这事。王为这事已费了许多精神，他实在不能解决，也就应许了婆罗门人的要求。第二天早晨，牧王把真假两个婆罗门人都招来，取出一个长颈瓶放在面前。他考问了一会儿，牧王说："好，够了，我明白你们的事由了。我现在立刻就要判断这案。这里有一个长颈瓶，你们当中如有能够钻进去的，我就判他是那房子的主人，母亲和妻子都是属于他的。我看你们当中谁能钻进去。"婆罗门人鄙夷地说："你是一个牧童假装的王，你真是与我开玩笑，做的都是牧童的事！哪里有一个人能够钻进那么小的瓶子里去呢？"牧王说："如果你不能钻进去，你就不是那房子的真正主人，母亲不是你的，妻子也不是你的。"他回过脸来对鬼灵说："你的意思怎样呢？如果你能钻进瓶子里去，那房子、母亲、妻子，都是你的。"鬼灵不迟疑地回答说："我自然能够钻进去。"他说完，身体渐渐缩小，不一会儿已经全身钻在瓶子里，好像一只小昆虫，牧王急把瓶口塞住，于是鬼灵就被禁在里面，不能再出来。他对婆罗门人说："把这瓶子扔进海里吧。回去认你的母亲和妻子。"婆罗门人照他的话去做，回到家里过着他愉快的生活。以后他生了些子女，在村里住了一辈子。

我的故事说到这里算完了，

那提耶棘也枯萎了。

那提耶呵，你为什么枯萎呢？

你的牛为什么要我用草来喂它？

牛呵，你为什么要人喂？

你的牧者，为什么不看护我？

牧者呵，你为什么不去看牛？

你的儿媳妇为什么不把米给我？

儿媳妇呵，你为什么不给米呢？

我的孩子为什么哭呢？

孩子呵，你为什么哭呢？

蚂蚁为什么要咬我呢？

蚂蚁呵，你为什么要咬人呢？

喀！喀！喀！

四　荒林乞士

从前有一个乞士来到国王面前求布施，国王没有东西给他。他知道国王望子心切，便对他说："因为你非常希望子息，现在我有一种药材奉送给王后。她把我的药吞下去不久便会怀孕，生下一对孪生的男子。不过我要请求你许我一件事，才能把药奉上。我的要求便是王后如生两个儿子，你必得赐一个给我做义子。"国王想着这条件未免苛刻一点，但他急于要求一个儿子来承继他的权位，若能从乞士得到生子良方，就是给他一个儿子也值得。他应许乞士如果是孪生的，必要将一个给他做儿子。乞士把药材递给国王就走了。

　　王后吞了药，果然怀孕生了一对孪生的男儿。两位王子一年一年长大了。过了许多年，总不见乞士来要他的儿子，王和王后想着大概那个老乞士是死了，所以他们都很放心。可是那老乞士没有死，他在计算着时日，要来要他的儿子咧。两位王子入了学堂，书算骑射，无不精通。他们又长得非常健美，所以人民都很爱戴他们。当他们十六岁的时候，老乞士忽然来到宫门，要求国王履行他从前所应许的事情。王和王后听见乞士来要求这事，心伤到极点。他们每在暗地里私下喜欢，因为他们以为老乞士已经死掉，现在忽然见他站在面前，一时实在想不出对付的方法。但悲伤也没用处，国王总得履行他所应许的条件。如果他不把一个儿子给那老乞士，灾祸必临到他和王后乃至全国的人民身上。可是要把哪一位王子给他呢？两位王子都是一样可爱，王和王后实在舍不得容哪一位随着乞士去。王和王后正在犹豫不定的时候，二位王子同时说："我随他去吧。"王次子对王长子说："你年纪长我一些，你是父王的宝贝。你留在宫中，容我随他去吧。"王长子回答说："你的年纪小一点。你是母亲最钟爱的，还是你留在宫中，容我随那乞士去好一些。"彼此争执了好些时间，各人都很悲伤。王后的衣服都被眼泪渗得湿透了。最后，还是王长子随着乞士去了。王长子在离开王宫之前，就在院子种了一棵树，对他的父母和弟弟说："这就是我生命的代表，你们如果看见这树的枝叶茂盛，颜色青绿时，便知道我还平安；如果你们看见这树凋零，便知道我身体有病；如果全树枯萎掉，就知道我是死了。"他说完便与父母兄弟一个一个搂着吻别，随即跟着乞士离开王宫。

王长子和乞士向着城外的密林走的时候，他们看见道旁有一群小狗。其中一只对母狗说："母亲，我愿意同那个美少年去。他定是一位王子。"母狗说："去吧。"小狗于是跟着王长子。王长子也很喜欢它。他们走不远，又看见道旁的树上有一群小鹰和一只母鹰歇着。其中一只小鹰对母鹰说："母亲，我愿意跟着那个美男子去。他定是国王的儿子。"母鹰也说："去吧。"小鹰于是飞下来

他每天早晨总得穿入密林里去采花回来给乞士

跟着王长子。现在在道上有乞士、王长子、小狗和小鹰四个生灵。他们最后来到一个远隔人烟的森林中，那里有一间小草舍，是乞士搭起来的。乞士对王长子说："你同我住在这小草舍里，这就是你的家了。你的主要工作就是每天早晨到林中去采取鲜花为我供献诸天之用。什么地方你都可以去，唯有北方你不能去。你若往北方去，厄运必临到你身上。林中的果子和根茎都可以随你的意采取来吃，喝的水可以从那边小溪汲取。"

王长子很不喜欢那孤寂的树林，更不喜欢乞士派给他的工作。他每天早晨总得穿入密林里去采花回来给乞士。那老人捧着花就到他礼拜的地方，一直到黄昏才回来。因此，王长子一天的工夫很闲。他时常带着他的小狗和小鹰在林中游行。有时他也用弓箭猎射野兽。林中的鹿很多，所以他唯一的生活便是用箭来射杀它们。有一天，他射中一只大鹿。鹿带着箭便往北飞跑，他忘记了乞士警告他的话，迈步便追。越追越远，至终不见那只大鹿。他穿过一所密林，只见一所非常美丽的房子在当前，他也不往前追鹿了。他走进大门，看见一个绝世的美人站在那里，身边还搁着一副骰子。女人看见王长子进来，见他只管站着用两只眼睛注视她，就对他说："客人，来吧，这是很好的机会使你来到我这里，在你未走之前，请与我掷掷骰子取乐吧。"王长子应许了她这样的要求，就坐在一边与她掷骰子。他们商议定了，如果女人输给王长子，她就得给他一只小鹰，如果王长子输了，也照样地给她。结果女人赢了，王长子就把小鹰给了她。王长子见把小鹰输了，于是要求再玩第二次，说如果她赢了，她可以得他的小狗。结果他又输了。结果王长子急起来，就求她再玩一次，说这次如果他输了他把全身给她，由她处置，如果她输了他也可以随意处置她。结果王长子又输了！她把小鹰、小狗和王长子分置在三个小洞里，用木板盖着他们。那女人本是一个罗刹所化的。她看见王长子，早已垂涎，不过她那天吃得很饱，所以留着他和他的两只小朋友，等到明天才来受用。

在王长子被拘的时候，宫中的树忽然凋谢起来，把父王和母后都惹哭了。王次子每天必要来观察那棵树，一看见树叶黄萎，知道他哥哥必有事故。他于是想跑去救他的哥哥。在离宫以前，他也种一棵树在院里。他也对他父母吩咐，如他哥哥从前所说的话一样。他从王的厩里选出一只很快的马，骑上去，就向树林奔来。在道上他看见一只母狗和一只小狗。那小狗看见王次子来，以为是从前带它哥哥走的人，就对他说："你从前把我的哥哥带走，现在也把我带走吧。"王次子理会他哥哥把小狗的哥哥带走，也就应许要与它同行。走不远，又遇见一只小鹰歇在道旁的树上，它看王次子也以为是从前那个人，就对他说："你从前把我的哥哥带走，现在也把我带走吧。"他于是又带着小鹰一同走。他同小鹰、小狗来到林中的草舍。不见他哥哥，也不见老乞士。他不晓得要怎么办，也不晓得要往哪里去才能找着他哥哥。他下了马，走进屋里去候着。到黄昏的时候，老乞士回来了。他看见王次子就对他说："你来了，我很高兴看见你。我对你哥哥说不要向树林北方去，他不听话，果然凶运临到他身上了。他到现在还没回来，一定是到北方被罗刹拿住了。那里住着一个罗刹女，时常伤害人畜，我想他一定在这时被吃掉了。我们没有法子救他。"

王次子听了，因为还有一点光明，就骑着马往北飞跑。他看见一只大鹿，就拔出箭来射它。鹿带着箭往前跑，王次子一直地追，追到一间美丽的房子，鹿也不见了。他下了马，走进门里，看见那个俊美的女人站在那里召呼他。她又请他掷骰子。王次子早已听过老乞士所说的话，知道她不是人。现在见她要求他耍骰子，就应许她，看她要耍什么手段。他们所议输赢的办法，都如与王长子所定的一样。第一次，王次子赢了，女人把鹰拿出来赔他。鹰兄见鹰弟自然非常喜欢。第二次女人又输了，她于是再把小狗拿出来赔他。第三次又是王次子赢，女人不能再找一个人与他一样，不得已便把王长子放出来。两兄弟相见非常喜悦。罗刹女知道王次子有非常的能力，就请求他说："求你不要杀我。我要告诉你一件秘密的事情是与你哥哥的性命有关的。"她于是告诉他们那老乞士是拜黑母迦梨的。她的庙就离草舍不远。老乞士是信与鬼魂交流的教派的，所以他已经杀过六个人为牺牲献给迦梨。他们的骷髅现在都挂在庵里。如果他再杀一个人为第七次的牺牲，他就能够完成他的圣事，成为一个完全的人。他要王长子，就是为做牺牲用的。罗刹女又叫王长子立刻到庙里去看是不是有六个骷髅挂在那里。

王长子一到庙里，果然看见六个骷髅。骷髅一见他进来，都发出奇怪的笑声。他对于这事很惊异，就问它们为什么笑。它们当中一个说："少年的王子，过几天，那乞士的修行就圆满了，你的头颅要在这庙里被他砍下来，为第七个牺牲，与我们同在一处。但是，你如不愿意，只有一条路可以避免，并且可以解救我们。"王长子问："哪一条路？请告诉我吧！我一定要尽我的所能来解救你们。"骷髅说："在乞士领你到这里来的时候，他必叫你先跪下，献你为活祭。他要叫你伏在迦梨面前，趁你不备，把你的头砍下来。我们告诉你，如果他叫你伏在迦梨面前，你就说你不懂，请他先做一次给你看。你说你是一个王子，不曾向什么人神俯过首，他自然要教你怎样做。你等他伏下的时候，就用刀把他的头割下来，那么，我们的生命就可以立刻恢复过来，乞士的愿望就永远不能成功。"王长子把骷髅对他说的记在心里，就和他弟弟回到乞士的草舍里。

过了几天，果然乞士要王长子同他到迦梨的庙里去礼拜，他也没把这次特别要带他去的理由说明，可是王长子早已知道了。他知道乞士一定要在那时用他为牺牲供献给迦梨。他们来到庙里，乞士就对王长子说："伏在女神面前礼拜她吧。"王长子回答说："我是一个王子，一向不曾向人行过伏拜礼，不晓得要怎样做。请你做一次给我看，我要照样地做。"乞士于是伏着做礼拜的姿势，王长子急用剑把他的头砍下来。六个骷髅在殿边立刻大笑起来。女神也赞赏王长子的功德，用她所许那乞士的福分转赐给他。他的功行算是圆成了。六个骷髅同时变成肉身。两个王子也回到他们的国里。

我的故事说到这里算完了，

那提耶棘也枯萎了。

那提耶呵，你为什么枯萎呢？

你的牛为什么要我用草来喂它？

牛呵，你为什么要人喂？

你的牧者，为什么不看护我？

牧者呵，你为什么不去看牛？

你的儿媳妇为什么不把米给我？

儿媳妇呵，你为什么不给米呢？

我的孩子为什么哭呢？

孩子呵，你为什么哭呢？

蚂蚁为什么要咬我呢？

蚂蚁呵，你为什么要咬人呢？

喀！喀！喀！

五

鬼
妻

从前有一个婆罗门人，娶了妻还与他母亲同住在一起。在他的房子附近有一个池子。池边有一棵树，一个女鬼散金尼住在那里。散金尼是一个白皙的女鬼魂，常于深夜站在树下，乍看见很像一幅白布悬着。有一晚上，婆罗门人的妻子因事到池边去。她经过树下，不意触犯了散金尼。女鬼于是对她发怒，就把她的喉咙叉着，到大树边，把她扔在树洞里头。妇人在洞里吓得几乎死去，动也不能动，只是躺着。女鬼把妇人的衣服脱下来，自己穿上，慢慢地来到婆罗门人家里。婆罗门人和他的母亲都不理会这个变故，他想着妻子是从池边来，他母亲还以为来的是她儿媳妇。

第二天早晨，母亲发现那女子不像她儿媳妇，她知道她儿媳妇的体格很弱，做事很慢。可是现在她完全改变了，她的身体也不见得疲弱，她做事很快，老婆子不作声，她不把这事告诉儿子，也不盘问她的儿媳妇，她只庆幸她儿媳妇已经变为一个新人。不到几天，老婆子的怀疑越来越大。不但她儿媳妇近来饭做得很快，即使叫她到隔屋去取东西，在平常人还没走到的时候，她已经取来了。因为鬼灵是不用走的，他要往远处取东西，只伸长手臂就可以。她的四肢都有伸缩的能力。她的身体也能够透过墙壁，不必从门户出入。她这样的行为，有一天被老婆子看见了。她叫儿媳妇拿一个盘子来。那盘子本离她很远，她无意中就伸长手臂去把它取来。她这

有一晚上，婆罗门人的妻子因事到池边去，当她经过树下时，不小心触犯了散金尼

样做了两三次。老婆子看见这怪事，也不作声。自此以后母子俩就很注意那妇人的行为。有一天，老婆子明知屋里没有火，她儿媳妇也没出去取火，很奇怪的是她看见有火焰从灶里冒出来。她跑进厨房，看见她儿媳妇并没用火煮饭，只把她的脚放在灶里，火焰就从那里冒出来。母亲把所见的告诉她儿子。于是他们断定那女人不是他们的媳妇，乃是一个鬼魂。

儿子也看出她不是一个人，他所看见的也和他母亲所见的一样。他就去请了一位驱鬼的巫师来。巫师要试验她是不是鬼灵，就用郁金香在她的鼻下烧着。这种试验是很准的，因为无论是男鬼或女鬼，都不能闻郁金香的烟味。巫师把郁金香点着，拿近她身边的时候，她便大声嚷起来，往外逃走。现在全屋的人都知道她若不是女鬼，便是被鬼灵附体的女人。巫师把她拿住，问她到底是什么人物。她最初不肯说出来，巫师就要用鞋底来打她。鬼说话时，声音常从鼻子发出来。这次她的声音完全带着鼻音，说她是住在池边树上的散金尼，她把婆罗门人的妻子扔在树洞里，因为在一天晚上，那女人触犯了她。她说现在若到树洞去把她扶出来，还可以使她复活。

婆罗门人赶快到树洞里将妻子救出来。她已经半死，不省人事，用了许久的工夫才把她救活了。女鬼被巫师用鞋底掌了很多下，用符咒来魇她，不许她再侵扰婆罗门人的家庭。她都发誓了，巫师才放她走。自此以后，婆罗门人的妻子渐渐强健起来。他们同住着，以后生了许多子息，同过愉快的日子。

我的故事说到这里算完了，

那提耶棘也枯萎了。

那提耶呵，你为什么枯萎呢？

你的牛为什么要我用草来喂它？

牛呵，你为什么要人喂？

你的牧者，为什么不看护我？

牧者呵，你为什么不去看牛？

你的儿媳妇为什么不把米给我？

儿媳妇呵，你为什么不给米呢？

我的孩子为什么哭呢？

孩子呵，你为什么哭呢？

蚂蚁为什么要咬我呢？

蚂蚁呵，你为什么要咬人呢？

喀！喀！喀！

六　鬼友

从前有一个地方住着一对穷婆罗门人夫妻。丈夫不能得着谋生之道，只以挨门挨户求乞度日。他们有时乞些米，再到田中捡些青菜回来煮着吃。过了些时间，他们所住的村落换了主人，婆罗门人想着到新地主那里去求乞，或者可以得着一点东西，在一个早晨，他就到地主那里去。那时，新地主正问着他的仆人村中一切的情形。仆人告诉他村外有一棵榕树，被群鬼所据，晚间没有一个人敢从那里经过。从前曾有些轻率的人夜间到那里去，他们的脖子都被群鬼扭断而死。自从那时，没有人敢在夜间到那里去，可是白天倒很平安，牧童们都在树下看牛。新地主很好奇，他出了一个赏格说，如果有人能在夜间把那榕树的枝砍一枝下来，他必要用一百亩地送他，不要他的田税，作为酬报。仆人中没有一个敢承领这事，他们都知道若在晚间到那里去，必定会被群鬼害死。婆罗门人坐在一边，听见地主发出这样的赏格，就自己说："我现在几乎饿得要死了。我自生来，未尝吃过一顿饱足的饭。如果我到榕树那里去，能够砍下一枝树枝来，我就可以得着一百亩不纳租税的田地，我就可以独立谋生了。如果群鬼把我害死，我也不觉得坏，与其挨饿而死，不如被鬼杀掉更为痛快。"他于是对地主说他愿意承纳这个赏格，要在夜间到榕树那里去砍一枝树枝来给他。地主又对他说，如果他能办得到，他一定画出一百亩不纳租税的地来给他。

全村的人听见婆罗门人要在夜间去砍树枝都为他悲悯。他们说他太笨，没来由自己跑去寻死。他的妻子也不赞同他的主意，但也没法阻止他。他说无论如何，他终归是要死的，这个机会，或者可以使他逃掉死亡的羁勒而成为一个独立生活的人。在日落后一小时，婆罗门人就出去了。他走到村外，也不害怕，一直来到一棵薄拘罗树下，那里离群鬼聚集的榕树只有一箭左右。他起首战栗，站在薄拘罗树下动也不能动。他的心上下跳动得很厉害，好像摇炒米的踏板一样。那棵薄拘罗树下也有一个婆罗摩戴特耶鬼灵。婆罗摩戴特耶是没曾结过婚而死的婆罗门人的鬼灵。那鬼灵看见婆罗门人在树下颤着，就对他说："婆罗门人，你害怕么？请你告诉我你愿意做什么事情，我要帮助你。我是一个婆罗摩戴特耶。"婆罗门人回答他说："多福的精灵呀，我愿意到那棵榕树下把它的枝砍一枝下来给村长。我若能办到这事，村长应许给我一百亩不纳租税的田地。可是现在我胆怯起来，走也走不动了。如果你能帮助我做这件事，我就很感谢你。"鬼灵回答他说："婆罗门人我自然要帮助你。到那树下去吧，我也陪你去。"婆罗门人靠着他那鬼友的力量一直往前走。婆罗摩戴特耶鬼灵为群鬼所敬畏，所以婆罗门人与他同行一定不会受群鬼的侵害。他到了树下就用刀砍树枝。他一砍下去的时候，许多鬼怪都集拥来难为他。群鬼看见婆罗摩戴特耶站在一边，都不敢十分嬲他，鬼灵对群鬼发出命令

他到树下砍下第一刀的时候，就有许多鬼怪过来要难为他

式的语言说："鬼灵，你们都听着。这是一个穷乏的婆罗门人。他要从榕树砍一枝来，那是于他很有用处的。我要你们容他砍一枝下来。"群鬼听见鬼灵的声音，都回答说："我们的主，我们依从你的意旨。在你的意思之下，我们愿意为你效劳。容那个婆罗门人歇着，我们替他砍下一枝来给他就是了。"说着，它们在一瞬间已把树枝砍下来交到婆罗门人手里。他得着树枝，乘夜飞跑进村里去见村长。村长和村人看见那树枝，都不觉得奇怪，后来，村长就说："好吧，到明天早晨我再去看看这是不是从那棵树上砍下来的。如果你真是从那树上把这枝砍下来，我当然要将所应许的田地给你。"

第二天早晨，村长就和仆人们一同到村外那棵榕树下。他们很惊讶地证实了昨晚上婆罗门人砍下来的树枝是属于那多鬼聚集的榕树的。村长对于这事很满意，就把一百亩田地给他。婆罗门人因此成为村里数一数二的富豪。

婆罗门人所得的一百亩地立刻就可以收成，因为田上的庄稼都已成熟了。他忽然得着那么些地，身边一个钱也没有，自然不能置备农具来收获。他要怎么办呢？他又跑到他的鬼友那里，说："婆罗摩戴特耶呀，我很失意。因你的恩惠，使我得着一百亩不纳租税的田地，可是田上的庄稼都已成熟，我没有一件农具，叫我怎样收获呢？我是一个穷人。我应当怎样办呢？"他的鬼友回答他说：

"婆罗门人哪，不要为这事伤悲。我不但可以使你看见庄稼都从田上收割下来，并且不费力地使它们送进仓里，把稻草也堆起来。你只要做一件事就可以。今晚上，你去向邻舍借一百把钩镰，把它们放在这树底下。你还要预备存贮五谷和堆积稻草的地方。"婆罗门人非常欢喜。他很容易就把一百把钩镰借出来，因为村人都看他为财主，凡他所求无不应许。黄昏以后，他把钩镰拿去放在薄拘罗树下，他又选择了存贮五谷和堆积稻草地方的。他把那些地方的牛粪和秽物洗刷干净以后，就回到自己的家里睡觉去了。

那一晚上，当所有的村人都回家歇息的时候，鬼友到榕树那里去叫一百个鬼灵收庄稼。他说："你们今晚当为婆罗门人收庄稼，他是我的朋友。他从村长那里领来的一百亩地已经到了收获的时候，可是他没有器具，也没有人工去做这事。今晚上你们必得为他去做。这里有一百把钩镰，你们每人拿一把到田里去为他收割。你们每人收割一亩，还要将庄稼搬到他所预备地方存贮起来，把稻草也堆起来。现在就去吧，不要耽误时间。你们在今夜须得把一切的事做得妥贴才好。"一百个鬼灵对鬼友说："凡我们的主所命令的，我们必要照办。"他们说完就到田里去。鬼友把婆罗门人的住处指示给群鬼知道，并且告诉那存放庄稼和稻草的地方。他又领他们到那一百亩田地那里去。他们于是都在田上工作起来。鬼灵的收获是与人不同的。人割一天鬼灵只要一分时间就可以。镰刀割截的声音在田中大响起来，不一会儿，所有稻秆都倒下来了。他们把五谷起来，一捆一捆放在背上，扛到婆罗门人所预备的地方。他们在那里立时把五谷打下来，再把稻草堆在一边。乘夜又为他盖了一座很大的仓廪。他们从收获到运谷入仓，只用了几小时的工夫，到太阳要出来以前两小时，一切的工作都完了。他们各自回到榕树那里歇息。第二天早晨，婆罗门人和他的妻子看见这奇事，自然喜出望外。他们把这事述说给全村的人听，并且指示他们那鬼盖的仓廪。村人都不明白这是什么缘故，他们以为是诸天的恩赐。

过了几天，婆罗门人又到薄拘罗树下去找他的鬼友，求他说："婆罗摩戴特耶呀，我还有一件事要求你帮助。因为诸天加我许多恩惠，我愿意供养一千个婆罗门人。现在我要求你为我预备些材料。"鬼友说："我很喜欢为你预备。我必要供给你足以供养一千个婆罗门人的材料，你只需指示我那存放物件的地方就可以。"婆罗门人于是预备一个库房，指示给他的鬼友知道。在宴会前一晚上，库房里忽然堆满了一切应用的东西。那里放着一百罐酥酪，一百罐糖，一百罐牛乳，一百罐酪浆，一百罐凝乳，一大堆面粉，还有许多吃的东西。那些食物足够供养一千以上的婆罗门人。第二天早晨，他又雇了一百个婆罗门制饼师来预备筵宴。所有的婆罗门人都吃得饱足，唯有主人一点也不吃，他想与他的鬼友一同吃。他的鬼友那天也在那里，不过人看不见他。鬼友对他说人鬼是不能同吃的，所以他只得自己吃了些。

他和鬼友投契的缘分已尽了。财神鸠　罗派车子来接鬼友上天去，他自此以后，就不做鬼了。婆罗门人在地上享受了很多年的愉快生活。他的子孙绕满膝前，一家人很安乐地住在村里。

我的故事说到这里算完了，

那提耶棘也枯萎了。

那提耶呵，你为什么枯萎呢？

你的牛为什么要我用草来喂它？

牛呵，你为什么要人喂？

你的牧者，为什么不看护我？

牧者呵，你为什么不去看牛？

你的儿媳妇为什么不把米给我？

儿媳妇呵，你为什么不给米呢？

我的孩子为什么哭呢？

孩子呵，你为什么哭呢？

蚂蚁为什么要咬我呢？

蚂蚁呵，你为什么要咬人呢？

喀！喀！喀！

七

绿

珠

绿珠是一种鹦鹉的名字。它是美丽的绿鹦鹉的一种，产于东印度摩洛迦岛，本地人叫它"希罗摩尼"，意思是"绿色的宝珠"。

　　从前有一个捕鸟的人与他的妻子同住在一起。妻子有一天对她的丈夫说："我亲爱的，我告诉你，我们时常陷在贫乏的境地的缘故是因为你把黏得的鸟都卖出去，如果你有时把自己获得的鸟宰来吃，你一定会逢着好运气。我请你今天出去胶鸟，无论得着什么种类，都不要拿去卖，我们留着自己吃。"丈夫听从他妻子的话，就出门到林中去胶鸟。他手里拿着一枚涂 的长竿，同他妻子从一个树林经过一个树林，都无所得，一天的工夫他们尽在树林里走来走去，一直到黄昏还胶不上半只鸟儿。他们很懊恼地向着归途前进。在道上恰巧给他们黏上一只美丽的绿珠鹦鹉。妻子把鸟拿在手里，心里非常不满足，说："这鸟是多么小！我们能够在它身上得着多少肉来吃呢？杀了它也是无用的。"绿珠对她说："母亲哪，求你不要杀我，把我送到王那里去卖，你们必定能够得着许多钱财。"夫妇听见鹦鹉的话说得很自然，知道是可贵的鸟，就问它他们应当要多少价。绿珠说："把这事交给我吧，你只把我送到王那里，如果王问你的价钱多少，你可以说，'这鸟自己会说出它的价值，'我就可以为你们要求许多钱财。"

　　捕鸟的人在第二天早晨就带着绿珠到王宫去卖。王看见那美丽的小鸟就问他要多少价钱。他说："大王，这鸟自己会说出它的价值。"王惊讶地问："什么！这鸟能够说话么？"捕鸟人说："不错，我的君主，请你问它的价值该得多少。"王一半当开玩笑，一半当真，就向着小鸟说："好吧，绿珠，你的代价是多少？"绿珠回答说："大王，我的代价是一万卢比。请你不要以为这价格太高，快把钱如数付给捕鸟人吧。我将要伺候你，为你做很大的事体。"王问它："你能为我做什么事呢？"绿珠回答说："大王，以后你便知道。"王觉得小鸟所说的话像很有知识的，就命人打开他的宝藏，取出一万卢比交给捕鸟人。

王有六位王后，自从得了鹦鹉以后，对于她们的情爱就淡薄了。他每日每夜都和绿珠在一块，不到王后们那里去。绿珠不但能够回答王所问一切的话，并且能够背诵印度神庙里三百三十兆位天神的名字。一个人有幸能够背诵和能够静听那么些名字实在是一种最敬信的功业。六位王后见王不大眷顾她们，自然妒嫉小鸟夺了她们从王得来的宠爱。她们立意要害死绿珠，可是老没得机会，因为它时常在王身边，片刻不离王的左右。

王的猎期到了，他得住在林中，要离宫两天。六位王后于是决定要利用这个机会来把绿珠杀死。王去了以后，她们彼此说："我们都到那小鸟面前去问它，我们当中谁是最丑的吧。如果它说哪个

071

最丑，哪一个就动手伤害它的性命，把它捏死。"她们于是来到王的屋里，那鹦鹉正挂在当中。绿珠见她们进来，便背诵三百三十兆位天神的名字，把她们的心都软化了。她们听了，各人现着慈心出来，没有实行她们进来屋里的原意。第二天，她们的恶念又复兴起，想着她们昨天实在太愚拙，被小鸟骗了。她们商定今天无论如何，总得把它害死，不然，王在明天就要回来了。她们来到屋里，一齐问它："绿珠，你是一只最聪明的鸟，我们听说你的判断是很准的。请你现在说在我们当中，谁是最美，谁是最丑的。"绿珠早知道她们不怀好意，就对她们说："我在笼里怎能回答你们的问题呢？如果要得着一个公正的判断，我必得出去把你们身体的上下前后仔细地观察一遍才可以。你们若是要得我的意见，就请放我出来，容我仔细地观察你们。"王后们起先怕放了它出来，它就飞走，后来她们想着不如把窗户都关起来，再把笼开了。绿珠四围一看，知道还有房角一条水道没有被她们堵住，它就从笼里安然走出来。诸位王后问了它好几次，它只是前后上下一个一个地观察她们。最后它说："你们当中，谁也不见得很美。你们的美丽远不如在七海十三河那边一位贵女的小脚趾那么可人哪。"六位王后听见它这样花言巧语，各人都愤怒起来，要把它拿来撕碎。绿珠眼快，不等她们的手伸到，它已从水道钻出去，飞到附近一个樵夫家里躲避起来。

第二天，王从猎场回宫，不见了绿珠，心里非常难过。他问几位王后绿珠往哪里去。她们都推脱说不知道。王为那小鸟哭了一日一夜，因为他非常喜爱它。宰相劝他不要过于伤心，国事比较重要得多。可是王时刻哭着说："绿珠，我的绿珠呀！你到哪里去了？"宰相见他如此，就请他出个赏格，希望可以再把那小鸟找回来。王于是布告四城及全国，如能把绿珠送回王宫来，他必得一万卢比的酬报。樵夫想着一个人独立的生活，于是把那小鸟送回王宫，得着他的报酬。王从绿珠探出日前的事，知道王后们存心要杀害他宝贝的小鸟，就很生气。他命人把六位王后驱逐出宫，把她们送到荒野里，不许人送东西给她们吃。王后们在荒野中，不到几天都被野兽吞噬了。

过了些日子，王偶然问起他的绿珠，说："绿珠，你说我那六位王后的美丽远不如住在七海十三河那边一位贵女的脚趾那么好看。你能够让我见见她么？我能得着那贵人么？"

绿珠回答说："我自然可以让你见着她。我可以领你到她所住的宫廷。不过你得听我的指导，我才有法子使你能够搂着她。"

王说："我一定听从你一切的指导。你愿意我做什么呢？"

"我们需要一匹天马。你如能得着这鸟王马种，就可以骑着它飞过七海十三河一直到那贵女的宫阙。"绿珠对王这样说。

王说："你知道我养了许多马，都在大马厩里拴着，我们就去看看那里有天马没有。"

王和绿珠走到马厩去相马。绿珠相了半天，看过许多好马，壮大的，美丽的，种种不等，都不满意。最后它看见一匹瘦弱并且长得很不好看的小马，就对王说："这就是我要找的天马。它是真正的鸟王马种，不过没人注意豢养它，致使它现出瘦弱的形态。你可以命人用精细食料养它，六个月后就能用了。"王就命人搜集国中一切饲马的精细食料来养那匹瘦马。小马一天强似一天，到了第六个月，果然是一匹天马。绿珠对王说天马已可应用，王还得命人预备许多银制的炒米。王于是命银匠加工赶造多量的银米。不久，一切都预备妥了。王骑在马上，绿珠歇在王的肩膀上。绿珠对王说："我没有什么要告诉你的了。只有一件事情要请你注意，就是这天马只许一鞭就可以到达那位贵女那里，如果你多鞭一下这马便要立刻停在中途，一步也走不动。我们回来的时候也是一鞭就够了。如果你多鞭它一下，它就在中途停住，我们和那贵女必要落在地上，走路回国。"王把绿珠所说的记住，带了银米就扬鞭启行。天马受了一鞭，便往空中飞行，好像风驰电掣一般。他们在一瞬间经过许多城邑国土，又经过七海十三河，到黄昏时分已来到一座宫门口。

那宫门的建筑是极华丽的。

在宫门附近有一棵很高的树。绿珠告诉王把马牵入宫外那间马厩里拴着，它和他爬上树顶去藏着。绿珠用喙把银米一粒一粒从口袋里啄出来，使它们落在树根上头。它又含着银米从树边一直散布到宫里，连那贵女的卧室前头也被碎银铺满了。它要用这事引起那美人的好奇心。做完之后，它便飞回王所藏的那棵高树上头去。在中夜的时候，住在贵女隔厢的侍女想去园里散步，就开了房门出来。她立刻发现地上满铺了银屑。她捡了些起来，因为不知道它们是从哪里来的，就拿进去问她的女主人。贵女觉得那些银米很可爱，立时同侍女出来捡。她们看见地上的银屑一直铺到很远，就循着那条道走，一直来到宫门外的树下。

美人一直到树下，王便听从绿珠的指导急从树上跳下来，把她搂住。王把她抱到马厩里，骑上天马，加上一鞭，马已在空中飞行，像闪电一般。绿珠歇在王的肩膀上，正在庆贺王的成功，王心急要回宫看看那美人的真面目，不意多鞭了一下。绿珠不及阻止，马已从空中落下来，不能再走了。绿珠嚷着说："大王，你干的什么事！我不是告诉过你，只要一鞭就够了么？现在你又鞭它一下，我们就不能往前走了！我们将要死在这里。"王已经做了，没法挽回，他不得已就抱着女人下了马。他们落下的地方正是一个大树林，四围一点人烟也没有。他们饿了就找树根和野果来吃，晚间就躺在地上睡。

第二天早晨，可巧那国的王出来打猎，他追一只带着箭的鹿来到王和贵女跟前。国王看见那样美丽的女子自然起了贪爱的心，把她抢去，他又把那在难中的王的双眼弄瞎了，容他在树林里活着。他的侍从很多，不一会儿都来到，拥着美人去了。王在林中，只靠着绿珠每天飞去采取食物来养他。

贵女和那匹天马被擒到宫里，那国的王要立她为后，但她应许六个月后才能答应他的要求。王不能违反这个风俗，就应许等她到六个月。她知道天马的鞭伤需要六个月才能复原，每天礼拜以后，就到厩里调护那匹天马。可是天马恢复了也不中用，因为她自己一个人很难离开宫里，宫中的人时刻都注意她的行为。她想着非得绿珠的帮助，她必不能脱离现在的景况。想了又想，她就命宫人去预备许多种饲鸟的材料，每天撒在庭园当中，为的是引动群鸟来啄食。所有附近树林的鸟都集聚在宫苑里享受贵女的布施。但她最注意的是要找出绿珠，看看它在不在鸟群里头啄食饲料。绿珠原来是她的鸟。它现在在林中伺候那位瞎眼的爱者，心里难受已极。它每天总要为王啄些果子，然后自己飞去觅食。

有一天，别的鸟看见绿珠那么忙碌，就对它说："绿珠呀，你为什么尽在林中自行觅食？这是多么苦恼呢？你为什么不飞到宫里去享受那贵女的施舍呢？她的庭院和房顶天天都撒满了东西来供给我们，你为什么不去呢？我们一早飞去，晚上才飞回来，一天同着千千万万的同类啄食，多么清闲，多么快乐啊！"绿珠听了，打算明早同群鸟飞到宫中享受贵女的布施，且希望能够带一点回来给它的瞎主人吃。

绿珠一飞到宫苑，就看见它的女主人。立刻飞到她身边，同她谈了很久。她和小鸟商量怎样才能够把王的眼睛治好，怎样才能逃脱。

天马的伤痕经过六个月已经恢复了。绿珠告诉王说他的眼睛只有毗韩笈摩的粪可以治。贵女宫门前头那棵树上现在住着一对那样的神鸟，可是隔着七海十三河的路途，怎么办呢？它想着它可以飞到那里去把神鸟的粪取来。第二天早晨，它对瞎主人说明白，一直飞到七海十三河外去含了一片叶子，裹着些有气味、鲜热的鸟粪，来把王的眼睛敷上。不一会儿，王的眼睛复明了。过了几天，贵女骑着天马飞到林中把王和绿珠带走。

他们很喜悦地回到自己的国土。不久，王便和她结婚，他们一同过了很长的愉快生活。绿珠也时常在他们身边解答一切的问题，并且背诵三百三十兆位天神的名字。

贵女、国王、绿珠和天马他们都很喜悦地平安回到国王的国土

我的故事说到这里算完了，

那提耶棘也枯萎了。

那提耶呵，你为什么枯萎呢？

你的牛为什么要我用草来喂它？

牛呵，你为什么要人喂？

你的牧者，为什么不看护我？

牧者呵，你为什么不去看牛？

你的儿媳妇为什么不把米给我？

儿妇媳呵，你为什么不给米呢？

我的孩子为什么哭呢？

孩子呵，你为什么哭呢？

蚂蚁为什么要咬我呢？

蚂蚁呵，你为什么要咬人呢？

喀！喀！喀！

八　红宝石

从前有一个国，国王死后留下王后和四位王子。王后极疼爱第四个王子。她用最华丽的衣服给他穿，把最驯良的马给他骑；做香馥的饭给他吃；供给最精致的器具给他用。其余三个王子看见他们的母后这么偏心，各人都很嫉妒第四个王子。他们商定把四弟和母亲都撵出宫，占据了他们一切的东西。

第四个王子被撵后，就与他母亲同住。因为王后太过娇养他，致使他对于一切的事情都很任性。有一天，他同王后到河里去洗澡。岸边泊着一只很大的空船，因为里头没人，四王子就爬上船，还叫他母亲也上去。他母亲认为他不应当上别人的船，叫他快点下来。他回答说："母亲，我不下来，我要照着这条水路出外去咧。你如果愿意同我去，就请快些上来，不然我在一瞬间就要起锚了。"王后一直走到船边叫他下来。他不听话，就到船头去起锚。王后急急地上船，不一会儿，船就离岸了。他驶着大船，顺流而下。船走得好像箭一般快，随着潮流一直出了洋海。在汪洋上越漂越远，最终他们驶近一个漩涡。王子看见许多红宝石在那漩涡的附近漂流着。那些红宝石都是非常大块的，世人不曾见过的。每颗宝石都值得七个王所拥的财产。王子捞了五六颗起来，放在船上。他的母亲说："我的宝贝，不要把那些红球捞起来，它们是属于别人的。也许是商船在此地沉没了，这是商人的货物，你拿了，人家必以我们为贼。”因为王后的劝勉，他就把捞得的宝石抛回海中，自己只留着一颗，暗藏在怀里。船走了一会儿，已经近岸他和母亲就上了岸。

　　船泊的地方乃是一所大城，是一国的王都。离宫廷不远的地方，王后和她儿子赁了一间第屋住下。王子还是一个孩子，所以很喜欢作石子戏。那国的王子有时也从宫里出来玩，我们的王子也和他们在一起。王子并没有大理石做的小球，他只好用捞得的那颗红宝石来玩。红宝石的质地很坚强，别的石球被它打中，没有不破的。王女有时也从宫里的壁厢看他们游戏。她看见王子所玩的那块红宝石，心里非常喜爱它，想把它要过来。她告诉她的父王，说街上那个孩子有一颗大红宝石，她非要来不可，不然她就要不吃而死。王本很疼爱他的女儿，听见她的要求，便命人把王子叫来。王子来到王面前，把红宝石给他看。王也很诧异他得着那么大的宝石，无怪他女儿非要过来不可。他真是不曾见过那么大的宝石。他也怀疑世界诸国的君王是否也曾拥有这样的宝贝。他问王子从什么地方得来的。王子说是从海上捞起来的。王给了一千卢比的价，要从他买过来。孩子不晓得宝石的价值，就答应了。他拿着一千卢比来给他母亲。母亲惊讶起来，以为他是到什么富人家去偷来的，后来她才相信那些钱是王付给他那红宝石的代价。

鹦鹉对公主说："你看哪里有一个公主只戴一颗红宝石在头上的？"

王女得着那红宝石就用来装饰她的头发，她的身边有一只驯熟的鹦鹉。王女问她的小鸟说："我的宝贝鹦鹉，我戴这红宝石在头上，衬着我的头发，是不是很好看呢？"鹦鹉回答她说："真好看！不过有一点不顺眼！你看哪里有一个公主只戴一颗红宝石在头上的？如果你再能得一颗，那就好看得多了。你最少得有两颗才可以。"王女听见鹦鹉的批评，心里觉得一颗宝石实在不够美丽。她于是跑到宫中的忧郁室里去，在那里，不吃也不喝。那国的王宫有一间忧郁室，凡宫里的人有什么不幸的境遇，不愿意将愁容对着别的宫人的，都到那里去发泄自己的悲哀。王一听见他的女儿到忧郁室去，立刻来到她跟前，问她为什么事悲伤。王女把鹦鹉的话告诉给王听，且说："父亲哪，你如果不能再得一颗这么大的宝石来给我，我就要在此地自杀。"王听见她的要求，心中自然很难过。他想他从哪里再能得着一颗那么大的红宝石呢？他怀疑世间还有第二颗那么大的红宝石。至终，他想着不如再把那孩子叫来，问他还有没有。

"少年人，你还有像前口卖给我那么大的红宝石么？"王这样问。

"没有了，我只有一颗。你真想再要一颗么？如果你要它，我可以拿许多块来给你。它们都在海上一个漩涡中漂流着咧。那漩涡离此地虽然很远，如果你真愿意要，我可以为你捞许多回来。"王子这样对王说。

王听见他的话，应许他如果他能再得着另一颗红宝石与前天他所卖的那颗一般大，他就要重重地赏他。

孩子回到家里，对他母亲说他必要再出海去采取红宝石。他母亲自然不许他去，可是他已经决定他的意志，没有人能阻止他。他自己上了原来那只船就出海去了。他把船驶到漩涡那里，看见许多红宝石还是漂流着。这次他把船驶到漩涡中心，看看红宝石到底是怎样出来的。他到漩涡中心的时候，看见当中有一个深洞达到海底。他从那里下去，由着那只船在水面旋转。

他到了海底，看见一所很华丽的宫阙，就走进去。在正殿当中坐着湿婆，闭着眼睛，像深入禅定的状态。在湿婆的头上几尺的距离有一个平台，那里躺着一个绝世的美人。

他上到平台去，才发现那美人的头是与身不相连的！他看见了，非常害怕，不晓得要怎样办。他理会从她的头的断处，一滴一滴的血不断地滴出来。血点滴在湿婆的头上，立刻变成很大的红宝石，一颗一颗浮上水面。不久，王子发现那美人的头旁边放着一支金杖和一支银杖。他拿起金杖来触那头颅，美人的身首忽然连合起。她坐起来，看见王子站在身边，就对她表示忧虑。她说："不

王子与那美人一同浮上海面，上了船，装上红宝石满载而归

幸的少年，快点离开这里吧。如果等到湿婆从他的禅定起来，他必用他的眼睛把你烧成白灰。"

王子虽然知道他有危险，可是他非要那美人同他一起走不可。他已经爱上了她，不能离开她。至终他与那美人一同浮上海面，上了船，把红宝石满载而归。他母亲得着那个美人来做儿媳妇，心里自然万分愉快。第二天早晨，王子命仆人把一大篮红宝石送到王宫去。王得着这样无价的礼物就非常喜欢。王女看见那少年拥有那么些红宝石，就请求父王把她配给王子。王子虽然有了从海底娶来的妻子，现在因为王的命令，又得再行一次婚礼。他同两个妻子住着，生子生孙，过了许多年的愉快生活。

　我的故事说到这里算完了，

　那提耶棘也枯萎了。

　那提耶呵，你为什么枯萎呢？

　你的牛为什么要我用草来喂它？

　牛呵，你为什么要人喂？

　你的牧者，为什么不看护我？

　牧者呵，你为什么不去看牛？

　你的儿媳妇为什么不把米给我？

儿媳妇呵，你为什么不给米呢？

我的孩子为什么哭呢？

孩子呵，你为什么哭呢？

蚂蚁为什么要咬我呢？

蚂蚁呵，你为什么要咬人呢？

喀！喀！喀！

九

豹
媒

从前有一个织工，他祖上的家境本来很富裕，但到他父亲手里就淫邪放纵起来，把所有的家财都花尽了。他出生的地方在一所很华美的房子，但现在他只住在一间破烂不堪的茅舍。他的父母已经死掉，也没有什么亲戚。离他的茅舍不远有一个豺的巢穴。那豺很聪明，知道织工的祖先本是很富裕的，它常对他现在的境遇表示同情。有一天它跑到织工跟前，对他说："织工，朋友，我觉得你现在的生活是很不幸的，我有意要让你的生活丰裕。我要让你和这国的公主结婚。"织工说："让我做国王的女婿么！如果太阳从西方升上，从东方下去，或者有我的福分！"豺见他不信，就说："你怀疑我的能力么？你等着吧，我必定为你办到这事。"

因为王城离豺的巢穴很远，所以豺在第二天一清早就启程到王宫去。在道上，它经一个种槟榔和蒌叶的园子。它采了些许蒌叶，含着往前走。一到王城，它就躲来躲去，所以人民没发现它来到王宫。在宫前有一个池子，王和宫人早晚都要到那里去沐浴。豺一到池边的道上就躺下。正在那时，王女和她的侍女出来洗澡。她看见豺横卧在道上，也不惊慌，只命侍女把它撵走。豺装作刚睡醒的样子站立起来，也不走，把方才带来的蒌叶放在嘴里大嚼起来。王女和侍女从来没见过畜生也会嚼槟榔和蒌叶的，现在看见豺这样做，自然非常诧异。他们心里想："这是一只多么不凡的豺呢！它

豺装作刚睡醒的样子站立起来，并把方才自己带来的姜叶放在嘴里大嚼起来

是从哪国来的呢？豺也会嚼蒌叶！从这事，就可以想象那国的人民一定是很富裕的，连豺也嚼起蒌叶来。它一定是从一个富裕的地方来的。"王女于是走到豺的面前问它："西婆卢，你是从哪一国来的？那国定然是很富裕，不然怎么连豺也能嚼蒌叶呢？""西婆卢"是印度人给豺的别名。它一听见公主这样问，便回答说："最敬爱的公主，我是从那出乳和蜜的国土来的。蒌叶和槟榔在我们的国里非常之多，好像你这国里田原上的杂草一样丰盛。在我们的国里，所有的畜生——牛、羊、狗、马等——都会嚼蒌叶。我们毋须再要别的好东西吃。"王女说："这样的国，实在是康乐呀。人民享受那么些天产还能够留给畜生们受用。那国的王统治一个丰盛的国土一定是加三倍的愉快。"豺说："我们的王是世界的王中最富有的。他的宫殿直如天上因陀罗的宫殿。我看你们现在住的宫廷，和我们王的住处比较起来，你们的直如草舍一般。"

王女的好奇心被激发起来，潦草地洗了一个澡，就跑到她母后那里去，对她述说方才池边那只豺所说的话。王后也很惊奇，就命人把豺带到她面前。豺一面走，一面嚼着蒌叶，故意显示它有这样阔绰的习惯。王后问它："我听说你是从一个丰盛的国土来的，我问你，你国的王曾娶过王后没？"豺很郑重地说："王后陛下，我们的王还不曾结婚，许多国王从远地遣使来要将公主许配他，他都把人家推辞了。如果哪一位得着我们国王的眷恋，她一定是世间一个极快乐的女人。"王后问它："西婆卢，你看我的女儿是不是好像天女一样俊美，她是不是该嫁给这世间最尊贵的王？"豺回答说："我也这样想。公主果真是非常俊美，我实在不曾见过一个女人像她那么好看。不过我不知道我们的王喜欢她不喜欢。"王后说："肯定喜欢我的女儿！你只要将你所见的对他说，他一定就爱上她。我的女儿，不用亲眼看见，凡听见她的美丽的，都要为爱而发狂，你晓得么？西婆卢，我实在地对你说，我很愿意我的女儿早一点嫁出去。从前也曾有许多王子来求婚，我都不愿意将她嫁给其中的无论哪一个，因为他们都不是大国国王的儿子。你的国王好像是一个大国的君王，如果他肯，我必愿意认他为女婿。"王后说完，命人去把王请来与豺会面。豺把它的国王的富裕和威权又重复说了一遍。王听了，也很愿意将女儿许配给他。他们都请豺去做媒。

豺回郊外，到织工那里去，对他说："织坊君主，你是世间最幸福的人！一切的事情我都为你办妥了，你不久就是国王的女婿了。我对他们说你是一位大国的王，所以你要显出一个国王应有的威仪。你当听我的指导，不然不但你的幸运来不到，连我们的性命也有危险。"织工答说："好，我一定听从你的指导。"豺在它心里已经有了介绍织工到宫里去的计划。过了几天，它又跑到王宫去，嚼着荄叶，躺在池边的道上。王和王后看见它来，都很欢喜，走来问它事情办得怎样。豺说："我已将这事对我们的王说了，看那样子，大概有九成可以成功。如果你知道我曾费了多少心神去鼓励我的国王与你的女儿结婚，你就应当不尽地感谢我。他起先不愿意，后来我极力劝他，他才应许了。现在你只要择定一个吉日举行大礼就成了。可是现在我要以朋友的身份告诉你一件事，我的君主是一个大国的王，如果他排列他的仪仗，领着他的侍从、他的象、马来到你这里，恐怕你的宫廷和都城都容不下。所以我要对我的主人劝说，请他不要用一切的仪仗，只是他自己一个人带几个侍从来到，作私下的探访，你可以用你的仪仗、象、马，去郊外迎接他到宫里来。"王说："有智的西婆卢，谢谢你的指导。在这小城里，我实在不能招待你的主人和他的侍从。如果他不排着仪仗来，那就更方便。我托你去请他私下地来到我国里，若不然我就要支应不起了。"豺回答说："我为你尽力去对他请求就是。"它随着要求国王选择一个吉日，它好去回信。国王把日子告诉它，它就慢慢地走回村里。

豺在道上忙着筹备大典，因为织工的衣服穿得很破烂，它叫他到村里洗衣店里去借一身白净的衣服。它又自己去见豺王，请它在某天领着一千豺类到某地方去。它又去见鸦王，求它遣派一千黑色的百姓到某地方去听候差使。禾雀王也应许它，遣派一千禾雀到它指定的那地方去。

行大典的日子到了。织工穿上从洗衣店借来的洁白衣服，豺媒人领着一千豺类、一千乌鸦和一千禾雀随着他走。那班禽兽构成了织工结婚的仪仗，它们一直在前进，一直到黄昏后，就来到距离王宫六里左右的地方。它们停住，豺媒命诸豺类犬吠起来，叫禾雀与乌鸦们都大噪起来。那种嘈杂的声音从很远就可以听见。它们发出的声音，大概从世界开辟以来没有闹过这样厉害的。它们正在发出声音时，豺媒立刻跑到王宫，说王的结婚仪仗已经到了，现在只离王宫六里左右的路程，问王到底要他们进城不要。王听见远地里一种嘈杂的声音送来，就很着急地说："这是不可能的。从这种声音听来，你的君主至少也带着十万侍从前来，我这小城怎样支应得起？我怎能供给那么些客人呢？请你再去游说一下，请你主人的侍从们都不必进城，只请新郎光临就够了。"豺媒说："好吧，我再为你去请求他吧，我最初便告诉你你不能供应我那位庄严的主人。我就照你的意旨去办吧。你命人预备一匹马去接他，我请他自己一个人穿便服入宫就是了。"

豺命织工骑上马，谢了那班豺类、乌鸦与禾雀，命它们各自回去，它和那位假王就进城去了。他来到宫门，新娘这边的人看见他只穿一身洁白衣服，又没有随从的仆役，都很失意。豺又向他们解释说这是国王的意思，因为他的主人如果把一切仪仗都带进城，恐怕这小城要容不下。不久，婚礼举行了，王宫的司祝为他们结了婚姻的结子。新郎不敢多说话，他完全听豺媒的指导，他恐怕说错了话，露出破绽，那时他们的性命就难保了。

那一晚上，新郎进了洞房。他躺在床上不会说什么话，也不会向公主献殷勤。他数着屋里的梁和椽，便很得意地说："这些梁一定可以做很好的织机，那些椽也可以做成很细密的梳子。"公主听见他的说话，起先很不介意，后来见他屡次说，像很认真的样子，她心里不由得不想那新郎到底是一个王还是一个织匠呢？看他的样子很像一个织匠，不然，他怎么屡次提起织机和机梳呢？她想，那人就是命运为她安排的么？第二天早晨，公主到她母亲那里，对她说昨晚她的新郎所说的话。王和王后于是又把豺叫来问它新郎到底是一个什么人。有智的豺媒，立刻想到织工说错了话，它就为他辩白说："大王，请你不要诧异我的主人所说的话。在他的宫廷周围有七百家织坊，做工的都是全世界最好的织匠。他赐地给他们，不要他们的租税。他也时常为一般织匠的幸福和利益着想。这也是他的慈心的一种表示。所以我请你不要因为他的话就惊讶起来。"

豺媒想着织工应当早些带着公主回家，不然，他一定会再闹出第二次笑话，结果要使它没法对付，他们的性命就有危险了。豺媒于是跑到王面前，对他说，王带着那么些侍从在郊外候着，一定不能在宫里久留，他必得与他的新婚的王后当天离宫。他的主人也不要一切仪仗送他，因为他愿意走路。王只要为公主预备一乘肩舆就可以。王和王后商量了许久，至终应许照它所说的去办。织工和豺媒领着公主的轿来到郊外，一直向他的村里走。一到村外，他便打发轿夫回去，他和公主徒步走进村里去。不一会儿已经到了织工的机房，豺媒便对公主说："贵夫人，这就是你丈夫的宫廷。"公主一听见它的话，便捶着自己的头说："唉，我的命！这就是司婚姻的神婆罗阇婆帝为我选择的丈夫么？死比这样的生活还要好一千倍呀！"

在那村里，别人也不晓得是怎么一回事，也没人去给国王报信，后来公主只认定她的命该如此，也就安居下去。她于是决定要让她丈夫致富，因为她知道致富的秘法。有一天，她命她丈夫去买一点面粉回来，她把面粉放进水里掺和起来，然后涂在她身上，用手指去按它使糊块黏在身上。糊块在身上干了以后，搓下来便成金粉。她天天这样做，在不久的时候已经积了许多金子。后来金子越积越多，一直积到与王的财产相当的数目。她用那些金子雇了一班瓦匠、泥匠、木匠，来盖一所世界里最美丽的宫廷。她又命人去找七百家最好的织工来村里围绕着她的宫廷住着。她写信去请她的父王来，说自她嫁了以后，他还没有来过，如果他肯来，她和他的女婿一定都很欢喜地接待他。王接到女儿的信，就定了日子要去探望他们。在国王来到之前，公主极力地把一切应用的东西预备妥当。她把一个小村变成了王都。四城都建立医院容纳病人和残废的牲口。她又叫所有的牲口在街道上，等王来到时，都嚼着槟榔和蒌叶。王所经过的街道都铺着迦湿弥罗的氆氇。她的丈夫的国土被她一整理，真是丰乐无匹。王和王后来到，看见一切的景况，自然非常羡慕他们女婿的富有，都点头说："不错，不错！"豺媒来到他们跟前，对王和王后说："我在先不都对你们说过么？"

我的故事说到这里算完了，

那提耶棘也枯萎了。

那提耶呵，你为什么枯萎呢？

你的牛为什么要我用草来喂它？

牛呵，你为什么要人喂？

你的牧者，为什么不看护我？

牧者呵，你为什么不去看牛？

你的儿媳妇为什么不把米给我?

儿媳妇呵，你为什么不给米呢?

我的孩子为什么哭呢?

孩子呵，你为什么哭呢?

蚂蚁为什么要咬我呢?

蚂蚁呵，你为什么要咬人呢?

喀! 喀! 喀!

十　新月王子

从前有一位国王娶了六位王后，个个都不能生育子女。国王曾为她们访问了一切的医生、圣人、仙人等，也命她们服了许多药，都没有功效。他为这事非常忧虑。大臣们都劝他再娶一位第七王后，或者还有希望，于是他便时常注意到再选一位王后的事。

在王城里住着一个很穷的老婆子，她每日到郊外的田原上去捡牛粪回来，将它们做成粪块，晒干后，拿到市场去卖给人做柴火。牛粪是印度的一种燃料，做这种事业的，都是极穷的人家。老婆子只是靠着这一样事业度日，但她有一个女儿长得非常俊美，凡见她的人都喜欢亲近她。因为她长得好看，性情又很率直，所以有许多贵女愿意与她做朋友。她有三个最好的朋友，一个是宰相的小姐，一个是富商的姑娘，一个是宫廷司祝的女儿。这三位贵女时常和卖牛粪的老婆子的女儿到离宫廷不远一个池子里去洗澡。她们四个人在洗澡的时候，彼此把各人的好处述说出来。

"姊姊，你看，将来做我丈夫的人一定是一个很有福分的，因为他不必为我买什么衣服。衣服一被我穿在身上，就永不会破裂，也不会陈旧，永远和新的一样。"宰相的小姐对富商的姑娘这样说。

富商的姑娘也对小姐说："我将来的丈夫也是一个很有福分的人，因为我烧的柴火，永远是着的，永远不会变成死灰。一把柴火给我用，可以用到许多年。"

"我将来的丈夫也是一个有福分的人，因为我煮的饭永远是有余的。我每顿煮的饭，吃饱了，饭仍是满锅，不见减少，留到下一顿吃，也不腐败。"司祝的女儿也这样对她的姊姊说。

　　老婆子的女儿没有她们三个人的特能，只说："我将来的丈夫也是很有福分的，因为我可以为他生产一对孪生的子女。我的女儿要长得像天神那么美丽。我儿子的额前必有一个新月，他的两个手掌上各有一颗明星，都能发出特异的光明。"

　　王因为要求第七位王后，时常微行，自己到女子们常到的地方去藏着，静静地选择。那天，他正在池边藏着，四个女孩子的话都被他听见。王心里这样想："那穿衣服永不破烂的女子于我有什么用呢？我又不是不能供给衣服给妻子穿。那能烧柴火不致变成死灰的女子于我也没有什么用处；就是那能使饭常满一锅的女子，我也不需要她；那第四个女孩，真是长得俊美！她说她能生产孪生的子女。她的女儿要长得像天神一样俊美；她的儿子的额前有一个光明的新月，手掌上有灿烂的明星。这个女孩子就是我所要的。我一定要立她为第七位王后。"

　　王回到宫里，就打听那第四个女子是谁，人家说她是一个卖牛粪老婆子的女儿。王因为爱她，虽然身份差得很远，定要立她为第七王后。那一天，他命人到老婆子家里传旨。老婆子听见王的使者来到，自然非常害怕。她想也许是她把王田原上的牛粪捡了，王派人来责罚她。王的使者站在茅屋外头，请她立刻进宫，因为王要问她话。老婆子战战栗栗地跟着她来到宫里。人又领她到内庭，王的寝室里去。王问她是不是有一个很美丽的女儿；她女儿是不是与宰相的小姐和司祝的女儿们做朋友。老婆子回答说："是。"王就对她说："我要立你的女儿为后。"老婆子起先以为她是听错了，哪里有一个王肯要一个卖牛粪的女儿为后的？王见她现出在犹豫的状态，又对她说明他一定要娶她的女儿。

不久全城的人都知道王要立卖牛粪老婆子的女儿为后。这消息传到六位王后耳边，她们自然很不喜悦。她们起先也不信王会做这事，后来王亲自对她们说过，她们就想着王必是疯了。她们对王说："王是多么笨，多么疯呢？你真要和一个连当我们的侍女也不够格的女子结婚！一个卖牛粪的女儿！你要待她与待我们一样！我们的主，你的性情真是改变了！"王已经决意要娶她，无论六位王后怎样怂恿，他都不听。他把王室的天文师叫来命他选择吉日。到时，王和卖牛粪老婆子的女儿就结上婚姻的结。她此后便成为最可爱的第七位王后。

他们结婚以后不久，王要到国内第二个都城去，在未动身以前，他把第七王后叫来，对她说："我要到第二个都城去办事，需要六个月以后才能回来。在这六个月中，我想你必要生产。现在我给你这个金钟，你拿去挂在你屋里，我知道你的仇家必要在你临盆的时候伤害你，所以到时你要我回来，无论我在什么地方，离此地多么远，我一听见这个钟声，立刻就要回来，站在你跟前保护你。你要记清楚了，若不是在你要生产的时候切不可敲这个金钟。"王把话吩咐明白，就启程到别的都城去了。

六位王后在王到第七王后屋里的时候，都伏在门外偷听他所说的话。第二天，她们都到第七王后屋里，故意问她说："好妹妹，这个金钟真好看呀！你从哪里得来的呢？你为什么把它挂在屋里呢？"第七王后不隐藏地对她们说："这是昨天我们的王所赐的。他说如果我有危急的事情一敲这金钟，他便立刻回到我跟前来。"六个王后显出怀疑的样子说："这是绝对办不到的！大概是你误会了王的意思吧。谁能够在百千里外听见这小小的钟声呢？即使听得见，王哪里能够在很远的地方，一瞬间就能跑回来？这大概是你听错了，不然，就是王欺骗你。如果你现在把钟敲起来，你就要立刻理会王是和你开玩笑。"六位王后怂恿她，命她试敲那个金钟。她原先不愿意，因为王再三叮咛她非到临产的时候才能敲。后来她被她们逼不过，只得拿钟锤来敲了几下。王正在道上，还没到第二个都城，一听见钟声，果然用起神术，不一会儿就回到宫里。他看见第七王后没有什么事，就问她为什么不听他的话，在没到临产的时候轻易地敲起金钟来。第七王后不愿意把六位王后怂恿她的事实说出来，只说她要试试看那钟声应验不应验。王听了就很生气，再吩咐她不到时候，不要随意敲打那个金钟。他说完又走了。

过了几十天，六位王后又来怂恿第七王后敲打那钟。她们说："你第一次敲钟的时候，王还没走许多路程，所以立刻能够回来。现在他已经在那很远的都城了，我们何不再试试，看他能在一瞬间回到你这里来不能。"她心里对于六位王后的要求很是犹豫，至终她又把钟敲了几下。王在很远的都城，正在坐朝判事，一听见钟声就速速地退朝。朝中的人都不明白他为什么忽然显出那么匆忙的样子。他们也听不见那钟的声音。王回到第七王后的屋里，看见她还是没有事情，就问她为什么又敲着钟来玩。她没把六位王后怂恿她说的话告诉给王知道，只说她还是怀疑，要试那钟声灵验不灵验。王于是非常愤怒，就对她说："因为你已经无缘无故地叫了我两次，自此以后，无论在什么危险当中，你所送的钟声我一定不听，一定不回来。你在生育的时候遇着什么危险，只看你的命运安排就是了。"王说完，就愤愤地走了。

过了不久，第七王后果然到了产期。她一觉得腹痛就敲起金钟，等了许久，总不见王回来。她敲了又敲，尽力地敲，总是无效！王并不是没听见，他不回来，因为他的气还没消尽。六位王后看见王不回来，就走到第七王后跟前，说宫中的规矩是不许任何女人在王的屋里生产的，她必得搬到靠近马厩那间特别为她预备的草舍去，等产后才可以回宫。她听见是宫中的规矩也就听从她们的安排。六位王后又买通了产婆，叫她在第七王后生产的时候，用方法把婴儿治死。第七王后在草舍里，果然生了一个男孩，额上戴着一个明亮的新月，手掌上各有一颗明星，又生了一个女孩，和天神一般俊美。产婆因为受了很重的贿赂，就预备了两只新生的小狗，把它们放在产母旁边。她对第七王后说："王后，你所生的是这两只小东西。"王后在产后精神本很恍惚，也不理会什么就昏沉地睡了。产婆把那对孪生的男女私下带出宫去。

王虽然对于第七王后的作为很生气，但他知道她的产期已到，在第二天就立刻回宫。他到时，王后把一对小狗抱出来，说这就是她生的，王的愤怒到这时候已达极度。他把第七王后废了，撵她出宫，命她穿着皮衣在市上撵乌鸦和野狗。她虽然在产后还不能行动，得着王的命令，也得把美丽的衣服脱下来，换上皮衣，到市场上去撵乌鸦和野狗。

再说产婆把两个婴孩放在一个土罐里头，想着要用一个好的方法来杀害他们。她不敢把他们扔在池子里，恐怕容易被人发现，她也不敢把他们埋掉，恐怕豺狼要把他们挖出来吃，人民就会发现她的行为。最好的方法，她想，就是把他们烧成灰，那就一点踪迹也没有。可是她自己一个人怎能办得到？在深夜中，她哪里去找那么多柴火来焚烧他们？她忽然想起一个好方法。在城外有一个瓦器匠，他白天在轮盘上把坯做好，到夜半才放进窑里烧到天明。她想不如把那个土罐拿到那里去混在坯里，等到天明，就能烧得一点痕迹也不露。她于是照所想的去办，把盛婴孩的土罐私下送进窑里。她看见窑里还没举火，瓦器匠还在睡着，就把燃料点着，然后走回家去。

那一晚上，赶巧瓦器匠和他的妻子睡过了平常的时候。一直到了天明，妻子才急急摇醒她丈夫说："唉，我的好人，我们睡得发昏了！现在已经天亮，我们还没曾把窑里的火点着咧。"她赶快起来，开门，离开他们的草舍到瓦窑去。她一见窑里的瓦器都已烧好，个个都很红，很滑。起先她以为是自己眼花，看错了，后来才理会这次自然烧得的比哪一次都烧得好。她明知她丈夫没起来举火，觉得这是他们的好运，就速速走到草舍里去叫她丈夫说："你快来看！"瓦器匠看了也觉得很奇怪。那些瓦器比平时烧得好得多。可是谁替他烧的呢？他想这一定是诸天的恩惠。正要把瓦器从窑里搬出来，他偶然发现了一个土罐里盛着两个新生的婴孩。他对妻子说："我所爱的,你一定很喜欢要一对这样俊美的婴儿。"他们急急把婴儿抱到家里,妇人装作产期已到,过几天就对邻舍说,她生了一对孪生的子女。他们真是一对俊美无比的婴儿。那一天,许多邻人都来贺喜。瓦器匠的妻子也不敢以生得一对俊美的婴儿为自己的功劳,只对众邻人说:"我本不希望生产,可是现在诸天加恩给我,使我为一对儿女的母亲,我愿意他们受你们诸位的祝福,使他们得着长寿。"

那对孪生的子女长大了,他们都很壮健。兄妹俩无论在哪一个地方玩,众人都很称赞,羡慕他们长得那般美丽。他们也艳羡瓦器匠夫妇的福分,能够生出一对这样的子女。当他们十二岁时,瓦器匠便得了重病,无论什么药也治不好。他在临终的时候,就对妻子说:"我所爱的,我快要离开世间了,我留给你的财产足够你用的,你好好地养育这两个孩子吧。"妇人对她的丈夫说:"你死了,我也不独自活着,我要像一切的好妻子,你死了,我也陪你去。你和我将要在同时火葬。至于孩子们,他们已经长大了,你已为他们留下充足的钱财,他们一定能够独立谋生去。"丈夫死了,妇人一意要殉她的丈夫,朋友们多方劝勉,也没功效。到火葬场去,她果然投身入火,跟着她丈夫一起烧死。

男孩子长大了常用头巾把额上的新月掩住,他很怕被人发现

那个孩子射箭时，无意中把头巾拨掉了，他额上的新月立时发射出光来

了他额上有特异的光明。他和他的妹妹把瓦窑收拾了，把一切剩下的货物如轮盘、土罐、瓦壶等都变卖了。兄妹们就到王城里的市场去。他们一到市场，个个都争着来看他们，因为所有的人都不曾见过那么美丽的男女。店里的人更是惊异，他们以为这两个少年男女一定是天神下凡来的。他们都用惊讶的眼神看着那一对小孩子，求他们就住在市场里头。市场里的众人为他们建筑了一所房子叫他们住下。

他们住在市场，一出来玩，便有一个穿皮衣的妇人在远地里跟着。那妇人就是被王废掉的第七王后，奉王命在市场赶乌鸦和野狗的。她有时也到他们所住的房子探望，可是不敢认他们。

孩子买了一匹马，时时骑着它到附近的树林去打猎，有一天，王也到那里去打猎，他看见一个孩子骑在马上，他只顾看他长得非常俊美，连眼前走过一只鹿也忘了发箭去射它。孩子看见一只鹿走过，也就急发一箭。他射时，无意中把头巾拨掉了，他额上的月光立时发射出来。王一看见，立时想到他的第七王后说过她生的儿子的额上有一个新月，掌上各有一颗明星。孩子把箭射了，不等王和他说话，就勒着马走了。王回到宫中，心里非常难过。他的悲伤是没有人能够劝解的。六位王后问他为什么那么悲哀。他就说曾在林中看见一个孩子，额上有一个新月，使他想起第七王后所生的儿

113

六位王后用尽许多方法要使国王愉快，都没有效果

子。六位王后用尽许多方法要使他愉快，终于无效。她们想着产婆已经把那对婴儿治死，哪里还有一个额上有新月的孩子活在树林里头？那一对孪生的子女还活着么？产婆不是说得千真万确，把他们烧成灰了么？她们于是命人去把产婆叫来问明底细。产婆赌着咒，说她真是把婴儿烧了，她出宫以后，立刻去访查那个额上戴着新月的孩子是谁，才理会当时没曾把他们烧死。产婆知道他们的住处，等孩子出去打猎的时候，就走到他们那里对女孩子说她是他们的姑母，自从他们生后，就很少与他们的父母往来。她又说她住在王宫附近，所以很少出城去探亲，现在打听得侄子、侄女也在城里，所以特地来相认。女孩子不知道她的家世，也信她是个真正姑母。她看见女孩那么美丽，心里就生出一个毒计，对她说："我的好女孩，你长得真美，你应当戴迦多奇花使你的美丽更能显露出来。你应当告诉你哥哥，叫他去把这种花拿来种在你的院子里。"女孩子问："那是什么花呢，姑母？我一向不曾见过那样的花。"产婆说："我的女儿，你哪能见得着？这里没有那种花，它长在隔海那边，被七百个罗刹守护着咧。"女孩子说："那么，我哥哥能够取得来么？"产婆说："他可以试试。你若是对他说，他一定能为你取来。"产婆心里的计划是希望孩子到隔洋去取花，被罗刹吃了，她可以卸责。

新月王子回来，他的妹妹告诉他方才姑母来到说如果他能做得到，就可以为她去取迦多奇花。王子很怀疑他们在这世间还有什么姑母，可是为要使他妹妹喜欢的缘故，他应许为她去把花取来，他知道那花只长在罗刹国里。第二天早晨，他便预备启程，并且告诉妹妹不要在他出外期间随意出门去游玩。他骑的是一匹天马，不一会儿，已经来到一个稠密的森林。他看见有些罗刹在那里找寻食物，于是走近一点，用箭射杀麋鹿和犀牛，献给它们。他对罗刹们说："可爱的姑母，可爱的姑母呀，你们的侄儿在这里。"当中一个长得非常庞大的罗刹走来对他说："噢，你就是那额上有新月，掌中有明星的少年。我们时常希望你来，可以把你吃掉。因为你叫我姑母，我就不吃你。你要什么呢？你带了什么能吃的东西来给我呢？"王子把麋鹿和犀牛献给她。她的嘴张得很大，不一会儿已经把所有的都吞下去了。她吃饱了，就问王子："你要什么呢？"王子说："我要为我的妹妹取些迦多奇花回去。"她告诉他那花很难得，因为是被七百个罗刹守护着的。但无论如何，他可以试试。第一步，他应当去见他住在林北的叔叔。王子听从她的指导，就勒着马往北走。在道上，他又射了些麋鹿、犀牛，把它们带着，一直到看见一个很庞大、很凶悍的罗刹男。他大声嚷说："叔叔，可爱的叔叔，你的侄子在这里。姑姑叫我来看你哪。"罗刹走到他面前，看看他，就对他说："你就是那额上有新月，掌中有明星的少年，我很愿意把你吃掉，不过你已叫我叔叔，又是你姑姑叫你来找我的，我就舍不得吃你了。现在你需要什么呢？"他把麋鹿和犀牛献给罗刹，等他吃完，然后向他要求。他问罗刹要迦多奇花。罗刹说："问我要迦多奇花么？很好，你试一试去取吧。你过了这个树林，就到了一个没有道路的迦支利林。你应当对迦支利林说：'迦支利母亲，请你为我开一条路，不然我就要死了。'那树林听见这声音，一定为你开一条道，容你通过。你过了迦支利林，就要到一个海岸。你应当对海说：'洋海母亲，请你为我开一条道，不然我就要死了。'洋海听见你的话，一定要为你开一条道，容你走过去。一过了洋海，你就到了迦多奇花林了。请吧，这就是你所要知道，我所能对你说的。"王子谢过他的罗刹叔叔，上了马，照着所指示的道路前进。走不远，果然来到一个不通行的迦支利林。林中枝叶极密，荆棘交错，简直没法通过。王子记得罗刹的话，便合掌对着树林说："迦支利母亲哪，请你为我开一条路，不然，我就要死了。"树林果然开了一条干净的道路，一直引他到海边。他看见当前的洋海，又合掌说："洋海母亲哪，请你为我开一条道，不然我就要死了。"洋海立时分开，两旁的水矗立起来，像两堵墙一样。王子从当中走过，一点也没沾着水。

他来到迦多奇花园了，一走进园门，他就觉得里面很空旷，像没有人居住一般。他进屋里，从一间到另一间，都不见有什么。后来走到一间房子，他就看见一个美人躺在一张金床上睡着。在她的床上有一支金杖和一支银杖。银杖是放在她的脚边的。金杖放在她头上。他把金银杖拿在手里，仔细地看着，不意金杖触着了那睡着的女子的脚。她立时醒过来。她睁眼一看，就对王子说："客人，你怎样走进处女的住处？噢，我知道你是谁，我知道你的生平。你是那额上有新月，掌中有明星的少年。快走吧，快离开此地吧。这是七百罗刹的住处，他们是守护那迦多奇花的。他们现在出去找吃的，到黄昏后就回来，如果他们看见你在此地，一定把你吃掉。我本是王女，被一个罗刹母带到这里来。我的名字叫普斯坡婆帝。她非常喜爱我，不许我离开她。每天早晨，她出去的时候，她把银杖触我，使我死在床上；到晚间她回来才用金杖触我，使我复活。这里只有我一个是人，其余的一来到都要被吃掉。快走吧，不然，你的性命就难保了。"

新月王子告诉王女他到这里是为他妹妹取迦多奇花而来。他又把怎样经过迦支利林和渡过洋海的情形说给她听。他又说他回去的时候，一定要把她带走，他们在那一天同在园里游玩，一直到黄昏后。罗刹们快要回来的时候，王子用银杖把王女触倒，自己就去藏在隔壁房间的迦多奇花堆里。日落后，王子听风声从远地越来越近，知道是七百罗刹回来了。罗刹走进王女的房里说："我闻见了人的气味，我闻见了人的气味。"少女回答她说："哪一个人能够来到这个地方呢？这里只有我一个是人。"母罗刹于是躺在地上命王女为她搓腿。她为罗刹搓腿的时候，故意把眼泪滴在女怪的腿上。罗刹问："我的宝贝，你为什么哭呢？"王女回答说："妈妈我没为什么，你使我在这里活得很愉快，我还有什么不舒服呢？不过我忽然想起你将来死后，我不晓得要怎么办。"罗刹说："我死么？我的儿，我会死么？不错，一切的生灵都有死期，可是罗刹是不容易死的。我的儿，你知道在这园中有一个池子吧。在池子的深处有一个木匣，里头藏着一只雌蜂和一只雄蜂。命运这样规定，说如果有一个额上有新月，掌中有明星的人能够来到此地，潜入池底，把那木匣拿起来，将那一对马蜂打死，我们的命也就同归于尽了。不过，杀蜂的时候，不能容一滴血滴在地上；那额上有新月，掌中有明星的人更是不容易遇见，所以我想要我们罗刹的性命是一件很难的事情。第一我断定世间决不会有一个额戴新月，掌持明星的人；第二，我想就是有，他也不能来到此地，被七百罗刹所守护的园子，隔着一个迦支利林和一个大海。他一来，不说我们这里的罗刹可以把他吃掉，在对岸树林里住着的罗刹早已把他吃了。即使他能到此地来，他也未必知道池中有一个木匣是我们的性命所寄托的。假使他知道，他杀害那对马蜂时，也不免要把血滴在地上。如果他把血滴在地上，我们不但不死，并且要把他的身体撕成七百块。我的儿，你看，我们实在是永远活着的。虽然不是意义上的不死，实际上我们是不死的。所以我劝你不要为这事忧心。"

第二天早晨，罗刹起来，用银杖触死王女，便随着同类们觅食去了。新月王子从花堆里出来，到王女房里。王女把罗刹的生命所寄托的秘密向他泄露出来。他立时要到池里去把那木匣取上来。在潜入水池之前他把几重很重的园门关起来，然后行事。他把木匣子拿上水面，一打开匣盖，果然有一对马蜂急着要飞出来。他速速地用手把它们搓碎。他掌上是有明星的，所以不怕蜂螫他。他把蜂血都涂在自己身上，所以一滴也滴不到地上，正当他做这事时，远地里一阵狂叫的声音飞送到园门外。罗刹们都躺在地上死了。王子把迦多奇花采了许多插在头上，又取了许多花种。他带着王女踏过一大堆的罗刹尸体一直来到海边。他照着原来的语言对洋海说了一遍，就平安地渡到了对岸。过迦支利林的时候，也是用去时的话向它请求，树林果然又为他开了一条道。他过了树林，和王女骑上天马一直飞到市场，他妹妹住的地方。

第二天早晨，王子又到林中去打猎，王又在那里。一只鹿走过，王子就发箭射它。他射时，又在无意中把头巾拨下来，露出额上的新月。王看见他头上发出光明，便命他停住，表示要与他做朋友。王子与他谈了一会儿，就将他的住址告诉他，并且请他去找他。王回宫后，立刻命人预备仪仗，因为他要到市场去探访那额上有新月的王子。新月王子还没回来，王到时，由他妻子普斯坡婆帝接见。普斯坡婆帝在罗刹国的时候，已知道新月王子的生平，这时见了她的公公，不免要把从前的事情告诉他。她对王说第七王后怎样被六位王后欺负；在她临生育时，怎样贿赂产婆用小狗把一对孪生的子女换了；产婆怎样把婴儿送到城外的窑里烧化；一切的经过，她都尽情述说出来。她又告诉国王新月王子怎样从罗刹国救她出来，和她与他现在的关系。王听了她的话，才恍然大悟。第二天，他命人把第七王后接回来，把六位王后活埋掉。自此，国王和第七王后，王子和普斯坡婆帝，大家住在宫里一同过着很愉快的日子。

　　我的故事说到这里算完了，
　　那提耶棘也枯萎了。
　　那提耶呵，你为什么枯萎呢？
　　你的牛为什么要我用草来喂它？

牛呵，你为什么要人喂？

你的牧者为什么不看护我？

牧者呵，你为什么不去看牛？

你的儿媳妇为什么不把米给我？

儿媳妇呵，你为什么不给米呢？

我的孩子为什么哭呢？

孩子呵，你为什么哭呢？

蚂蚁为什么要咬我呢？

蚂蚁呵，你为什么要咬人呢？

喀！喀！喀！

十一
鬼役

从前有一个剃头匠，家里只有一个妻子，并无子女。他们的生活很困难，所以妇人时常骂她的男子不中用，致使她每顿吃不饱。每夜临睡时，妻子必在枕边把丈夫申斥一顿才能安歇。她常埋怨她穷困的丈夫说："如果你养不起一个妻子，为什么你要娶妻？一个男子若不能供养他的妻子，他就不配娶妻，他也不要梦想家庭的快乐。当我在我父母家里的时候，吃得饱，穿得好，一到你家，我好像是为禁食而来的！世间只有寡妇是常时禁食的，我现在简直是一个有丈夫的活寡妇！"不但如此，她一生起气来，白天男子出去没奈何，等到晚间丈夫回来，常用扫帚来打他出气。丈夫被妻子欺负得这么厉害，心里又是惭愧，又是痛苦。他因为怕打的缘故，便带着他的工具，发誓若不发财就誓不回家。他从一村走过另一村为人家剃发。晚间没地方住，他就一直走到树林里去。他躺在一棵树下休息，在那里长吁短叹。

正巧他躺下的地方树上住着一个鬼灵。鬼看见一个人躺在树下，就下来要把他害死。它从树上跳下来，长着怪脸，伸着那可怕的手，对剃头匠说："剃头匠，现在我要杀害你，谁能够保护你呢？"剃头匠的腿虽然哆嗦得很厉害，他的毛发也立起来，但他却有一点急智，不慌不忙地躺在地上，对鬼灵说："噢，鬼灵，你想伤害我么？你等一等，我要把我今晚上拿着的鬼灵给你看，叫你算

那个鬼长着怪脸，伸着那可怕的手，对剃头匠说："现在我要杀害你，谁能够保护你呢？"

算它们有多少个。我很欢喜在此地遇见你，因为我可以把你也拿住，放在我的口袋里。"他说着就从装工具的口袋里取出一面镜子。镜子是个个剃头匠都有的，它和剃刀、刀石等，都是重要的工具。他拿着镜子向鬼灵一照说，"你看见里面有一个鬼没有？它也是我方才拿住放在里面的。待一会儿我休息够了，就把你也装在里头与它做伴。"鬼灵从镜中看见一个形象，不知道是自己的相貌，以为剃头匠真是有捉鬼的本领。它起首害怕，请求他不要把它收入镜里。它说："剃头匠先生，请求你不要把我装进去，你要我做什么，我一定为你做去。你若缺乏什么，我一定为你取去。"剃头匠还装作不依的样子说："鬼是最无信的，我信不过你。你们应许了的事，你们常不去做，所以我还是要把你收入这里面。"鬼灵恳切地求他说："求你开恩，我一定照我所应许的去做，万求你不要把我收入你的口袋里。"剃头匠说："好吧，你现在立刻去为我取一千个金钱来，明天晚上再为我盖一间谷仓，还要里面贮满了白米。立刻去把一千金钱取来吧，不然，我就要把你装入口袋里去。"鬼灵认为取一千金钱是很容易的，它好像遇见大赦一般，去了不久，果然把金子取来放在剃头匠面前。他收了金子，心中暗自喜欢，又吩咐它明天晚上一定要为他去盖一间充满了白米的仓廪。

第二天早晨，剃头匠扛着一大堆的金子回到家中。他妻子一开门认为他一夜没回来，想是到别处干不正经的事去了，不由分说，拿起扫帚便要打下去。她丈夫眼快，闪了一闪，便把金子奉献给她。她也没问明是怎样得的，见了金子，就把从前对待丈夫的态度都改变了。

那天晚上，鬼灵果然到他家里为他盖了一间仓库。它正在扛米进仓的时候，在道上遇见第二个鬼灵，是它的叔叔。鬼叔问它要扛到哪里，它就把事情的原委说给它听。鬼叔说："你真是愚拙！你想那剃头匠真能把你收掉么？他是一个狡猾的人，他骗了你。你实在是笨，会受他的欺骗。"鬼灵说："你怀疑那剃头匠的能力么？跟着我来看吧。我亲眼看见他所收的鬼灵哪。"鬼叔不信，就跟着它来到剃头匠的家。剃头匠知道另有一个鬼灵从窗户探头进来，便拿起镜子向外一照说："来吧，现在我就要把你装在里头。"鬼叔看见自己的相貌也害怕起来。它也应许要为他盖一间充满了五谷的仓廪。这样，在两晚上，那个穷到不得了的剃头匠立刻变成富人。他和他妻子一同过着平安的日子。妻子也不打他，不骂他了。他们后来生了些子女，过着很愉快的生活。

我的故事说到这里算完了，

那提耶棘也枯萎了。

那提耶呵，你为什么枯萎呢？

你的牛为什么要我用草来喂它？

牛呵，你为什么要人喂？

你的牧者，为什么不看护我？

牧者呵，你为什么不去看牛？

你的儿媳妇为什么不把米给我？

儿媳妇呵，你为什么不给米呢？

我的孩子为什么哭呢？

孩子呵，你为什么哭呢？

蚂蚁为什么要咬我呢？

蚂蚁呵，你为什么要咬人呢？

喀！喀！喀！

十二　骨原

从前有一位王子结了三个朋友，一个是宰相的公子。一个是巡查官的儿子，一个是王城里最富商人的儿子。这四个朋友很相投契，时常同出同入。有一天，他们想到国外去看看，各人约定时候，一同上马启程。他们一早就离开王城，一直到过了中午，走进一个森林。他们下马休息，把马拴在树边，容它们吃附近的草叶。歇了一会儿，他们又上马前进。那森林非常大，走了一天，还没走到尽头。黄昏到了，他们还在森林的深密处徘徊着。忽然前面露出一个庙宇，他们一看见就非常喜欢，立意晚上要在那里过一夜。一到庙里，他们看见只有一个修士在里面坐禅，他们进来，他也没理会。四位朋友也不惊动他，把马拉到殿后拴好，各自悄悄地在殿上找一个安歇的地方。黑暗把全个森林都盖住了，在殿中还有一点光明发射出来。因为那森林里有许多野兽，那庙又没有门，所以他们商定每三小时换一人守夜，三个人就在殿中的走廊上睡。第一个守夜的是商人的儿子，他自晚六时守到九时。到了九时，他看见一件奇事。他看见修士拿起一块白骨头在手里，口中念些咒语。不一会儿，庙的四围发出些声音，他看见从森林四处来了许多白骨，堆在修士面前。因为他的时间已经到了，他把方才修士所念的咒记住就睡觉去了。

　　第二个守夜的是巡查官的儿子。他一起来，就看见那修士还跌坐着，深入禅定，不过面前多了一大堆白骨。他不明白那堆白骨是从哪里来的，注意了许久，也不见有什么动静。夜深了，沉静的森林时时被狼吠虎啸的声音撩动得成为一个恐怖的世界。他很怕野兽在没提防的时候进到庙里来。到他的守夜时间快完的时候，他看见那修士注视着他面前一大堆白骨。他口中念出咒语，不一会儿，那堆骨就发出移动的声音，他又继续他的咒语说："各样的骨归到各类，是一身所属的骨都连回去。"他看见方才那一大堆白骨，现在已成为一副完全的骨骼在修士面前排列得整整齐齐。他本想看下去，可是他的时间已到，他也疲乏了。他把方才修士所念的咒语记住，把公子叫醒自己便安睡去。

公子起来，揉着他的眼睛，来到廊外。那时正是一群野鬼恶灵猖狂的时候，虽然狼吠虎啸的声音渐次减少了，而静默的森林还是静默得可怕。他从门中往外一看那黑漆漆的森林，使他的毛发都竖起来。他看见修士还在坐禅，只是他面前多了一副兽类骨骼排列着。一直等到他的守夜时间快要完毕的时候，才看见那修士念着咒语："血和肉附在骨上吧，用皮肤把它们裹上吧。"不久，那副骨骼已变成一只野兽，躺在原地，看不出它有什么生气。他看见修士做完这件事，他的守夜时间已完了。他去把王子摇醒，也没对他说什么，自己便安歇去了。

王子出来，看见修士还在静坐，面前躺着一只野兽，但是没有生气，动也不动一下。王子因为睡足了，精神比较好，又因为夜里没出什么危险，所以他就注意到天空的颜色。夜已快过去了，天色渐渐地从深蓝变成灰白。他忽然听见殿里有声音发出来，就把望天的眼移注在修士身上。他见修士口中念着咒语："呼吸吧，活吧，站起来走吧。"那躺在地上没有气息的野兽一听见咒语，立刻站起来往门外蹿进森林里去了。不一会儿，晨鸦噪起来了，王子见天已大明，就去把三位朋友叫起来。他们各人骑上马再上旅途。各人在马上都想着各人昨夜所见的奇事，却都静默无言，谁也没对谁说什么。

他们在密林里走，到处随时都要小心，所以很不宜于对谈。一直到了正午，他们走到一个小池边。各人下了马，在树下小憩。他们摘了些野果，又从池里取水，各人拿出些干粮，就在那里吃午饭。王子对他的三位朋友说："朋友，你们昨晚在殿里看见那修士做了些什么事？我要对你们说我所见的。"他对着商人的儿子说，"现在就请你先说吧，我们照着昨晚守夜的次序说。"

商人的儿子说："听吧，朋友们，我所见的是这样。那修士把一块白骨拿在手里，口中念着咒语，不一会儿，就有许多骨从森林的四围跑来堆积在他面前。他所用的咒语，我现在还记得。不过我看到白骨堆起来以后，就去睡了。以后的事，我不知道。"

巡查官的儿子说："他睡了，我就起来守夜。我所见的是这样。那修士静坐了很久，忽然念起咒语。那咒语我现在还记得很明白。他念完的时候，那堆白骨就各自找寻各个连属的关节，变成一副兽类的骨骼，躺在他面前。以后我就不知道了。"

公子说："我到廊上的时候，只见修士还在坐禅。夜静极了，我很害怕。那修士忽然睁开眼望着那些排好的骨骼，口中念着咒语。他一念完，那些骨骼便长上肌肉和皮毛！我看到这里就去叫王子出来替我，所以后来的事，我不知道。不过我还记得当时他所念的咒语。"

王子接着说："朋友们，从现在所听的，你们一定能够猜出我所见的是怎么一回事。我看见修士对着那没有生气的野兽念了些咒语。一念完，它便站立起来，向森林里跑去。我当时看得很清楚，那站起来的，是一只很好看的鹿，正要多看一会儿，可惜它已跑了。那时晨鸦已经啼得很嘈杂，我就去把你们叫醒。"

各人听了各人所见的事情，都很欢喜各人能把当时修士所用的咒语记住。他们想那些咒语是具有超自然的能力，很有用处的。可是他们很怀疑他们自己一说出来能否得着与修士一样的结果，他们彼此都愿意试试那有趣的咒语到底灵验不灵验。在树下恰巧有一

133

块骨头，他们不管那是属于什么生灵的，一捡起来就递给商人的儿子。商人的儿子拿起骨来照修士所念的咒念了一遍，果然，有许多骨片从森林的四围来到跟前，堆在树下。巡查官的儿子于是注目看着那堆骨头，念着他昨晚听来的咒语。不一会儿，各块骨片已自连成一副骨骼，他们理会那是一副走兽的骨骼。公子走到那副骨骼旁边，念起咒语，立刻理会那野兽的肌肉和皮毛都长起来。他们看见是一只老虎，身子比平常的还要大，就都惊慌起来。三位朋友都求王子不要再往下试验。恐怕老虎一活起来，他们的性命难保。可是王子还没有把他所听见的说出来，不晓得应验不应验，一定要亲自试试。他对三位朋友说："你们所得的咒语已经应验，证明是真而可用的了。可是我所得的，能用与否，还不能断定。所以我一定要试验一下。我们自然也不值得为试验这事丢了我们的性命。你们都先爬上树顶去吧，我念完了，也立刻爬上去，看看它的动静怎样。"三位朋友苦劝王子不要再往下试验，可是无论如何他还不依，不得已，各人都爬上树去。王子见他们都爬到树梢，自己也爬到树当中，注视着地上的死老虎，大声念起咒语来。老虎果然站起来，咆哮得很凶恶。王子也顾不得什么，急急地爬到树梢藏着。那老虎向上望着四个人，大发起它的野性，幸亏它不能上树，它只把四匹马咬的咬死，吃的吃掉，慢慢地向密林里奔去，它一面走一面还是咆哮着。四位朋友在树上听见它的声音已经离开他们那里很远，知道危险已经过去，就都下地。一到地上，他们看见马已经被害，只得徒步往前走。好在那里离海边已经很近，他们随着波涛的声音来到岸边。海上正有一只船从岸边驶过，他们就扬着手帕要求船上的人搭救。船上的人看见有人在荒寂的岸边站着求渡，也就把船泊到岸边容他们上船去。船主对他们说，船上的食料很缺乏，所以到第一个埠头，他们就得上岸再作计划。船走了四五天来到一个城，四个朋友看见那城建筑得很雄壮，有很大的宫阙，有很高的楼台，他们就一齐上了岸。

他们从岸边一直走，走到大街上。两边的树木很是繁茂，所以走到很远也不觉得恼热。大街的尽头，露出一个市场。他们进去，总不见有人，才想起来方才在道上也没见过一个人来往。他们看见店里的货物都排列得非常整齐。糖铺里的糖食一堆一堆地堆起来，只是没有人在那里卖。铁铺里的铁器一件一件安排得很有次序，也没有铁匠在里头。杂货店里的咸菜和酱料，颜色和气味都很香馥，也是没有半个人影在那里管着。满城是空无居民的，连牲口也没有！有车放在路边，可是不见牛，也不见马。他走到城的内部街道，各家的门户都开放着，只是没有人住在里面。这像是一个死城。所有的人和牲口都死掉了。他们一直来到那最高的楼台，大概

他们四个朋友一起来到一座建筑得很雄壮的城市

是一所王宫。走进去，也没有人来拦阻他们。他们看一切武器，如盾剑、枪、刀之类，都悬在守卫室里，可没有卫兵来用它们。宫里也是空的。他们到马厩里一看，只见马的饲料很多，却不见有马。一直进到深宫里去，他们都没遇见一个人。他们从第一院一直进到第六院都不见什么，再进到第七院，才看见有人，那里有四个很美丽的女子，一见他们来，都迎出来，叫他们丈夫。她们说她们都是王女，很喜欢他们能够来到这里相会，她们在宫里等了他们许久了。她们把四个朋友带到内宫去，为他们预备吃的和喝的。他们问四个王女为什么城中一个人也没有。王女们告诉他们先不要问，以后自然知道。他们吃完，各人同一位王女到各人的私室去了。

王子与那女子同在一个屋里的时候，女孩子忽然哭出来。王子问她为什么悲伤。她说："王子呀！我很怜爱你。从你的面貌看起来，你一定是在王家生长的一个王子。我现在要告诉你我在此地的生活景况。那三个女人装饰得与我一样的并不是人类乃是罗刹。我自小就在这宫里住。我父亲是这国的王。不幸，有一年，罗刹种类来到此地，把所有的人民连我的父母兄弟、姊妹、亲属都吃了。凡是活物都被她们吃净了。你来的时候已经明白这个，满城都没有人民，也没有牲口。他们都是被那三个罗刹，就是现在你的三位朋友的妻子吃掉的。她们把我留住，大概也不能长久，多大会儿她们要把我吃掉，我也不知道。方才她们看见你们来，就喜欢到了不得，因为它们许久没尝过人肉了。她们打算在一两天就动手伤害你们。"

王子说："如果她们是罗刹，我怎能证明你不是一个罗刹？你想自己把我吃掉，用计把我的保卫者调开，也未可知。"

王女说："你自然不信我的话。只有一件事请你注意，罗刹和我不同的地方就是她们食量的宏大。罗刹是吃生东西的，她们在平常人类的席上一定是吃不饱的，到晚间一定要出外去求食。你如果叫你那三位朋友留心观察他们各人的妻子，看她们在半夜里出去不出去就知道了。她们不能在这城里求食，必得走到很远的地方去。你如果不相信我，只看我的生活是否与你一样。我夜里也不离开你。我还要请你小心提防被罗刹们听见这些话。如果她们听见了，不但我的性命难保，连你们都难免于死亡。"

第二天，王子真个把三位朋友叫来，私下对他们说，并且叫他们务必要守秘密。他叫他们在夜间看他们的妻子是否出去，他自己也在那晚上假睡，窥探那王女到底是不是人类。他的三位朋友果然发现他们各人的妻子都在他们睡熟的时候私自出去了，一直到天快亮的时候才回来。王子的妻子倒是整夜睡在他身边。三位朋友又理会他们各人的妻子要睡到晌午才起床。从这些迹象看来，四个王女当中三个是罗刹的断定就不错了。

王女后来又告诉王子说，罗刹吃剩的骨头都扔在城北的原野上，他们有工夫可以去看看，四位朋友果然到城北去，看见一堆一堆的骨头积聚得像山一样。他们越发信服王女的话，回来就商量要怎样逃脱这一场灾厄。

他们都知道三个罗刹每天总要睡到过午才起来的。王女叫他们到海边去看看有船经过没有。如果有，就约定船上的人在早晨来接他们逃走。王女自然是要跟着她的丈夫去的。她把一切首饰、珠宝都放在一个小箱里，预备机会来到，可以脱离那个荒凉的城市。有一天早晨他们看见有一只船从远处漂来，他们就在岸上招呼求渡。船泊近岸边，四个朋友和王女都上去。王女鼓励舵工和水手们尽力地驾驶，她将来要重重地酬报他们。她知道罗刹一醒过来，必要追到海边，那船若能离开岸边二百四十里就可以得着平安，因为罗刹的身体可以伸长到十由旬①。船上的人都尽力地摇，一面挂起风帆来驶着。一直到了黄昏，从远地传来一种怪声。不久，他们看见三个罗刹从岸上伸长她们的头一直到离船很近的海面。那船已经离岸二百四十多里，只差一点，船舷就被那三张大嘴咬住。那三个怪脸向着船上的人说："哦，我的姊妹，你这样办，就是要自己把他们

① 1由旬相当于约8英里。——编者注

139

王女自己一人在那里等了许久，知道她是被人怀疑是个罗刹，被他们舍弃了

吃掉。"王子的三位朋友本来怀疑王女也是一个罗刹，现在听了这话心中更加害怕。王子到这时心里也怀疑起来，不过他没露出惊惶的神色。

　　船主告诉四位朋友说他是要到远国去采金的，所以如遇有海港，他们就得上岸，各自计划各的行程。船主也很怀疑王女是个罗刹，所以也不愿意容留他们。好几天，总见不着海港，一直到一天的黄昏，船才靠近一个岸边。四位朋友和王女一同上了岸。他们徒步走了很远。王女因为不惯走路，到了一个荒野，就不能再走。她说她又饿又疲乏，非得歇一歇不可。王子们看见附近像有人烟，就命商人的儿子去为她买一些东西回来吃，他去了很久，总不见回来。王子又叫了巡查官的儿子去看看到底是怎么一回事。他去了，也没回来！他们都想着王女是个罗刹，现在正是逃脱的机会，所以一去不回头。公子不久也去了。他们都不回来！至终王子叫他妻子自己在那里等着，他去为她买些东西回来吃。原来那里离市场不远，王子一到，就看见他的三位朋友都在那里。他们看见他来，一定不让他回去。王子也不回到王女那里去了！王女自己一人在那里等了许久，知道她是被人怀疑是个罗刹，没奈何，只得自己走到市场来。王子们已经回到他们的本国去了。

　　原来那地离王子们的国土不远。王女就在市场附近找了一个地方住下。她和一个穷妇人住在一起，从她打听到王城的路径。过了几天，她就启程向王子们的城邑前进。一到王城，她便把贵重的首饰如珍珠、宝石之类卖了一些，赁了一间很华丽的房子住下，并宣扬自己是个天生的赌博家，如果城中有人能胜过她，她必要用一万卢比来酬报他，如果对手输了，也得如数赔她。她又得着国王的应许，凡输给她而不能付款的，她可以把那人拘禁在她家里。王子的三位朋友各自以为是赌博的老手，听见了这个消息，就去与她掷骰子。他们不认得她，因为她化了装。她赢了三位朋友。他们输给她好几十万卢比，一直到他们不能再付款的时候，她就把他们拘禁起来。王子听见三位朋友被那女赌博家拘禁了，自己想去救他们出来。他的赌术是很好的。他到王女那里求对赌，头一次，她容他赢了，以后每次都叫他输了。王子也输到不能再付现款的地步。她又把他留下了。在那时候，她便详细地对王子说明她是谁。王子深自后悔当时不该把她舍弃。她把三位从地窖下放出，彼此相认，都非常欢喜。这次，他们不再怀疑她是一个罗刹了。国王知道王子的妃子来到，也就为他预备筵席，接她入宫居住。

王女在宫中，个个人都很喜欢她。她没有忘记她的国土和父母是被罗刹所害的。她知道他们的骨骼都被罗刹们放弃在城北的原野上。因为王子曾对她说过，他和三位朋友有使枯骨生肉的法术，很想请他们去试试，把她全国的人都救活过来。不过那三个罗刹还在那里，救活也不中用。四位朋友想着那修士既然能给生命，一定也能毁生命。王子于是再来到森林的庙宇里，求他赐给他们从远地毁坏生命的法术。他们把事情的原委说给修士知道，修士可怜那国的人民，就将咒术教给他们。他看见有一只鹿走过，便掬了一掬水，向着它念些咒语，然后把水向它一洒，它立刻倒在地上死了。鹿死了不久，他又念了些咒语使它复活。这些咒语，王子都熟记在心头，辞了修士回到宫里。

王子夫妇和他三位朋友到他岳父的国去。他们到时，三个罗刹正要伸长脖来把他们吃掉，被王子念了咒语，用水向它们一洒，它们立刻倒在地上死掉。他们于是走到城北的骨原，各人按顺序念所会的咒语，到最后，王子把他们都救活了。王女那时再与她父母、兄弟、姊妹和人民相见，她的愉快，实在难以形容。她愉快的眼泪不歇地从眼睛流出。他们在那国里住了好几天，备受国王和人民的供养，以后就回到他们的本国来。四位朋友的友谊延长到有生之年，王子夫妇俩同过着极乐的生活。

我的故事说到这里算完了，

那提耶棘也枯萎了。

那提耶呵，你为什么枯萎呢？

你的牛为什么要我用草来喂它？

牛呵，你为什么要人喂？

你的牧者，为什么不看护我？

牧者呵，你为什么不去看牛？

你的儿媳妇为什么不把米给我？

儿媳妇呵，你为什么不给米呢？

我的孩子为什么哭呢？

孩子呵，你为什么哭呢？

蚂蚁为什么要咬我呢？

蚂蚁呵，你为什么要咬人呢？

喀！喀！喀！

十三　禿妻

有一个人娶了两个没有多少头发的妻子。他比较爱那年轻的，不爱那年长的。年轻妻子的头发是分两股梳起来的，年长的妻子只有一股。男子出外去做买卖，留下两个妻子在家同住。她们彼此互相怨恨，年轻的妻子靠着丈夫偏爱她，时常欺负那年长的。她叫年长的妻子做家中一切的工作，从早到晚，不容她歇着，又不叫她吃饱，用种种方法来虐待她。

　　有一天，年轻的妻子对年长的说："来把我头上的虱子都拿掉。"她正在为年轻的妻子找虱子的时候，不经意把她的头发拨掉了许多。头发本是自己掉下来的，女人生气起来，不由分说，把年长妻子那一股头发用力揪下来，并且撵她出去。年长妻子的头完全秃了。她想到森林里去寻死，无论是饿死或是被野兽吃掉，她都愿意。她在道上走着，经过一块种棉花的土地。她看见棉花的四围很脏，便住步，捡起一根小棍子做成一把扫帚，把地上扫干净。棉花很喜欢她这样做就赐福给她。她一直走，又到了一棵芭蕉树下。她看见树下很脏，又用扫帚把它扫干净。芭蕉也赐福给她。走的时候，她又看见一间很脏的牛圈，那是圣牛住的。她走进去，把牛圈打扫干净。圣牛也很喜欢，就赐福给她。她走不远，又来到一棵兜罗树下。她用扫帚把树下的垃圾扫掉。兜罗树也赐福给她。她又往前走，看见一间草屋，里面有一个修道士趺坐着，像入了很深的禅

她一从水里出来，觉得全身都改变了，她变成了一个非常美丽的女人

定一般。她走进前，站在他后面。修士说："无论你是谁，不要站在我背后，不然，我就要把你化成灰。"妇人怕得哆嗦起来，赶快走到他面前。修士说："你要求什么？"妇人回答他："仁者，因为你是知一切的，你自然也知道我是一个何等不幸的人。我的丈夫不爱我。他的第二个妻子欺负我，把我的头发都揪掉，还将我撵出来。仁者，求你可怜我！"修士说："到你现在所见的那个池里去吧。你先去把你的全身泡进水里一次，再来我这里。"

妇人走到池里去洗一个澡，照着修士的话，把全身泡入水中，立刻上来。她一出水，觉得全身都改变了！她的头上长满了很长的头发，长到垂到她的脚跟。她的容貌变得非常美丽。她喜欢极了，一直跑到修士面前，五体投地，向他顶礼。修士说："妇人你起来，你到草屋里去，那里有许多柳篮，你愿意拿哪一个就拿哪一个出来。"妇人进到屋里，挑上一个最好看的篮子，拿到修士面前。修士说，"打开那篮子吧。"她于是把篮盖揭开，发现里面装满了金珠、宝石之类。修士说，"妇人，你把这篮子带去吧。这篮子里的宝贝是取不尽的。你把这里头的珠宝拿起来，盖上盖子，不一会儿，它又充满许多珠宝。你取出的次数越多，它的出产也越多。在它里头的珠宝是永远取不尽的。女儿，平安地回去吧。"妇人又向他深深地顶礼，过了一会儿，就回家去了。

她拿着那篮子来到兜罗树下。兜罗树对她说："好孩子，平安地回去吧，你的丈夫一定要热烈地爱你。"她又往前走，来到圣牛那里。圣牛把缠在角上的贝串给她说："女儿，把这贝串拿去吧，把它缠在你臂上，你要用多少贝串，只要一摆手臂就可以得着。"她拿了那贝串，又向前来到芭蕉树下。芭蕉给她一片蕉叶说："孩子，把这块蕉叶拿去吧，你若把这片叶子一摇，不但可以得着很好吃的香蕉，并且能够摇出许多别样好吃的东西来。"她又把蕉叶带着，来到棉花旁边。棉花给她一枝花枝，说："女儿，你把这枝拿去吧，你摇着这枝，不但可以得着棉布，还可以得着丝绸。你就在我面前摇摇它，看应验不应验。"妇人把花枝一摇，果然摇出好些匹丝绸来。她把丝披在身上，把贝串摇出几串来装饰身体，又从篮子里取出些珠宝来戴上。她带着一切东西回到家里，年轻的妻子正在门外。她乍一看见，心里没想到那是秃妻，后来才理会出来。改变了！一个秃妻变成一个俊美的女人中的王后！她看见**秃妻**现在比她强，又有钱，自然要奉承她。**秃妻**待她很好。她穿什么，她也给她什么穿。她吃什么，她也给她什么吃。但年轻的妻子还是妒嫉她。她听人说**秃妻**的福分是树林里一个修士赐给她的，她也要去请求。

　　年轻的妻子问明路途就要到林中去求那修士赐福给她。她走过棉花园，也没为它做什么。她走过芭蕉树下、牛圈和兜罗树下都不理会它们。最后，她来到修士面前。修士叫她到池子里去洗澡，叫她只把身体全泡进水里就起来，到他那里。她到池中泡了一次，站起来，果然全身的肌肤都润滑起来，头发也长长到脚跟，很是光泽。她想再泡一下，不更好么？她再泡了一下，站起来，头发都掉了，皮肤也皱起来了！她的样子变得更难看。她哭着来到修士面前。修士撵她说："去吧，离开此地吧。你是一个不听话的女人。你不能从我这里得着什么福分了。"她很伤心，垂着头回家去了。

丈夫从远国做买卖回来，看见他的大妻子那么俊美，自然加倍爱护她。他热烈地爱她。后来知道年轻的妻子虐待她，致她得着许多法宝，就更敬慕她。他把年轻的妻子降为奴婢。他们一同过着很愉快的生活。

我的故事说到这里算完了，

那提耶棘也枯萎了。

那提耶呵，你为什么枯萎呢？

你的牛为什么要我用草来喂它？

牛呵，你为什么要人喂？

你的牧者为什么不看护我？

150

牧者呵，你为什么不去看牛？

你的儿媳妇为什么不把米给我？

儿媳妇呵，你为什么不给米呢？

我的孩子为什么哭呢？

孩子呵，你为什么哭呢？

蚂蚁为什么要咬我呢？

蚂蚁呵，你为什么要咬人呢？

喀！喀！喀！

FOLK–TALES OF BENGAL

Lal Behari Day

PREFACE

In my *Peasant Life in Bengal* I make the peasant boy Govinda spend some hours every evening in listening to stories told by an old woman, who was called Sambhu's mother, and who was the best story-teller in the village. On reading that passage, Captain R. C. Temple, of the Bengal Staff Corps, son of the distinguished Indian administrator S. Richard Temple, wrote to me to say how interesting it would be to get a collection of those unwritten stories which old women in India recite to little children in the evenings, and to ask whether I could not make such a collection. As I was no stranger to the Mährchen of the Brothers Grimm, to the *Norse Tales* so admirably told by Dasent, to Arnason's *Icelandic Stories* translated by Powell, to the *Highland Stories* done into English by Campbell, and to the fairy stories collected by other writers, and as I believed that the collection suggested would be a contribution, however slight, to that daily increasing literature of folk lore and comparative mythology which, like comparative philosophy, proves that the swarthy and half-naked peasant on the banks of the Ganges is a cousin, albeit of the hundredth remove, to the fair-skinned and well-dressed Englishman on the banks of the Thames, I readily caught up the idea and cast about for materials. But where was an old story-telling woman to be got? I had myself, when a little boy, heard hundreds—it would be no exaggeration to say thousands— of fairy tales from that same old woman, Sambhu's mother—for she was no fictitious person; she actually lived in the flesh and bore that name; but I had nearly forgotten those stories, at any rate they had all got confused in my head, the tail of one story being joined to the head of another, and the head of a third to the tail of a fourth. How I wished that poor Sambhu's mother had been alive! But she had gone long, long ago, to that bourne from which no traveller returns, and her son Sambhu, too, had followed her thither. After a great deal of search I found my Gammer Grethel—though not half so old as the Frau Viehmännin of Hesse-Cassel—in the person of a Bengali Christian woman, who, when a little girl and living in her heathen home, had heard many stories from her old grandmother. She was a good story-teller, but her stock was not large; and after I had heard ten from her I had to look about for fresh sources. An old Brahman told me two stories; an old barber, three; an old servant of mine told me two; and the rest I heard from another old Brahman. None of my authorities knew English; they all told the stories in Bengali, and I translated them into English when I came home. I heard many more stories than those contained in the following pages; but I rejected a great many, as they appeared to me to contain spurious additions to the original stories which I had heard when a boy. I have reason to believe that the stories given in this book area genuine sample of the old stories told by old Bengali women from age to age through a hundred generations.

Sambhu's mother used always to end every one of her stories—and every orthodox Bengali story-teller does the same—with repeating the following formula—

Thus my story endeth,
The Natiya-thorn withereth.
"Why, O Natiya-thorn, dost wither?"
"Why does thy cow on me browse?"
"Why, O cow, dost thou browse?"
"Why does thy neatherd not tend me?"
"Why, O neatherd, dost not tend the cow?"
"Why does thy daughter-in-law not give me rice?"
"Why, O daughter-in-law, dost not give rice?"
"Why does my child cry?"
"Why, O child, dost thou cry?"
"Why does the ant bite me?"

"Why, O ant, dost thou bite?"

Koot! Koot! Koot!

What these lines mean, why they are repeated at the end of every story, and what the connection is of the several parts to one another, I do not know. Perhaps the whole is a string of nonsense purposely put together to amuse little children.

LAL BEHARI DAY.

HOOGHLY COLLEGE,

February 27, 1883.

CHAPTER I
STRIKE BUT HEAR

Once upon a time there reigned a king who had three sons. His subjects one day came to him and said, "O incarnation of justice! The kingdom is infested with thieves and robbers. Our property is not safe. We pray your majesty to catch hold of these thieves and punish them." The king said to his sons, "O my sons, I am old, but you are all in the prime of manhood. How is it that my kingdom is full of thieves? I look to you to catch hold of these thieves." The three princes then made up their minds to patrol the city every night. With this view they set up a station in the outskirts of the city, where they kept their horses. In the early part of the night the eldest prince rode upon his horse and went through the whole city, but did not see a single thief. He came back to the station. About midnight the second prince got upon his horse and rode through every part of the city, but he did not see or hear of a single thief. He came also back to the station. Some hours after midnight the youngest prince went the rounds, and when he came near the gate of the palace where his father lived, he saw a beautiful woman coming out of the palace. The prince accosted the woman, and asked who she was and where she was going at that hour of the night. The woman answered, "I am Rajlakshmi[①], the guardian deity of this palace. The king will be killed this night. I am therefore not needed here. I am going away." The prince did not know what to make of this message. After a moment's reflection he said to the goddess, "But suppose the king is not killed tonight, then have you any objection to return to the palace and stay there?" "I have no objection," replied the goddess. The prince then begged the goddess to go in, promising to do his best to prevent the king from being killed. Then the goddess entered the palace again, and in a moment went the prince knew not whither.

The prince went straight into the bedroom of his royal father. There he lay immersed in deep sleep. His second and young wife, the stepmother of our prince, was sleeping in another bed in the room. A light was burning dimly. What was his surprise when the prince saw a huge cobra going round and round the golden bedstead on which his father was sleeping. The prince with his sword cut the serpent in two. Not satisfied with killing the cobra, he cut it up into a hundred pieces, and put them inside the pan dish[②] which was in the room. While the prince was cutting up the serpent a drop of blood fell on the breast

---

① The tutelary goddess of a king's household.

② A vessel, made generally of brass, for keeping the *pan* leaf together with betel-nut and other spices.

of his stepmother who was sleeping hard by. The prince was in great distress. He said to himself, "I have saved my father but killed my mother." How was the drop of blood to be taken out of his mother's breast? He wrapped round his tongue a piece of cloth sevenfold, and with it licked up the drop of blood. But while he was in the act of doing this, his stepmother woke up, and opening her eyes saw that it was her stepson, the youngest prince. The young prince rushed out of the room. The queen, intending to ruin the youngest prince, whom she hated, called out to her husband, "My lord, my lord, are you awake? Are you awake? Rouse yourself up. Here is a nice piece of business." The king on awaking inquired what the matter was. "The matter, my lord? Your worthy son, the youngest prince, of whom you speak so highly, was just here. I caught him in the act of touching my breast. Doubtless he came with a wicked intent. And this is your worthy son!" The king was horror-struck. The prince went to the station to his brothers, but told them nothing.

Early in the morning the king called his eldest son to him and said, "If a man to whom I intrust my honour and my life prove faithless, how should he be punished?" The eldest prince replied, "Doubtless such a man's head should be cut off, but before you kill, you should see whether the man is really faithless." "What do you mean?" inquired the king. "Let your majesty be pleased to listen," answered the prince.

"Once on a time there lived a goldsmith who had a grown-up son. And this son had a wife who had the rare faculty of understanding the language of beasts, but neither her husband nor anyone else knew that she had this uncommon gift. One night she was lying in bed beside her husband in their house, which was close to a river, when she heard a jackal howl out, 'There goes a carcase floating on the river; is there anyone who will take off the diamond ring from the finger of the dead man and give me the corpse to eat?' The woman understood the jackal's language, got up from bed and went to the river-side. The husband, who was not asleep, followed his wife at some distance so as not to be observed by her. The woman went into the water, tugged the floating corpse towards the shore, and saw the diamond ring on the finger. Unable to loosen it with her hand, as the fingers of the dead body had swelled, she bit it off with her teeth, and put the dead body upon land. She then went to her bed, whither she had been preceded by her husband. The young goldsmith lay beside his wife almost petrified with fear, for he concluded after what he saw that his wife was not a human being but a Rakshasi. He spent the rest of the night in tossing in his bed, and early in the morning spoke to his father in the following manner: 'Father, the woman whom thou hast given me to wife is not a real woman but a Rakshasi. Last night as I was lying in bed with her, I heard outside the house, towards the river-side, a jackal set up a fearful howl. On this she, thinking that I was asleep, got up from bed, opened the door, and went out to the river-side. Surprised to see her go out alone at the dead hour of night, I suspected evil and followed her, but so that she could not see me. What did she do, do you think? O horror of horrors! She went into the stream, dragged towards the shore the dead body of a man which was floating by, and began to eat it! I saw this with mine own eyes. I then returned home while she was feasting upon the carcase, and jumped into bed. In a few minutes she also returned, bolted the door, and lay beside me. O my father, how can I live with a Rakshasi? She will certainly kill me and eat me up one night.' The old goldsmith was not a little shocked to hear this account. Both father and son agreed that the woman should be taken into the forest and there left to be devoured by wild beasts. Accordingly the young goldsmith spoke to his wife thus: 'My dear love, you had better not cook much this morning; only boil rice and burn a brinjal, for I must take you today to see your father and mother, who are dying to see you.' At the mention of her father's house she became full of joy, and finished the cooking in no time. The husband and wife snatched a hasty breakfast and started on their journey. The way lay through a dense jungle, in which the goldsmith bethought himself of leaving his wife alone to be eaten up by wild beasts. But while they were passing through this jungle the woman heard a serpent hiss, the meaning of which hissing, as understood by her, was as follows: 'O passer-by, how thankful should I be to you if you would catch hold of that croaking frog in yonder hole, which is full of gold and precious stones, and give me the frog to swallow, and you take the gold and precious stones.' The woman forthwith made for the frog, and began digging the hole with a stick. The young goldsmith was now quaking with fear, thinking his Rakshasi-wife was about to kill him. She called out to him and said, 'Husband, take up all this large quantity of gold and these precious stones.' The goldsmith, not knowing what to make of it, timidly went to the place, and to his infinite surprise saw the gold and the precious stones. They took up as much as they could. On the husband's asking his wife how she came to know of the existence of all this riches, she said that she understood the language of animals, and that the snake coiled up hard by had informed her of it. The goldsmith, on finding out what an accomplished wife he was blessed with, said to her, 'My love, it has got very late today; it would be impossible to reach your father's house before nightfall, and we may be devoured by wild beasts in the jungle; I propose therefore that we both return home.' It took them a long time to reach home, for they were laden with a large quantity of gold and precious stones. On coming near the house, the goldsmith said to his wife, 'My dear, you go by the back door, while I go by the front door and see my father in his shop and show him all this gold and these precious stones.' So she entered the house by the back door, and the moment she entered she was met by the old goldsmith, who had come that minute into the house for some purpose with a hammer in his hand. The old goldsmith, when he saw his Rakshasi daughter-in-law, concluded in his mind that she had killed and swallowed up his son. He therefore struck her on the head with the hammer, and she immediately died. That moment the son came into the house, but it was too late. Hence it is that I told your majesty that before you cut off a man's head you should inquire whether the man is really guilty."

The king then called his second son to him, and said, "If a man to whom I intrust my honour and my life prove faithless, how should he be punished?" The second prince replied, "Doubtless such a man's head should be cut off, but before you kill you should see whether the man is really faithless." "What do you mean?" inquired the king. "Let your majesty be pleased to listen," answered the prince.

"Once on a time there reigned a king who was very fond of going out a-hunting. Once while he was out hunting his horse took him into a dense forest far from his followers. He rode on and on, and did not see either villages or towns. He became very thirsty, but he could see neither pond, lake, nor stream. At last he found something dripping from the top of a tree. Concluding it to be rain-water which had rested in some cavity of the tree, he stood on horseback under the tree and caught the dripping contents in a small cup. It was, however, no rain-water. A huge cobra, which was on the top of the tree, was dashing in rage its fangs against the tree; and its poison was coming out and was falling in drops. The king, however, thought it was rain-water; though his horse knew better. When the cup was nearly filled with the liquid snake-poison, and the king was about to drink it off, the horse to save the life of his royal master, so moved about that the cup fell from the king's hand and all the liquid spilled about. The king became very angry with his horse, and with his sword gave a cut to the horse's neck, and the horse died immediately. Hence it is that I told your majesty that before you cut off a man's head you should inquire whether the man is really guilty."

The king then called to him his third and youngest son, and said, "If a man to whom I intrust my honour and my life prove faithless, how should he be punished?" The youngest prince replied, "Doubtless such a man's head should be cut off, but before you kill you should see whether the man is really faithless." "What do you mean?" inquired the king. "Let your majesty be pleased to listen," answered the prince.

"Once on a time there reigned a king who had in his palace a remarkable bird of the Suka species. One day as the Suka went out to the fields for an airing, he saw his dad and dam, who pressed him to come and spend some days with them in their nest in some far-off land. The Suka answered he would be very happy to come, but he could not go without the king's leave; he added that he would speak to the king that very day, and would be ready to go the following morning if his dad and dam would come to that very spot. The Suka spoke to the king, and the king gave leave with reluctance as he was very fond of the bird. So the next morning the Suka met his dad and dam at the place appointed, and went with them to his paternal nest on the top of some high tree in a far-off land. The three birds lived happily together for a fortnight, at the end of which period the Suka said to his dad and dam, 'My beloved parents, the king granted me leave only for a fortnight, and today the fortnight is over, tomorrow I must start for the city of the king.' His dad and dam readily agreed to the reasonable proposal, and told him to take a present to the king. After laying their heads together for some time they agreed that the present should be a fruit of the tree of Immortality. So early next morning the Suka plucked a fruit off the tree of Immortality, and carefully catching it in his beak, started on his aërial journey. As he had a heavy weight to carry, the Suka was not able to reach the city of the king that day, and was benighted on the road. He took shelter in a tree, and was at a loss to know where to keep the fruit. If he kept it in his beak it was sure, he thought, to fall out when he fell asleep. Fortunately he saw a hole in the trunk of the tree in which he had taken shelter, and accordingly put the fruit in it. It so happened that in that hole there was a snake; in the course of the night the snake darted its fangs on the fruit, and thus besmeared it with its poison. Early before crow-cawing the Suka, suspecting nothing, took up the fruit of Immortality in its beak, and began his aërial voyage. The Suka reached the palace while the king was sitting with his ministers. The king was delighted to see his pet bird come again, and greatly admired the beautiful fruit which the Suka had brought as a present. The fruit was very fair to look at; it was the loveliest fruit in all the earth; and as its name implies it makes the eater of it immortal. The king was going to eat it, but his courtiers said that it was not advisable for the king to eat it, as it might be a poisonous fruit. He accordingly threw it to a crow which was perched on the wall; the crow ate a part of it; but in a moment the crow fell down and died. The king, imagining that the Suka had intended to take away his life, took hold of the bird and killed it. The king ordered the stone of the deadly fruit, as it was thought to be, to be planted in a garden outside the city. The stone in course of time became a large tree bearing lovely fruit. The king ordered a fence to be put round the tree, and placed a guard lest people should eat of the fruit and die. There lived in that city an old Brahman and his wife, who used to live upon charity. The Brahman one day mourned his hard lot, and told his wife that instead of leading the wretched life of a beggar he would eat the fruit of the poisonous tree in the king's garden and thus end his days. So that very night he got up from his bed in order to get into the king's garden. His wife, suspecting her husband's intention, followed him, resolved also to eat of the fruit and die with her husband. As at that dead hour of night the guard was asleep, the old Brahman plucked a fruit and ate it. The woman said to her husband, 'If you die what is the use of my life? I'll also eat and die.' So saying she plucked a fruit and ate it. Thinking that the poison would take some time to produce its due effect, they both went home and lay in bed, supposing that they would never rise again. To their infinite surprise next morning they found themselves to be not only alive, but young and vigorous. Their neighbours could scarcely recognize them—they had become so changed. The old Brahman had become handsome and vigorous, no grey hairs, no wrinkles on his cheeks; and as for his wife, she had become as beautiful as any lady in the king's household. The king, hearing of this wonderful change, sent for the old Brahman, who told him all the circumstances. The king then greatly lamented the sad fate of his pet bird, and blamed himself for having killed it without fully inquiring into the case."

"Hence it is," continued the youngest prince, "that I told your Majesty that before you cut off a man's head you should inquire whether the man is really guilty. I know your Majesty thinks that last night I entered your chamber with wicked intent. Be pleased to hear me before you strike. Last night as I was on my rounds, I saw a female figure come out of the palace. On challenging her she said that she was Rajlakshmi, the guardian deity of the palace; and that she was leaving the palace as the king would be killed that night. I told her to come in, and that I would prevent the king from being killed. I went straight into your bed-room, and saw a large cobra going round and round your golden bedstead. I killed the cobra, cut it up into a hundred pieces, and put them in the *pan* dish. But while I was cutting up the snake, a drop of its blood fell on the breast of my mother; and then I thought that while I had saved my father I had killed my mother. I wrapped round my tongue a piece of cloth sevenfold and licked up the drop of blood. While I was licking up the blood, my mother opened her eyes and noticed me. This is what I have done, now cut off my head if your Majesty wishes it."

The king filled with joy and gratitude embraced his son, and from that time loved him more even than he had loved him before.

Thus my story endeth,
The Natiya- thorn withereth, &c.

CHAPTER II
THE ADVENTURES OF TWO THIEVES AND OF
THEIR SONS

PART I

Once on a time there lived two thieves in a village who earned their livelihood by stealing. As they were well-known thieves, every act of theft in the village was ascribed to them whether they committed it or not; they therefore left the village, and, being resolved to support themselves by honest labour, went to a neighbouring town for service. Both of them were engaged by a householder; the one had to tend a cow, and the other to water a *champaka* plant. The elder thief began watering the plant early in the morning, and as he had been told to go on pouring water till some of it collected itself round the foot of the plant he went on pouring bucketful after bucketful, but to no purpose. No sooner was the water poured on the foot of the plant than it was forthwith sucked up by the thirsty earth; and it was late in the afternoon when the thief, tired with drawing water, laid himself down on the ground, and fell asleep. The younger thief fared no better. The cow which he had to tend was the most vicious in the whole country. When taken out of the village for pasturage it galloped away to a great distance with its tail erect; it ran from one paddy-field to another, and ate the corn and trod upon it; it entered into sugar-cane plantations and destroyed the sweet cane;— for all which damage and acts of trespass the neatherd was soundly rated by the owners of the fields. What with running after the cow from field to field, from pool to pool; what with the abusive language poured not only upon him, but upon his forefathers up to the fourteenth generation, by the owners of the fields in which the corn had been destroyed,—the younger thief had a miserable day of it. After a world of trouble he succeeded about sunset in catching hold of the cow, which he brought back to the house of his master. The elder thief had just roused himself from sleep when he saw the younger one bringing in the cow. Then the elder said to the younger—"Brother, why are you so late in coming from the fields?"

Younger.—"What shall I say, brother? I took the cow to that part of the meadow where there is a tank, near which there is a large tree. I let the cow loose, and it began to graze about without giving the least trouble. I spread my *gamchha*[①] upon the grass

---

① A towel used in bathing.

under the tree; and there was such a delicious breeze that I soon fell asleep, and I did not wake till after sunset; and when I awoke I saw my good cow grazing contentedly at the distance of a few paces. But how did you fare, brother?"

Elder.—"Oh, as for me, I had a jolly time of it. I had poured only one bucketful of water on the plant, when a large quantity rested round it. So my work was done, and I had the whole day to myself. I laid myself down on the ground; I meditated on the joys of this new mode of life; I whistled; I sang; and at last fell asleep. And I am up only this moment."

When this talk was ended, the elder thief, believing that what the younger thief had said was true, thought that tending the cow was more comfortable than watering the plant; and the younger thief, for the same reason, thought that watering the plant was more comfortable than tending the cow: each therefore resolved to exchange his own work for that of the other.

Elder.—"Well, brother, I have a wish to tend the cow. Suppose tomorrow you take my work, and I yours. Have you any objection?"

Younger.—"Not the slightest, brother. I shall be glad to take up your work, and you are quite welcome to take up mine. Only let me give you a bit of advice. I felt it rather uncomfortable to sleep nearly the whole of the day on the bare ground. If you take a *charpoy*① with you, you will have a merry time of it."

Early the following morning the elder thief went out with the cow to the fields, not forgetting to take with him a *charpoy* for his ease and comfort; and the younger thief began watering the plant. The latter had thought that one bucketful, or at the outside two bucketfuls, of water would be enough. But what was his surprise when he found that even a hundred bucketfuls were not sufficient to saturate the ground around the roots of the plant. He was dead tired with drawing water. The sun was almost going down, and yet his work was not over. At last he gave it up through sheer weariness.

The elder thief in the fields was in no better case. He took the cow beside the tank which the younger thief had spoken of, put his *charpoy* under the large tree hard by, and then let the cow loose. As soon as the cow was let loose it went scampering about in the meadow, jumping over hedges and ditches, running through paddy-fields, and injuring sugar-cane plantations. The elder thief was not a little put about. He had to run about the whole day, and to be insulted by the people whose fields had been trespassed upon. But the worst of it was, that our thief had to run about the meadow with the *charpoy* on his head, for he could not put it anywhere for

___

① A sort of bed made of rope, supported by posts of wood.

fear it should be taken away. When the other neatherds who were in the meadow saw the elder thief running about in breathless haste after the cow with the *charpoy* on his head, they clapped their hands and raised shouts of derision. The poor fellow, hungry and angry, bitterly repented of the exchange he had made. After infinite trouble, and with the help of the other neatherds, he at last caught hold of the precious cow, and brought it home long after the village lamps had been lit.

When the two thieves met in the house of their master, they merely laughed at each other without speaking a word. Their dinner over, they laid themselves to rest, when there took place the following conversation:—

Younger. —"Well, how did you fare, brother?"

Elder.—"Just as you fared, and perhaps some degrees better."

Younger.—"I am of opinion that our former trade of thieving was infinitely preferable to this sort of honest labour, as people call it."

Elder.—"What doubt is there of that? But, by the gods, I have never seen a cow which can be compared to this. It has no second in the world in point of viciousness."

Younger.—"A vicious cow is not a rare thing. I have seen some cows as vicious. But have you ever seen a plant like this *champaka* plant which you were told to water? I wonder what becomes of all the water that is poured round about it. Is there a tank below its roots?"

Elder.—"I have a good mind to dig round it and see what is beneath it."

Younger.—"We had better do so this night when the good man of the house and his wife are asleep."

At about midnight the two thieves took spades and shovels and began digging round the plant. After digging a good deal the younger thief lighted upon some hard thing against which the shovel struck. The curiosity of both was excited. The younger thief saw that it was a large jar; he thrust his hand into it and found that it was full of gold mohurs. But he said to the elder thief—"Oh, it is nothing; it is only a large stone." The elder thief, however, suspected that it was something else, but he took care not to give vent to his suspicion. Both agreed to give up digging as they had found nothing, and they went to sleep. An hour or two after, when the elder thief saw that the younger thief was asleep, he quietly got up and went to the spot which had been digged. He saw the jar filled with gold mohurs. Digging a little near it, he found another jar also filled with gold mohurs. Overjoyed to find the treasure, he resolved to secure it. He took up both the jars, went to the tank which was near, and from which water used to be drawn for the plant, and buried them in the mud of its bank. He then returned to the house, and quietly laid himself down beside the younger thief, who was then fast asleep. The younger thief, who had first found the jar of gold mohurs, now woke, and softly stealing out of bed, went to secure the treasure he had seen. On going to the spot he did not see any jar; he therefore naturally thought that his companion the elder thief had secreted it somewhere. He went to his sleeping partner, with a view to discover if possible by any marks on his body the place where the treasure had been hidden. He examined the person of his friend with the eye of a detective, and saw mud on his feet and near the ankles. He immediately concluded the treasure must have been concealed somewhere in the tank. But in what part of the tank? On which bank? His ingenuity did not forsake him here. He walked round all the four banks of the tank. When he walked round three sides, the frogs on them jumped into the water, but no frogs jumped from the fourth bank. He therefore concluded that the treasure must have been buried on the fourth bank. In a little he found the two jars filled with gold mohurs; he took them up, and going into the cow-house brought out the vicious cow he had tended, and put the two jars on its back. He left the house and started for his native village.

When the elder thief at crow-cawing got up from sleep, he was surprised not to find his companion beside him. He hastened to the tank and found that the jars were not there. He went to the cow-house, and did not see the vicious cow. He immediately concluded the younger thief must have run away with the treasure on the back of the cow. And where could he think of going? He must be going to his native village. No sooner did this process of reasoning pass through his mind than he resolved forthwith to set out and overtake the younger thief. As he passed through the town, he invested all the money he had in a costly pair of shoes covered with gold lace. He walked very fast, avoiding the public road and making short cuts. He descried the younger thief trudging on slowly with his cow. He went before him in the highway about a distance of 200 yards, and threw down on the road one shoe. He walked on another 200 yards and threw the other shoe at a place near which was a large tree; amid the thick leaves of that tree he hid himself. The younger thief coming along the public road saw the first shoe and said to himself—"What a beautiful shoe that is! It is of gold lace. It would have suited me in my present circumstances now that I have got rich. But what shall I do with one shoe?" So he passed on. In a short time he came to the place where the other shoe was lying. The younger thief said within himself—"Ah, here is the other shoe! What a fool I was, that I did not pick up the one I first saw! However it is not too late. I'll tie the cow to yonder tree and go for the other shoe." He tied the cow to the tree, and taking up the second shoe went for the first, lying at a distance of about 200 yards. In the meantime the elder thief got down from the tree, loosened the cow, and drove it towards his native village avoiding the king's highway. The younger thief on returning to the tree found that the cow was gone. He of course concluded that it could have been done only by the elder thief. He walked as fast as his legs could carry him, and reached his native village long before the elder thief with the cow. He hid himself near the door of the elder thief's house. The moment the elder thief arrived with the cow, the younger thief accosted him, saying—"So you are come safe, brother. Let us go in and divide the money." To this proposal the elder thief readily agreed. In the inner yard of the house the two jars were taken down from the back of the cow; they went to a room, bolted the door, and began dividing. Two mohurs were taken up by the hand, one was put in one place, and the other in another; and they went on doing that till the jars became empty. But last of all one gold mohur remained. The question was—who was to take it? Both agreed that it should be changed the next morning, and the silver cash equally divided. But with whom was the single mohur to remain? There was not a little wrangling about the matter. After a great deal of yea and nay, it was settled that it should remain with the elder thief, and that next morning it should be changed and equally divided.

At night the elder thief said to his wife and the other women of the house, "Look here, ladies, the younger thief will come tomorrow morning to demand the share of the remaining gold mohur, but I don't mean to give it to him. You do one thing tomorrow. Spread a cloth on the ground in the yard. I will lay myself on the cloth pretending to be dead; and to convince people that I am dead, put a *tulasi*[①] plant near my head. And when you see the younger thief coming to the door, you set up a loud cry and lamentation. Then he will of course go away, and I shall not have to pay his share of the gold mohur." To this proposal the women readily agreed. Accordingly the next day, about noon, the elder thief laid himself down in the yard like a corpse with the sacred basil near his head. When the younger thief was seen coming near the house, the women set up a loud cry, and when he came nearer and nearer, wondering what it all meant, they said, "Oh, where did you both go? What did you bring? What did you do to him? Look, he is dead!" So saying they rent the air with their cries. The

---

① The sacred basil.

younger thief, seeing through the whole, said, "Well, I am sorry my friend and brother is gone. I must now attend to his funeral. You all go away from this place, you are but women. I'll see to it that the remains are well burnt." He brought a quantity of straw and twisted it into a rope, which he fastened to the legs of the deceased man, and began tugging him, saying that he was going to take him to the place of burning. While the elder thief was being dragged through the streets his body was getting dreadfully scratched and bruised, but he held his peace, being resolved to act his part out, and thus escape giving the share of the gold mohur. The sun had gone down when the younger thief with the corpse reached the place of burning. But as he was making preparations for a funeral pile, he remembered that he had not brought fire with him. If he went for fire leaving the elder thief behind, he would undoubtedly run away. What then was to be done? At last he tied the straw rope to the branch of a tree, and kept the pretended corpse hanging in the air, and he himself climbed into the tree and sat on that branch, keeping tight hold of the rope lest it should break, and the elder thief run away. While they were in this state, a gang of robbers passed by. On seeing the corpse hanging, the head of the gang said, "This raid of ours has begun very auspiciously. Brahmans and Pandits say that if on starting on a journey one sees a corpse, it is a good omen.

Well, we have seen a corpse, it is therefore likely that we shall meet with success this night. If we do, I propose one thing: on our return let us first burn this dead body and then return home." All the robbers agreed to this proposal. The robbers then entered into the house of a rich man in the village, put its inmates to the sword, robbed it of all its treasures, and withal managed it so cleverly that not a mouse stirred in the village. As they were successful beyond measure, they resolved on their return to burn the dead body they had seen. When they came to the place of burning they found the corpse hanging as before, for the elder thief had not yet opened his mouth lest he should be obliged to give half of the gold mohur. The thieves dug a hollow in the ground, brought fuel, and laid it upon the hollow. They took down the corpse from the tree, and laid it upon the pile; and as they were going to set it on fire, the corpse gave out an unearthly scream and jumped up. That very moment the younger thief jumped down from the tree with a similar scream. The robbers were frightened beyond measure. They thought that a *Dana*(evil spirit) had possessed the corpse, and that a ghost jumped down from the tree. They ran away in great fear, leaving behind them the money and the jewels which they had obtained by robbery. The two thieves laughed heartily, took up all the riches of the robbers, went home, and lived merrily for a long time.

PART II

The elder thief and the younger thief had one son each. As they had been so far successful in life by practising the art of thieving, they resolved to train up their sons to the same profession. There was in the village a Professor of the Science of Roguery, who took pupils, and gave them lessons in that difficult science. The two thieves put their sons under this renowned Professor. The son of the elder thief distinguished himself very much, and bade fair to surpass his father in the art of stealing. The lad's cleverness was tested in the following manner. Not far from the Professor's house there lived a poor man in a hut, upon the thatch of which climbed a creeper of the gourd kind. In the middle of the thatch, which was also its topmost part, there was a splendid gourd, which the man and his wife watched day and night. They certainly slept at night, but then the thatch was so old and rickety that if even a mouse went up to it bits of straw and particles of earth used to fall inside the hut, and the man and his wife slept right below the spot where the gourd was, so that it was next to impossible to steal the gourd without the knowledge of its owners. The Professor said to his pupils—for he had many—that anyone who stole the gourd without being caught would be pronounced the dux of the school.

Our elder thief's son at once accepted the offer. He said he would steal away the gourd if he were allowed the use of three things namely, a string, a cat, and a knife. The Professor allowed him the use of these three things. Two or three hours after nightfall, the lad, furnished with the three things mentioned above, sat behind the thatch under the eaves, listening to the conversation carried on by the man and his wife lying in bed inside the hut. In a short time the conversation ceased. The lad then concluded that they must both have fallen asleep. He waited half an hour longer, and hearing no sound inside, gently climbed up on the thatch. Chips of straw and particles of earth fell upon the couple sleeping inside. The woman woke up, and rousing her husband said, "Look there, someone is stealing the gourd!" That moment the lad squeezed the throat of the cat, and puss immediately gave out her usual "Mew! Mew! Mew!" The husband said, "Don't you hear the cat mewing? There is no thief, it is only a cat." The lad in the meantime cut the gourd from the plant with his knife, and tied the string which he had with him to its stalk. But how was he to get down without being discovered and caught, especially as the man and the woman were now awake? The woman was not convinced that it was only a cat; the shaking of the thatch, and the constant falling of bits of straw and particles of dust, made her think that it was a human being that was upon the thatch. She was telling her husband to go out and see whether a man was not there, but he maintained that it was only a cat. While the man and woman were thus disputing with each other, the lad with great force threw down the cat upon the ground, on which the poor animal purred most vociferously; and the man said aloud to his wife, "There it is, you are now convinced that it was only a cat." In the meantime, during the confusion created by the clamour of the cat and the loud talk of the man, the lad quietly came down from the thatch with the gourd tied to the string. Next morning the lad produced the gourd before his teacher, and described to him and to his admiring comrades the manner in which he had committed the theft. The Professor was in ecstasy, and remarked, "The worthy son of a worthy father." But the elder thief, the father of our hopeful genius, was by no means satisfied that his son was as yet fit to enter the world. He wanted to prove him still further. Addressing his son he said, "My son, if you can do what I tell you, I'll think you fit to enter the world. If you can steal the gold chain of the queen of this country from her neck, and bring it to me, I'll think you fit to enter the world." The gifted son readily agreed to do the daring deed.

The young thief—for so we shall now call the son of the elder thief—made a reconnaissance of the palace in which the king and queen lived. He reconnoitred all the four gates, and all the outer and inner walls as far as he could; and gathered incidentally a good deal of information, from people living in the neighborhood, regarding the habits of the king and queen, in what part of the palace they slept, what guards there were near the bedchamber, and who, if any, slept in the antechamber. Armed with all this knowledge the young thief fixed upon one dark night for doing the daring deed. He took with him a sword, a hammer and some large nails, and put on very dark clothes. Thus accoutred he went prowling about the Lion gate of the palace. Before the zenana[①] could be got at, four doors, including the Lion gate, had to be passed; and each of these doors had a guard of sixteen stalwart men. The same men, however, did not remain all night at their post. As the king had an infinite number of soldiers at his command, the guards at the doors were relieved every hour; so that once every hour at each door there were thirty-two men present, consisting of the relieving party and of the relieved. The young thief chose that particular moment of time for entering each of the four doors. At the time of relief when he saw the Lion gate crowded with thirty-two men, he joined the crowd without being taken notice of; he then spent the hour preceding the next relief in the large open space and garden between two doors; and he could not be taken notice of, as the night

---

① Zenana is not the name of a proyince in India, as the good people of Scotland the other day took it to be, but the innermost department of a Hindu or Mohammedan house which the women occupy.

as well as his clothes was pitch dark. In a similar manner he passed the second door, the third door, and the fourth door. And now the queen's bedchamber stared him in the face. It was in the third loft; there was a bright light in it; and a low voice was heard as that of a woman saying something in a humdrum manner. The young thief thought that the voice must be the voice of a maidservant reciting a story, as he had learnt was the custom in the palace every night, for composing the king and queen to sleep. But how to get up into the third loft? The inner doors were all closed, and there were guards everywhere. But the young thief had with him nails and a hammer: why not drive the nails into the wall and climb up by them? True, but the driving of nails into the wall would make a great noise which would rouse the guards, and possibly the king and queen,— at any rate the maidservant reciting stories would give the alarm. Our erratic genius had considered that matter well before engaging in the work. There is a water-clock in the palace which shows the hours; and at the end of every hour a very large Chinese gong is struck, the sound of which is so loud that it is not only heard all over the palace, but over most part of the city; and the peculiarity of the gong, as of every Chinese gong, was that nearly one minute must elapse after the first stroke before the second stroke could be made, to allow the gong to give out the whole of its sound. The thief fixed upon the minutes when the gong was struck at the end of every hour for driving nails into the wall. At ten o'clock when the gong was struck ten times, the thief found it easy to drive ten nails into the wall. When the gong stopped, the thief also stopped, and either sat or stood quiet on the ninth nail catching hold of the tenth which was above the other. At eleven o'clock he drove into the wall in a similar manner eleven nails, and got a little higher than the second story; and by twelve o'clock he was in the loft where the royal bedchamber was. Peeping in he saw a drowsy maid-servant drowsily reciting a story, and the king and queen apparently asleep. He went stealthily behind the story-telling maid-servant and took his seat. The queen was lying down on a richly furnished bedstead of gold beside the king. The massive chain of gold round the neck of the queen was gleaming in candlelight. The thief quietly listened to the story of the drowsy maid-servant. She was becoming more and more sleepy. She stopped for a second, nodded her head, and again resumed the story. It was plain she was under the influence of sleep. In a moment the thief cut off the head of the maid-servant with his sword, and himself went on reciting for some minutes the story which the woman was telling. The king and queen were unconscious of any change as to the person of the story-teller, for they were both in deep sleep. He stripped the murdered woman of her clothes, put them on himself, tied up his own clothes in a bundle, and walking softly, gently took off the chain from the neck of the queen. He then went through the rooms down stairs, ordered the inner guard to open the door, as she was obliged to go out of the palace for purposes of necessity. The guards, seeing that it was the queen's maid-servant, readily allowed her to go out. In the same manner, and with the same pretext, he got through the other doors, and at last out into the street. That very night, or rather morning, the young thief put into his father's hand the gold chain of the queen. The elder thief could scarcely believe his own eyes. It was so like a dream. His joy knew no bounds. Addressing his son he said—"Well done, my son, you are not only as clever as your father, but you have beaten me hollow. The gods give you long life, my son."

Next morning when the king and queen got up from bed, they were shocked to see the maid-servant lying in a pool of blood. The queen also found that her gold chain was not round her neck. They could not make out how all this could have taken place. How could any thief manage to elude the vigilance of so many guards? How could he get into the queen's bedchamber? And how could he again escape? The king found from the reports of the guards that a person calling herself the royal maid-servant had gone out of the palace some hours before dawn. All sorts of inquiries were made, but in vain. Proclamation was made in the city, a large reward was offered to anyone who would give information tending to the apprehension of the thief and murderer. But no one responded to the call. At last the king ordered a camel to be brought to him. On the back of the animal was placed two large bags filled with gold mohurs. The man taking charge of the bags upon the camel was ordered to go through every part of the city making the following challenge: —"As the thief was daring enough to steal away a gold chain from the neck of the queen, let him further show his daring by stealing the gold mohurs from the back of this camel." Two days and nights the camel paraded through the city, but nothing happened. On the third night as the camel-driver was going his rounds he was accosted by a *sannyasi*[①], who sat on a tiger's skin before a fire, and near whom was a monstrous pair of tongs. This *sannyasi* was no other than the young thief in disguise. The *sannyasi* said to the camel driver—"Brother, why are you going through the city in this manner? Who is there so daring as to steal from the back of the king's camel? Come down, friend, and smoke with me." The camel-driver alighted, tied the camel to a tree on the spot, and began smoking. The mendicant supplied him not only with tobacco, but with *ganja* and other intoxicating drugs, so that in a short time the camel-driver became quite intoxicated and fell asleep. The young thief led

---

① A religious mendicant.

away the camel with the treasure on its back in the dead of night, through narrow lanes and bye-paths to his own house. That very night the camel was killed, and its carcase buried in deep pits in the earth, and the thing was so managed that no one could discover any trace of it.

The next morning when the king heard that the camel-driver was lying drunk in the street, and that the camel had been made away with together with the treasure, he was almost beside himself with anger. Proclamation was made in the city to the effect that whoever caught the thief would get the reward of a *lakh* of rupees. The son of the younger thief—who, by the way, was in the same school of roguery with the son of the elder thief, though he did not distinguish himself so much— now came to the front and said that he would apprehend the thief. He of course suspected that the son of the elder thief must have done it— for who so daring and clever as he? In the evening of the following day the son of the younger thief disguised himself as a woman, and coming to that part of the town where the young thief lived, began to weep very much, and went from door to door saying—"O sirs, can any of you give me a bit of camel's flesh, for my son is dying, and the doctors say nothing but eating camel's meat can save his life. O for pity's sake, do give me a bit of camel's flesh." At last he went to the house of the young thief, and begged of the wife—for the young thief himself was out—to tell him where he could get hold of camel's flesh, as his son would assuredly perish if it could not be got. Saying this he rent the air with his cries, and fell down at the feet of the young thief's wife. Woman as she was, though the wife of a thief, she felt pity for the supposed woman, and said—"Wait, and I will try and get some camel's flesh for your son." So saying, she secretly went to the spot where the dead camel had been buried, brought a small quantity of flesh, and gave it to the party. The son of the younger thief was now entranced with joy. He went and told the king that he had succeeded in tracing the thief, and would be ready to deliver him up at night if the king would send some constables with him. At night the elder thief and his son were captured, the body of the camel dug out, and all the treasures in the house seized. The following morning the king sat in judgment. The son of the elder thief confessed that he had stolen the queen's gold chain, and killed the maid-servant, and had taken away the camel; but he added that the person who had detected him, and his father—the younger thief—were also thieves and murderers, of which fact he gave undoubted proofs. As the king had promised to give a *lakh* of rupees to the detective, that sum was placed before the son of the younger thief. But soon after he ordered four pits to be dug in the earth in which were buried alive, with all sorts of thorns and thistles, the elder thief and the younger thief, and their two sons.

Here my story endeth,
The Natiya-thorn withereth, &c.

CHAPTER III
THE GHOST–BRAHMAN

Once on a time there lived a poor Brahman, who not being a Kulin, found it the hardest thing in the world to get married. He went to rich people and begged of them to give him money that he might marry a wife. And a large sum of money was needed, not so much for the expenses of the wedding, as for giving to the parents of the bride. He begged from door to door, flattered many rich folk, and at last succeeded in scraping together the sum needed. The wedding took place in due time, and he brought home his wife to his mother. After a short time he said to his mother—"Mother, I have no means to support you and my wife, I must therefore go to distant countries to get money somehow or other. I may be away for years, for I won't return till I get a good sum. In the meantime I'll give you what I have; you make the best of it, and take care of my wife." The Brahman receiving his mother's blessing set out on his travels. In the evening of that very day, a ghost assuming the exact appearance of the Brahman came into the house. The newly married woman, thinking it was her husband, said to him—"How is it that you have returned so soon? You said you might be away for years, why have you changed your mind?" The ghost said—"Today is not a lucky day, I have therefore returned home; besides, I have already got some money." The mother did not doubt but that it was her son. So the ghost lived in the house as if he was its owner, and as if he was the son of the old woman and the husband of the young woman. As the ghost and the Brahman were exactly like each other in everything, like two peas, the people in the neighborhood all thought that the ghost was the real Brahman. After some years the Brahman returned from his travels; and what was his surprise when he found another like him in the house. The ghost said to the Brahman—"Who are you? What businesses have you to come to my house?" "Who am I?" replied the Brahman, "let me ask who you are. This is my house; that is my mother, and this is my wife." The ghost said—"Why herein is a strange thing. Everyone knows that this is my house, that is my wife, and yonder is my mother; and I have lived here for years. And you pretend this is your house, and that woman is your wife. Your head must have got turned, Brahman." So saying the ghost drove away the Brahman from his house. The Brahman became mute with wonder. He did not know what to do. At last he bethought himself of going to the king and of laying his case before him. The king saw the ghost-Brahman as well as the Brahman, and the one was the picture of the other; so he was in a fix, and did not know how to decide the quarrel. Day after day the Brahman went to the king and besought him to give him back his house, his wife, and his mother; and the king, not knowing what to say every time, put him off to the following day. Every day the king tells him to—"Come tomorrow", and every day the Brahman goes away from the palace weeping and striking his forehead with the palm of his hand, and saying—"What a wicked world this is! I am driven from my own house, and another fellow has taken possession of my house and of my wife! And what a king this is! He does not do justice."

Now, it came to pass that as the Brahman went away everyday from the court outside the town, he passed a spot at which a great many cow-boys used to play. They let the cows graze on the meadow, while they themselves met together under a large tree to play. And they played at royalty. One cow-boy was elected king; another, prime minister or vizier; another, *kotwal,* or prefect of the police; and others, constables. Every day for several days together they saw the Brahman passing by weeping. One day the cow-boy king asked his vizier whether he knew why the Brahman wept every day. On the vizier not being able to answer the question, the cow-boy-king ordered one of his constables to bring the Brahman to him. One of them went and said to the Brahman—"The king requires your immediate attendance." The Brahman replied— "What for? I have just come from the king, and he put me off till tomorrow. Why does he want me again?" "It is our king that wants you—our neatherd king," rejoined the constable. "Who is neatherd king?" asked the Brahman. "Come and see," was the reply. The neatherd king then asked the Brahman why he every day went away weeping. The Brahman then told him his sad story. The neatherd king, after hearing the whole, said, "I understand your case; I will give you again all your rights. Only go to the king and ask his permission for me to decide your case." The Brahman went back to the king of the country and begged his Majesty to send his case to the neatherd king, who had offered to decide it. The king, whom the case had greatly puzzled, granted the permission sought. The following morning was fixed for the trial. The neatherd king, who saw through the whole, brought with him next day a phial with a narrow neck. The Brahman and the ghost-Brahman both appeared at the bar. After a great deal of examination of witnesses and of speech-making, the neatherd king said—"Well, I have heard enough. I'll decide the case at once. Here is this phial. Whichever of yon will enter into it shall be declared by the court to be the rightful owner of the house the title of which is in dispute. Now, let me see, which of you will enter." The Brahman said—"You are a neatherd, and your intellect is that of a neatherd. What man can enter into such a small phial?" "If you cannot enter," said the neatherd king, "then you are not the rightful owner. What do you say, sir, to this?" turning to the ghost-Brahman and addressing him. "If you can enter into the phial, then the house and the wife and the mother become yours." "Of course I will enter," said the ghost. And true to his word, to the wonder of all, he made himself into a small creature like an insect, and entered into the phial. The neatherd king forthwith corked up the phial, and the ghost could not get out. Then, addressing the Brahman, the neatherd king said, "Throw this phial into the bottom of the sea, and take possession of your house, wife, and mother." The Brahman did so, and lived happily for many years and begat sons and daughters.

Here my story endeth,
The Natiya-thorn withereth, &c.

CHAPTER IV
THE MAN WHO WISHED TO BE PERFECT

Once on a time a religious mendicant came to a king who had no issue, and said to him, "As you are anxious to have a son, I can give to the queen a drug, by swallowing which she will give birth to twin sons; but I will give the medicine on this condition, that of those twins you will give one to me, and keep the other yourself." The king thought the condition somewhat hard, but as he was anxious to have a son to bear his name, and inherit his wealth and kingdom, he at last agreed to the terms. Accordingly the queen swallowed the drug, and in due time gave birth to two sons. The twin brothers became one year old, two years old, three years old, four years old, five years old, and still the mendicant did not appear to claim his share; the king and queen therefore thought that the mendicant, who was old, was dead, and dismissed all fears from their minds. But the mendicant was not dead, but living; he was counting the years carefully. The young princes were put under tutors, and made rapid progress in learning, as well as in the arts of riding and shooting with the bow; and as they were uncommonly handsome, they were admired by all the people. When the princes were sixteen years old the mendicant made his appearance at the palace gate, and demanded the fulfilment of the king's promise. The heart of the king and of the queen were dried up within them. They had thought that the mendicant was no more in the land of the living; but what was their surprise when they saw him standing at the gate in flesh and blood, and demanding one of the young princes for himself. The king and queen were plunged into a sea of grief. There was nothing for it, however, but to part with one of the princes; for the mendicant might by his curse turn into ashes, not only both the princes, but also the king, queen, palace, and the whole of the kingdom to boot. But which one was to be given away? The one was as dear as the other. A fearful struggle arose in the heart of the king and queen. As for the young princes, each of them said, "I'll go," "I'll go." The younger one said to the elder, "You are older, if only by a few minutes; you are the pride of my father; you remain at home, I'll go with the mendicant." The elder said to the younger, "You are younger than I am; you are the joy of my mother; you remain at home, I'll go with the mendicant." After a great deal of yea and nay, after a great deal of mourning and lamentation, after the queen had wetted her clothes with her tears, the elder prince was let go with the mendicant. But before the prince left his father's roof he planted with his own hands a tree in the courtyard of the palace, and said to his parents and brother, "This tree is my life. When you see the tree green and fresh, then know that it is well with me; when you see the tree fade in some parts, then know that I am in an ill case; and when you see the whole tree fade, then know that I am dead and gone." Then kissing and embracing the king and queen and his brother, he followed the mendicant.

As the mendicant and the prince were wending their way towards the forest they saw some dog's whelps on the road-side. One of the whelps said to its dam—"Mother, I wish to go with that handsome young man, who must be a prince." The dam said—"Go," and the prince gladly took the puppy as his companion. They had not gone far when upon a tree on the roadside they saw a hawk and its young ones. One of the young ones said to its dam—"Mother, I wish to go with that handsome young man who must be the son of a king." The hawk said—"Go," and the prince gladly took the young hawk as his companion. So the mendicant, the prince with the puppy and the young hawk went on their journey. At last they went into the depth of the forest far away from the houses of men, where they stopped before a hut thatched with leaves. That was the mendicant's cell. The mendicant said to the prince—"You are to live in this hut with me. Your chief work will be to cull flowers from the forest for my devotions. You can go on every side except the north. If you go towards the north evil will betide you. You can eat whatever fruit or root you like; and for your drink, you will get it from the brook." The prince disliked neither the place nor his work. At dawn he used to cull flowers in the forest and give them to the mendicant; after which the mendicant went away somewhere the whole day and did not return till sundown; so the prince had the whole day to himself. He used to walk about in the forest with his two companions—the puppy and the young hawk. He used to shoot arrows at the deer, of which there was a great number; and thus made the best of his time. One day as he pierced a stag with an arrow, the wounded stag ran towards the north, and the prince, not thinking of the mendicant's behest, followed the stag, which entered into a fine-looking house that stood close by. The prince entered, but instead of finding the deer he saw a young woman of matchless beauty sitting near the door with a dice-table set before her. The prince was rooted to the spot while he admired the heaven-born beauty of the lady. "Come in, stranger," said the lady, "chance has brought you here, but don't go away without having with me a game of dice." The prince gladly agreed to the proposal. As it was a game of risk they agreed that if the prince lost the game he should give his young hawk to the lady; and that if the lady lost it, she should give to the prince a young hawk just like that of the prince. The lady won the game; she therefore took the prince's young hawk and kept it in a hole covered with a plank. The prince offered to play a second time, and the lady agreeing to it, they fell to it again, on the condition that if the lady won the game she should take the prince's puppy, and if she lost it she should give to the prince a puppy just like that of the prince. The lady won again, and stowed away the puppy in another hole with a plank upon it. The prince offered to play a third time, and the wager was that, if the prince lost the game, he should give himself up to the lady to be done to by her anything she pleased; and that if he won, the lady should give him a young man exactly like himself. The lady won the game a third time; she therefore caught hold of the prince and put him in a hole covered over with a plank. Now, the beautiful lady was not a woman at all; she was a Rakshasi who lived upon human flesh, and her mouth watered at the sight of the tender body of the young prince. But as she had had her food that day she reserved the prince for the meal of the following day.

Meantime there was great weeping in the house of the prince's father. His brother used every day to look at the tree planted in the courtyard by his own hand. Hitherto he had found the leaves of a living green colour, but suddenly he found some leaves fading. He gave the alarm to the king and queen, and told them how the leaves were fading. They concluded that the life of the elder prince must be in great danger. The younger prince therefore resolved to go to the help of his brother, but before going he planted a tree in the courtyard of the palace, similar to the one his brother had planted, and which was to be the index of the manner of his life. He chose the swiftest steed in the king's stables, and galloped towards the forest. In the way he saw a dog with a puppy, and the puppy thinking that the rider was the same that had taken away his fellow-cub—for the two princes were exactly like each other—said, "As you have taken away my brother, take me also with you." The younger prince understanding that his brother had taken away a puppy, he took up that cub as a companion. Further on, a young hawk, which was perched on a tree on the road-side, said to the prince, "You have taken away my brother, take me also, I beseech you;" on which the younger prince readily took it up. With these companions he went into the heart of the forest, where he saw a hut which he supposed to be the mendicant's. But neither the mendicant nor his brother was there. Not knowing what to do or where to go, he dismounted from his horse, allowed it to graze, while he himself sat inside the house. At sunset the mendicant returned to his hut, and seeing the younger prince said—"I am glad to see you, I told your brother never to go towards the north, for evil in that case would betide him; but it seems that, disobeying my orders, he has gone to the north and has fallen into the toils of a Rakshasi who lives there. There is no hope of rescuing him, perhaps he has already been devoured." The younger prince forthwith went towards the north, where he saw a stag which he pierced with an arrow. The stag ran into a house which stood by, and the younger prince followed it. He was not a little astonished when instead of seeing a stag he saw a woman of exquisite beauty. He immediately concluded from what he had heard from the mendicant that the pretended woman was none other than the Rakshasi in whose power his brother was. The lady asked him to play a game of dice with her. He complied with the request, and on the same conditions on which the elder prince had played. The younger prince won; on which the lady produced the young hawk from the hole and gave it to the prince. The joy of the two hawks on meeting each other was great. The lady and the prince played a second time, and the prince won again. The lady therefore brought to the prince the young puppy lying in the hole. They played a third time and the prince won a third time. The lady demurred to producing a young man exactly like the prince, pretending that it was impossible to get one, but on the prince insisting upon the fulfilment of the condition his brother was produced. The joy of the two brothers on meeting each other was great. The Rakshasi said to the princes, "Don't kill me, and I will tell you a secret which will save the life of the elder prince." She then told them that the mendicant was a worshipper of the goddess Kali, who had a temple not far off; that he belonged to that sect of Hindus who seek perfection from intercourse with the spirits of departed men; that he had already sacrificed at the altar of Kali six human victims whose skulls could be seen in niches inside her temple; that he would become perfect when the seventh victim was sacrificed; and that the elder prince was intended for the seventh victim. The Rakshasi then told the prince to go immediately to the temple to find out the truth of what she had said. To the temple they accordingly went. When the elder prince went inside the temple, the skulls in the niches laughed a ghastly laugh. Horror-struck at the sight and sound, he inquired the cause of the laughter; and the skulls told him that they were glad because they were about to get another added to their number. One of the skulls, as spokesman of the rest, said—"Young prince, in a few days the mendicant's devotions will be completed, and you will be brought into this temple and your head will be cut off, and you will keep company with us. But there is one way by which you can escape that fate and do us good." "Oh, do tell me," said the prince, "what that way is, and I promise to do you all the good I can." The skull replied—"When the mendicant brings you into this temple to offer you up as a sacrifice, before cutting off your head he will tell you to prostrate yourself before Mother Kali, and while you prostrate yourself he will cut off your head. But take our advice, when he tells you to bow down before Kali, you tell him that as a prince you never bowed down to any one, that you never knew what bowing down was, and that the mendicant should show it to you by himself doing it in your presence. And when he bows down to show you how it is done, you take up your sword and separate his head from his body. And when you do that we shall all be restored to life, as the mendicant's vows will be unfulfilled." The elder prince thanked the skulls for their advice, and went into the hut of the mendicant along with his younger brother.

In the course of a few days the mendicant's devotions were completed. On the following day he told the prince to go along with him to the temple of Kali, for what reason he did not mention, but the prince knew it was to offer him up as a victim to the goddess. The younger prince also went with them, but he was not allowed to go inside the temple. The mendicant then stood in the presence of Kali and said to the prince—"Bow down to the goddess." The prince replied, "I have not, as a prince, bowed to any one; I do not know how to perform the act of prostration. Please show me the way first, and I'll gladly do it." The mendicant then prostrated himself before the goddess; and while he was doing so the prince at one stroke of his sword separated his head from his body. Immediately the skulls in the niches of the temple laughed aloud, and the goddess herself became propitious to the prince and gave him that virtue of perfection which the mendicant had sought to obtain. The skulls were again united to their respective bodies and became living men, and the two princes returned to their country.

Here my story endeth,
The Natiya-thorn withereth, &c.

CHAPTER V
A GHOSTLY WIFE

Once on a time there lived a Brahman who had married a wife, and who lived in the same house with his mother. Near his house was a tank, on the embankment of which stood a tree, on the boughs of which lived a ghost of the kind called *Sankchinni*[①]. One night the Brahman's wife had occasion to go to the tank, and as she went she brushed by a *Sankchinni* who stood near; on which the she-ghost got very angry with the woman, seized her by the throat, climbed into her tree, and thrust her into a hole in the trunk. There the woman lay almost dead with fear. The ghost put on the clothes of the woman and went into the house of the Brahman. Neither the Brahman not his mother had any inkling of the change. The Brahman thought his wife returned from the tank, and the mother thought that it was her daughter-in-law.

Next morning the mother-in-law discovered some change in her daughter-in-law. Her daughter-in-law, she knew, was

---

① *Sankchinnis* or *Sankhachurnis* are female ghosts of white complexion. They usually stand at the dead of night at the foot of trees, and look like sheets of white cloth.

constitutionally weak and languid, and took a long time to do the work of the house. But she had apparently become quite a different person. All of a sudden she had become very active. She now did the work of the house in an incredibly short time. Suspecting nothing, the old woman said nothing either to her son or to her daughter-in-law; on the contrary, she inly rejoiced that her daughter-in-law had turned over a new leaf. But her surprise became every day greater and greater. The cooking of the household was done in much less time than before. When the mother-in-law wanted the daughter-in-law to bring anything from the next room, it was brought in much less time than was required in walking from one room to the other. The ghost instead of going inside the next room would stretch a long arm—for ghosts can lengthen or shorten any limb of their bodies—from the door and get the thing. One day the old woman observed the ghost doing this. She ordered her to bring a vessel from some distance, and the ghost unconsciously stretched her hand to several yards' distance, and brought it in a trice. The old woman was struck with wonder at the sight. She said nothing to her, but spoke to her son. Both mother and son began to watch the ghost more narrowly. One day the old woman knew that there was no fire in the house, and she knew also that her daughter-in-law had not gone out of doors to get it; and yet, strange to say, the hearth in the kitchen-room was quite in a blaze. She went in, and, to her infinite surprise, found that her daughter-in-law was not using any fuel for cooking, but had thrust into the oven her foot, which was blazing brightly. The old mother told her son what she had seen, and they both concluded that the young woman in the house was not his real wife but a she-ghost. The son witnessed those very acts of the ghost which his mother had seen. An *Ojha*[①] was therefore sent for. The exorcist came, and wanted in the first instance to ascertain whether the woman was a real woman or a ghost. For this purpose he lighted a piece of turmeric and set it below the nose of the supposed woman. Now this was an infallible test, as no ghost, whether male or female, can put up with the smell of burnt turmeric. The moment the lighted turmeric was taken near her, she screamed aloud and ran away from the room. It was now plain that she was either a ghost or a woman possessed by a ghost. The woman was caught hold of by main force and asked who she was. At first she refused to make any disclosures, on which the *Ojha* took up his slippers and began belaboring her with them. Then the ghost said with a strong nasal accent—for all ghosts speak through the nose—that she was a *Sankchinni*, that she lived on a tree by the side of the tank, that she had seized the young Brahmani and put

---

① An exorcist, one who drives away ghosts from possessed persons.

her in the hollow of her tree because one night she had touched her, and that if any person went to the hole the woman would be found. The woman was brought from the tree almost dead; the ghost was again shoe-beaten, after which process on her declaring solemnly that she would not again do any harm to the Brahman and his family, she was released from the spell of the *Ojha* and sent away, and the wife of the Brahman recovered slowly. After which the Brahman and his wife lived many years happily together and begat many sons and daughters.

Thus my story endeth,
The Natiya-thorn withereth, &c.

CHAPTER VI
THE STORY OF A BRAHMADAITYA[①]

Once on a time there lived a poor Brahman who had a wife. As he had no means of livelihood, he used every day to beg from door to door, and thus got some rice which they boiled and ate, together with some greens which they gleaned from the fields. After some time it chanced that the village changed its owner, and the Brahman bethought himself of asking some boon of the new laird. So one morning the Brahman went to the laird's house to pay him court. It so happened that at that time the laird was making inquiries of his servants about the village and its various parts. The laird was told that a certain banyan-tree in the outskirts of the village was haunted by a number of ghosts; and that no man had ever the boldness to go to that tree at night. In bygone days some rash fellows went to the tree at night, but the necks of them all were wrung, and they all died. Since that time no man had ventured to go to the tree at night, though in the day some neatherds took their cows to the spot. The

---

① The ghost of a Brahman who dies unmarried.

new laird on hearing this, said that if anyone would go at night to the tree, cut one of its branches and bring it to him, he would make him a present of a hundred *bighas*[①] of rent-free land. None of the servants of the laird accepted the challenge, as they were sure they would be throttled by the ghosts. The Brahman, who was sitting there, thought within himself thus—"I am almost starved to death now, as I never get my bellyful. If I go to the tree at night and succeed in cutting off one of its branches I shall get one hundred *bighas* of rent-free land, and become independent for life. If the ghosts kill me, my case will not be worse, for to die of hunger is no better than to be killed by ghosts." He then offered to go to the tree and cut off a branch that night. The laird renewed his promise, and said to the Brahman that if he succeeded in bringing one of the branches of that haunted tree at night he would certainly give him one hundred *bighas* of rent-free land.

In the course of the day when the people of the village, heard of the laird's promise and of the Brahman's offer, they all pitied the poor man. They blamed him for his foolhardiness, as they were sure the ghosts would kill him, as they had killed so many before. His wife tried to dissuade him from the rash undertaking, but in vain. He said he would die in any case; but there was some

---

① A *bigha* is about the third part of an acre.

chance of his escaping, and of thus becoming independent for life. Accordingly, one hour after sundown, the Brahman set out. He went to the outskirts of the village without the slightest fear as far as a certain *vakula*-tree (Mimusops Elengi), from which the haunted tree was about one rope distant. But under the *vakula*-tree the Brahman's heart misgave him. He began to quake with fear, and the heaving of his heart was like the upward and downward motion of the paddy-husking pedal. The *vakula*-tree was the haunt of a Brahmadaitya, who, seeing the Brahman stop under the tree, spoke to him, and said, "Are you afraid, Brahman? Tell me what you wish to do, and I'll help you. I am a Brahmadaitya." The Brahman replied, "O blessed spirit, I wish to go to yonder banyan-tree, and cut off one of its branches for the zemindar, who has promised to give me one hundred *bighas* of rent-free land for it. But my courage is failing me. I shall thank you very much for helping me." The Brahmadaitya answered, "Certainly I'll help you, Brahman. Go on towards the tree, and I'll come with you." The Brahman, relying on the supernatural strength of his invisible patron, who is the object of the fear and reverence of common ghosts, fearlessly walked towards the haunted tree, on reaching which he began to cut a branch with the bill which was in his hand. But the moment the first stroke was given, a great many ghosts rushed towards the Brahman, who would have been torn to pieces but for the interference of the Brahmadaitya. The Brahmadaitya said in a commanding tone, "Ghosts, listen. This is a poor Brahman. He wishes to get a branch of this tree which will be of great use to him. It is my will that you let him cut a branch." The ghosts, hearing the voice of the Brahmadaitya, replied, "Be it according to thy will, lord. At thy bidding we are ready to do anything. Let not the Brahman take the trouble of cutting; we ourselves will cut a branch for him." So saying, in the twinkling of an eye, the ghosts put into the hands of the Brahman a branch of the tree, with which he went as fast as his legs could carry him to the house of the zemindar. The zemindar and his people were not a little surprised to see the branch; but he said, "Well, I must see tomorrow whether this branch is a branch of the haunted tree or not; if it be, you will get the promised reward."

Next morning the zemindar himself went along with his servants to the haunted tree, and found to their infinite surprise that the branch in their hands was really a branch of that tree, as they saw the part from which it had been cut off. Being thus satisfied, the zemindar ordered a deed to be drawn up, by which he gave to the Brahman for ever one hundred *bighas* of rent free land. Thus in one night the Brahman became a rich man.

It so happened that the fields, of which the Brahman became

the owner, were covered with ripe paddy, ready for the sickle. But the Brahman had not the means to reap the golden harvest. He had not a pice in his pocket for paying the wages of the reapers. What was the Brahman to do? He went to his spirit-friend the Brahmadaitya, and said, "Oh, Brahmadaitya, I am in great distress. Through your kindness I got the rent-free land all covered with ripe paddy. But I have not the means of cutting the paddy, as I am a poor man. What shall I do?" The kind Brahmadaitya answered, "Oh, Brahman, don't be troubled in your mind about the matter. I'll see to it that the paddy is not only cut, but that the corn is threshed and stored up in granaries, and the straw piled up in ricks. Only you do one thing. Borrow from men in the village one hundred sickles, and put them all at the foot of this tree at night. Prepare also the exact spot on which the grain and the straw are to be stored up."

The joy of the Brahman knew no bounds. He easily got a hundred sickles, as the husbandmen of the village, knowing that he had become rich, readily lent him what he wanted. At sunset he took the hundred sickles and put them beneath the *vakula*-tree. He also selected a spot of ground near his hut for his magazine of paddy and for his ricks of straw; and washed the spot with a solution of cow-dung and water. After making these preparations he went to sleep.

In the meantime, soon after nightfall, when the villagers had all retired to their houses, the Brabmadaitya called to him the ghosts of the haunted tree, who were one hundred in number, and said to them, "You must tonight do some work for the poor Brahman whom I am befriending. The hundred *bighas* of land which he has got from the zemindar are all covered with standing ripe corn. He has not the means to reap it. This night you all must do the work for him. Here are, you see, a hundred sickles; let each of you take a sickle in hand and come to the field I shall show him. There are a hundred of you. Let each ghost cut the paddy of one *bigha*, bring the sheaves on his back to the Brahman's house, thresh the corn, put the corn in one large granary, and pile up the straw in separate ricks. Now, don't lose time. You must do it all this very night." The hundred ghosts at once said to the Brahmadaitya, "We are ready to do whatever your lordship commands us." The Brahmadaitya showed the ghosts the Brahman's house, and the spot prepared for receiving the grain and the straw, and then took them to the Brahman's fields, all waving with the golden harvest. The ghosts at once fell to it. A ghost harvest-reaper is different from a human harvest-reaper. What a man cuts in a whole day, a ghost cuts in a minute. *Mash, mash, mash*, the sickles went round, and the long stalks of paddy fell to the ground. The reaping over, the ghosts

217

took up the sheaves on their huge backs and carried them all to the Brahman's house. The ghosts then separated the grain from the straw, stored up the grain in one huge store-house, and piled up the straw in many a fantastic rick. It was full two hours before sunrise when the ghosts finished their work and retired to rest on their tree. No words can tell either the joy of the Brahman and his wife when early next morning they opened the door of their hut, or the surprise of the villagers, when they saw the huge granary and the fantastic ricks of straw. The villagers did not understand it. They at once ascribed it to the gods.

A few days after this the Brahman went to the *vakula*-tree, and said to the Brahmadaitya, "I have one more favour to ask of you, Brahmadaitya. As the gods have been very gracious to me, I wish to feed one thousand Brahmans; and I shall thank you for providing me with the materials of the feast." "With the greatest pleasure," said the polite Brahmadaitya, "I'll supply you with the requirements of a feast for a thousand Brahmans; only show me the cellars in which the provisions are to be stored away." The Brahman improvised a store-room. The day before the feast the store-room was overflowing with provisions. There were one hundred jars of *ghi* (clarified butter), one hill of flour, one hundred jars of sugar, one hundred jars of milk, curds, and congealed milk, and the other thousand and one things required in a great Brahmanical feast. The next morning one hundred Brahman pastrycooks were employed; the thousand Brahmans ate their fill; but the host, the Brahman of the story, did not eat. He thought he would eat with the Brahmadaitya. But the Brahmadaitya, who was present there though unseen, told him that he could not gratify him on that point, as by befriending the Brahman the Brahmadaitya's allotted period had come to an end, and the *pushpaka*[1] chariot had been sent to him from heaven. The Brahmadaitya, being released from his ghostly life, was taken up into heaven; and the Brahman lived happily for many years, begetting sons and grandsons.

Here my story endeth,
The Natiya-thorn withereth, &c.

---

[1] The chariot of Kuvera, the Hindu god of riches.

CHAPTER VII
THE STORY OF A HIRAMAN[1]

There was a fowler who had a wife. The fowler's wife said to her husband one day, "My dear, I'll tell you the reason why we are always in want. It is because you sell every bird you catch by your rods, whereas if we sometimes eat some of the birds you catch, we are sure to have better luck. I propose therefore that whatever bird or birds you bag today we do not sell, but dress and eat." The fowler agreed to his wife's proposal, and went out a-bird-catching. He went about from wood to wood with his limed rods, accompanied by his wife, but in vain. Somehow or other they did not succeed in catching any bird till near sundown. But just as they were returning homewards they caught a beautiful hiraman. The fowler's wife taking the bird in her hand and feeling it all over, said, "What a small bird this is! How much meat can it have? There is no use in killing it." The hiraman said, "Mother, do not kill me,

---

[1] "*Hiraman* (from *harit*, green, and *mani*, a gem), the name of a beautiful species of parrot, a native of the Molucca Islands (*Psittacus sinensis*)."——CAREY'S *Dictionary of the Bengalee Language*, vol. ii. Part iii. p. 1,537.

but take me to the king, and you will get a large sum of money by selling me." The fowler and his wife were greatly taken aback on hearing the bird speak, and they asked the bird what price they should set upon it. The hiraman answered, "Leave that to me; take me to the king and offer me for sale; and when the king asks my price, say, 'The bird will tell its own price,' and, then I'll mention a large sum." The fowler accordingly went the next day to the king's palace, and offered the bird for sale. The king, delighted with the beauty of the bird, asked the fowler what he would take for it. The fowler said, "O great king, the bird will tell its own price." "What! Can the bird speak?" asked the king. "Yes, my lord; be pleased to ask the bird its price," replied the fowler. The king, half in jest and half in seriousness, said, "Well, hiraman, what is your price?" The hiraman answered, "Please your majesty, my price is ten thousand rupees. Do not think that the price is too high. Count out the money for the fowler, for I'll be of the greatest service to your majesty." "What service can you be of to me, hiraman?" asked the king. "Your majesty will see that in due time," replied the hiraman. The king, surprised beyond measure at hearing the hiraman talk, and talk so sensibly, took the bird, and ordered his treasurer to tell down the sum of ten thousand rupees to the fowler.

The king had six queens, but he was so taken up with the bird that he almost forgot that they lived; at any rate, his days and nights were spent in the company, not of the queens, but of the bird. The hiraman not only replied intelligently to every question the king put, but it recited to him the names of the three hundred and thirty millions of the gods of the Hindu pantheon, the hearing of which is always regarded as an act of piety. The queens felt that they were neglected by the king, became jealous of the bird, and determined to kill it. It was long before they got an opportunity, as the bird was the king's inseparable companion. One day the king went out a-hunting, and he was to be away from the palace for two days. The six queens determined to avail themselves of the opportunity and put an end to the life of the bird. They said to one another, "Let us go and ask the bird which of us is the ugliest in his estimation, and she whom he pronounces the ugliest shall strangle the bird." Thus resolved, they all went into the room where the bird was; but before the queens could put any questions the bird so sweetly and so piously recited the names of the gods and goddesses, that the hearts of them all were melted into tenderness, and they came away without accomplishing their purpose. The following day, however, their evil genius returned, and they called themselves a thousand fools for having been diverted from their purpose. They therefore determined to steel their hearts against all pity, and to kill the bird without delay. They all went into the room, and said to the bird, "O hiraman, you are a very wise bird, we hear, and your judgments are all right; will you please tell us which of us is the handsomest and which the ugliest?" The bird, knowing the evil design of the queens, said to them, "How can I answer your questions remaining in this cage? In order to pronounce a correct judgment I must look minutely on every limb of you all, both in front and behind. If you wish to know my opinion you must set me free." The women were at first afraid of setting the bird free lest it should fly away; but on second thoughts they set it free after shutting all the doors and windows of the room. The bird, on examining the room, saw that it had a water-passage through which it was possible to escape. When the question was repeated several times by the queens, the bird said, "The beauty of not one of you can be compared to the beauty of the little toe of the lady that lives beyond the seven oceans and the thirteen rivers." The queens, on hearing their beauty spoken of in such slighting terms, became exceedingly furious, and rushed towards the bird to tear it in pieces; but before they could get at it, it escaped through the water-passage, and took shelter in a wood cutter's hut which was hard by.

The next day the king returned home from hunting, and not finding the hiraman on its perch became mad with grief. He asked the queens, and they told him that they knew nothing about it. The king wept day and night for the bird, as he loved it much. His ministers became afraid lest his reason should give way, for he used every hour of the day to weep, saying, "O my hiraman! O my hiraman! Where art thou gone?" Proclamation was made by beat of drum throughout the kingdom to the effect that if any person could produce before the king his pet hiraman he would be rewarded with ten thousand rupees. The woodcutter, rejoiced at the idea of becoming independent for life, produced the precious bird and obtained the reward. The king, on hearing from the parrot that the queens had attempted to kill it, became mad with rage. He ordered them to be driven away from the palace and put in a desert place without food. The king's order was obeyed, and it was rumoured after a few days that the poor queens were all devoured by wild beasts.

After some time the king said to the parrot, "Hiraman, you said to the queens that the beauty of none of them could be compared to the beauty of even the little toe of the lady who lives on the other side of the seven oceans and thirteen rivers. Do you know of any means by which I can get at that lady?"

Hiraman.—"Of course I do. I can take your majesty to the door of the palace in which that lady of peerless beauty lives; and if your majesty will abide by my counsel I will undertake to put that lady into your arms."

King.——"I will do whatever you tell me. What do you wish me to do?"

Hiraman.—"What is required is a *pakshiraj*[①]. If you can procure a horse of that species, you can ride upon it, and in no time we shall cross the seven oceans and thirteen rivers, and stand at the door of the lady's palace."

King.—"I have, as you know, a large stud of horses; we can now go and see if there are any *pakshirajes* amongst them."

The king and the hiraman went to the royal stables and examined all the horses. The hiraman passed by all the fine-looking horses and those of high mettle, and alighted upon a wretched-looking lean pony, and said, "Here is the horse I want. It is a horse of the genuine *pakshiraj* breed, but it must be fed full six months with the finest grain before it can answer our purpose." The king accordingly put that pony in a stable by itself and himself saw every day that it was fed with the finest grain that could be got in the kingdom. The pony rapidly improved in appearance, and at the end of six months the hiraman pronounced it fit for service. The parrot then told the king to order the royal silversmith to make

---

① Winged horse, literally, the *king of bird*.

some *khais*[①] of silver. A large quantity of silver *khais* was made in a short time. When about to start on their aërial journey the hiraman said to the king, "I have one request to make. Please whip the horse only once at starting. If you whip him more than once, we shall not be able to reach the palace, but stick mid-way. And when we return homewards after capturing the lady, you are also to whip the horse only once; if you whip him more than once, we shall come only half the way and remain there." The king then got upon the *pakshiraj* with the hiraman and the silver *khais*, and gently whipped the animal once. The horse shot through the air with the speed of lightning, passed over many countries, kingdoms, and empires, crossed the oceans and thirteen rivers, and alighted in the evening at the gate of a beautiful palace.

Now, near the palace-gate there stood a lofty tree. The hiraman told the king to put the horse in the stable hard by, and then to climb into the tree and remain there concealed. The hiraman took the silver *khais*, and with its beak began dropping *khai* after *khai* from the foot of the tree, all through the corridors and passages, up to the door of the bedchamber of the lady of peerless beauty. After doing this, the hiraman perched upon the tree where the king was concealed. Some hours after midnight, the maid-servant of the lady,

---

① *Khai* is fried paddy.

who slept in the same room with her, wishing to come out, opened the door and noticed the silver *khais* lying there. She took up a few of them, and not knowing what they were, showed them to her lady. The lady, admiring the little silver bullets, and wondering how they could have got there, came out of her room and began picking them up. She saw a regular stream of them apparently issuing from near the door of her room, and proceeding she knew not how far. She went on picking up in a basket the bright, shining *khais* all through the corridors and passages, till she came to the foot of the tree. No sooner did the lady of peerless beauty come to the foot of the tree than the king, agreeably to instructions previously given to him by the hiraman, alighted from the tree and caught hold of the lady. In a moment she was put upon the horse along with himself. At that moment the hiraman sat upon the shoulder of the king, the king gently whipped the horse once, and they all were whirled through the air with the speed of lightning. The king, wishing to reach home soon with the precious prize, and forgetful of the instructions of the hiraman, whipped the horse again; on which the horse at once alighted on the outskirts of what seemed a dense forest. "What have you done, O king?" shouted out the hiraman. "Did I not tell you not to whip the horse more than once? You have whipped him twice, and we are done for. We may meet with our death here." But the thing was done, and it could not be helped. The *pakshiraj* became powerless; and the party could not proceed homewards. They dismounted; but they could not see anywhere the habitations of men. They ate some fruits and roots, and slept that night there upon the ground.

Next morning it so chanced that the king of that country came to that forest to hunt. As he was pursuing a stag, whom he had pierced with an arrow, he came across the king and the lady of peerless beauty. Struck with the matchless beauty of the lady, he wished to seize her. He whistled, and in a moment his attendants flocked around him. The lady was made a captive, and her lover, who had brought her from her house on the other side of the seven oceans and thirteen rivers, was not put to death, but his eyes were put out, and he was left alone in the forest—alone, and yet not alone, for the good hiraman was with him.

The lady of peerless beauty was taken into the king's palace, as well as the pony of her lover. The lady said to the king that he must not come near her for six months, in consequence of a vow which she had taken, and which would be completed in that period of time. She mentioned six months, as that period would be necessary for recruiting the constitution of the *pakshiraj*. As the lady professed to engage every day in religious ceremonies, in consequence of her vow, a separate house was assigned to her, where she took the *pakshiraj* and fed him with the choicest grain. But everything would be fruitless if the lady did not meet the hiraman. But bow is she to get a sight of that bird? She adopted the following expedient. She ordered her servants to scatter on the roof of her house heaps of paddy, grain, and all sorts of pulse for the refreshment of birds. The consequence was, that thousands of the feathery race came to the roof to partake of the abundant feast. The lady was every day on the lookout for her hiraman. The hiraman, meanwhile, was in great distress in the forest. He had to take care not only of himself, but of the now blinded king. He plucked some ripe fruits in the forest, and gave them to the king to eat, and he ate of them himself. This was the manner of hiraman's life. The other birds of the forest spoke thus to the parrot—"O hiraman, you have a miserable life of it in this forest. Why don't you come with us to an abundant feast provided for us by a pious lady, who scatters many maunds of pulse on the roof of her house for the benefit of our race? We go there early in the morning and return in the evening, eating our fill along with thousands of other birds." The hiraman resolved to accompany them next morning, shrewdly suspecting more in the lady's charity to birds than the other birds thought there was in it. The hiraman saw the lady, and had a long chat with her about the health of the blinded king, the means of curing his blindness, and about her escape. The plan adopted was as follows: The pony would be ready for aërial flight in a short time—for a great part of the six months had already elapsed; and the king's blindness could be cured if the hiraman could procure from the chicks of the bihangama and bihangami birds who had their nest on the tree at the gate of the lady's palace beyond the seven oceans and thirteen rivers, a quantity of their ordure, fresh and hot, and apply it to the eyeballs of the blinded king. The following morning the hiraman started on his errand of mercy, remained at night on the tree at the gate of the palace beyond the seven oceans and thirteen rivers, and early the next morning waited below the nest of the birds with a leaf on his beak, into which dropped the ordure of the chicks. That moment the hiraman flew across the oceans and rivers, came to the forest, and applied the precious balm to the sightless sockets of the king. The king opened his eyes and saw. In a few days the *pakshiraj* was in proper trim. The lady escaped to the forest and took the king up; and the lady, king, and hiraman all reached the king's capital safe and sound. The king and the lady were united together in wedlock. They lived many years together happily, and begat sons and daughters; and the beautiful hiraman was always with them reciting the names of the three hundred and thirty millions of gods.

Here my story endeth,
The Natiya-thorn withereth, &c.

CHAPTER VIII
THE ORIGIN OF RUBIES

There was a certain king who died leaving four sons behind him with his queen. The queen was passionately fond of the youngest of the princes. She gave him the best robes, the best horses, the best food, and the best furniture. The other three princes became exceedingly jealous of their youngest brother, and conspiring against him and their mother, made them live in a separate house, and took possession of the estate. Owing to over-indulgence, the youngest prince had become very wilful. He never listened to any one, not even to his mother, but had his own way in everything. One day he went with his mother to bathe in the river. A large boat was riding there at anchor. None of the boatmen were in it. The prince went into the boat, and told his mother to come into it. His mother besought him to get down from the boat, as it did not belong to him. But the prince said, "No, mother, I am not coming down; I mean to go on a voyage, and if you wish to come with me, then delay not but come up at once, or I shall be off in a trice." The queen besought the prince to do no such thing, but to come down instantly. But the prince gave no heed to what she said, and began to take up the anchor. The queen went up into the boat in great haste; and the moment she was on board the boat started, and falling into the current passed on swiftly like an arrow. The boat went on and on till it reached the sea. After it had gone many furlongs into the open sea, the boat came near a whirlpool, where the prince saw a great many rubies of monstrous size floating on the waters. Such large rubies no one had ever seen, each being in value equal to the wealth of seven kings. The prince caught hold of half a dozen of those rubies, and put them on board. His mother said, "Darling, don't take up those red balls; they must belong to somebody who has been shipwrecked, and we may be taken up as thieves." At the repeated entreaties of his mother the prince threw them into the sea, keeping only one tied up in his clothes. The boat then drifted towards the coast, and the queen and the prince arrived at a certain port where they landed.

The port where they landed was not a small place; it was a large city, the capital of a great king. Not far from the palace, the queen and her son hired a hut where they lived. As the prince was yet a boy, he was fond of playing at marbles. When the children of the king came out to play on a lawn before the palace, our young prince joined them. He had no marbles, but he played with the ruby which he had in his possession. The ruby was so hard that it broke every taw against which it struck. The daughter of the king, who used to watch the games from a balcony of the palace, was astonished to see a brilliant red ball in the hand of the strange lad, and wanted to take possession of it. She told her father that a boy of the street had an uncommonly bright stone in his possession which she must have, or else she would starve herself to death. The king ordered his servants to bring to him the lad with the precious stone. When the boy was brought, the king wondered at the largeness and brilliancy of the ruby. He had never seen anything like it. He doubted whether any king of any country in the world possessed so great a treasure. He asked the lad where he had got it. The lad replied that he got it from the sea. The king offered a thousand rupees for the ruby, and the lad not knowing its value readily parted with it for that sum. He went with the money to his mother, who was not a little frightened, thinking that her son had stolen the money from some rich man's house. She became quiet, however, on being assured that the money was given to him by the king in exchange for the red ball which he had picked up in the sea.

The king's daughter, on getting the ruby put it in her hair, and, standing before her pet parrot, said to the bird, "Oh, my darling parrot, don't I look very beautiful with this ruby in my hair?" The parrot replied, "Beautiful! You look quite hideous with it! What princess ever puts only one ruby in her hair? It would be somewhat feasible if you had two at least." Stung with shame at the reproach cast in her teeth by the parrot, the princess went into the grief-chamber of the palace and would neither eat nor drink. The king was not a little concerned when he heard that his daughter had gone into the grief-chamber. He went to her, and asked her the cause of her grief. The princess told the king what her pet parrot had said, and added, "Father, if you do not procure for me another ruby like this, I'll put an end to my life by mine own hands." The king was overwhelmed with grief. Where was he to get another ruby like it? He doubted whether another like it could be found in the whole world. He ordered the lad who had sold the ruby to be brought into his presence. "Have you, young man," asked the king, "another ruby like the one you sold me?" The lad replied, "No, I have not got one more. Why, do you want another? I can give you lots, if you wish to have them. They are to be found in a whirlpool in the sea, far, far away. I can go and fetch some for you." Amazed at the lad's reply, the king offered rich rewards for procuring only another ruby of the same sort.

The lad went home and said to his mother that he must go to

sea again to fetch some rubies for the king. The woman was quite frightened at the idea, and begged him not to go. But the lad was resolved on going, and nothing could prevent him from carrying out his purpose. He accordingly went alone on board that same vessel which had brought him and his mother, and set sail. He reached the whirlpool, from near which he had formerly picked up the rubies. This time, however, he determined to go to the exact spot whence the rubies were coming out. He went to the centre of the whirlpool, where he saw a gap reaching to the bottom of the ocean. He dived into it, leaving his boat to wheel round the whirlpool. When he reached the bottom of the ocean he saw there a beautiful palace. He went inside. In the central room of the palace there was the god Siva, with his eyes closed, and absorbed apparently in intense meditation. A few feet above Siva's head was a platform, on which lay a young lady of exquisite beauty. The prince went to the platform and saw that the head of the lady was separated from her body. Horrified at the sight, he did not know what to make of it. He saw a stream of blood trickling from the severed head, falling upon the matted head of Siva, and running into the ocean in the form of rubies. After a little two small rods, one of silver and one of gold, which were lying near the head of the lady, attracted his eyes. As he took up the rods in his hands, the golden rod accidentally fell upon the head, on which the head immediately joined itself to the body, and the lady got up. Astonished at the sight of a human being, the lady asked the prince who he was and how he had got there. After hearing the story of the prince's adventures, the lady said, "Unhappy young man, depart instantly from this place; for when Siva finishes his meditations he will turn you to ashes by a single glance of his eyes." The young man, however, would not go except in her company, as he was over head and ears in love with the beautiful lady. At last they both contrived to run away from the palace, and coming up to the surface of the ocean they climbed into the boat near the centre of the whirlpool, and sailed away towards land, having previously laden the vessel with a cargo of rubies. The wonder of the prince's mother at seeing the beautiful damsel may be well imagined. Early next morning the prince sent a basin full of big rubies, through a servant. The king was astonished beyond measure. His daughter, on getting the rubies, resolved on marrying the wonderful lad who had made a present of them to her. Though the prince had a wife, whom he had brought up from the depths of the ocean, he consented to have a second wife. They were accordingly married, and lived happily for years, begetting sons and daughters.

Here my story endeth,
The Natiya-thorn withereth, &c.

CHAPTER IX
THE MATCH–MAKING JACKAL

Once on a time there lived a weaver, whose ancestors were very rich, but whose father had wasted the property which he had inherited in riotous living. He was born in a palace-like house, but he now lived in a miserable hut. He had no one in the world, his parents and all his relatives having died. Hard by the hut was the lair of a jackal. The jackal, remembering the wealth and grandeur of the weaver's forefathers, had compassion on him, and one day coming to him, said, "Friend weaver, I see what a wretched life you are leading. I have a good mind to improve your condition. I'll try and marry you to the daughter of the king of this country." "I become the king's son-in-law!" replied the weaver; "that will take place only when the sun rises in the west." "You doubt my power?" rejoined the jackal, "you will see, I'll bring it about."

The next morning the jackal started for the king's city, which was many miles off. On the way he entered a plantation of the Piper betel plant, and plucked a large quantity of its leaves. He reached the capital, and contrived to get inside the palace. On the premises of the palace was a tank in which the ladies of the king's household performed their morning and afternoon ablutions. At the entrance of that tank the jackal laid himself down. The daughter of the king happened to come just at the time to bathe, accompanied by her maids. The princess was not a little struck at seeing the jackal lying down at the entrance. She told her maids to drive the jackal away. The jackal rose as if from sleep, and instead of running away, opened his bundle of betel-leaves, put some into his mouth, and began chewing them. The princess and her maids were not a little astonished at the sight. They said among themselves, "What an uncommon jackal is this! From what country can he have come? A jackal chewing betel-leaves! Why thousands of men and women of this city cannot indulge in that luxury. He must have come from a wealthy land." The princess asked the jackal, "Sivalu[①]! From what country do you come? It must be a very prosperous country where the jackals chew betel-leaves. Do other animals in your country chew betel-leaves?" "Dearest princess," replied the jackal, "I come from a land flowing with milk and honey. Betel-leaves are as plentiful in my country as the grass in your fields. All animals in my country—cows, sheep, dogs—chew betel-leaves. We want

---

① A name for a jackal, not unlike Reynard in Europe.

no good thing." "Happy is the country," said the princess, "where there is such plenty, and thrice happy the king who rules in it!" "As for our king," said the jackal, "he is the richest king in the world. His palace is like the heaven of Indra. I have seen your palace here; it is a miserable hut compared to the palace of our king." The princess, whose curiosity was excited to the utmost pitch, hastily went through her bath, and going to the apartments of the queen-mother, told her of the wonderful jackal lying at the entrance of the tank. Her curiosity being excited, the jackal was sent for. When the jackal stood in the presence of the queen. He began munching the betel-leaves. "You come," said the queen, "from a very rich country. Is your king married?" "Please your majesty, our king is not married. Princesses from distant parts of the world tried to get married to him, but he rejected them all. Happy will that princess be whom our king condescends to marry!" "Don't you think, Sivalu," asked the queen, "that my daughter is as beautiful as a Pori and that she is fit to be the wife of the proudest king in the world?" "I quite think," said the jackal, "that the princess is exceedingly handsome; indeed, she is the handsomest princess I have ever seen; but I don't know whether our king will have a liking for her." "Liking for my daughter!" said the queen, "you have only to paint her to him as she is, and he is sure to turn mad with love. To be serious, Sivalu, I am anxious to get my daughter married. Many princes have sought her hand, but I am unwilling to give her to any of them, as they are not the sons of great kings. But your king seems to be a great king. I can have no objection to making him my son-in-law." The queen sent word to the king, requesting him to come and see the jackal. The king came and saw the jackal, heard him describe the wealth and pomp of the king of his country, and expressed himself not unwilling to give away his daughter in marriage to him.

The jackal after this returned to the weaver and said to him, "O lord of the loom, you are the luckiest man in the world; it is all settled; you are to become the son-in-law of a great king. I have told them that you are yourself a great king, and you must behave yourself as one. You must do just as I instruct you, otherwise your fortune will not only not be made, but both you and I will be put to death." "I'll do just as you bid me," said the weaver. The shrewd jackal drew in his own mind a plan of the method of procedure he should adopt, and after a few days went back to the palace of the king in the same manner in which he had gone before, that is to say, chewing betel-leaves and lying down at the entrance of the tank on the premises of the palace. The king and queen were glad to see him, and eagerly asked him as to the success of his mission. The jackal said, "In order to relieve your minds I may tell you at once that my mission has been so far successful. If you only knew the infinite trouble I have had in persuading his Majesty, my sovereign, to make up his mind to marry your daughter, you would give me no end of thanks. For a long time he would not hear of it, but gradually I brought him round. You have now only to fix an auspicious day for the celebration of the solemn rite. There is one bit of advice, however, which I, as your friend, would give you. It is this. My master is so great a king that if he were to come to you in state, attended by all his followers, his horses and his elephants, you would find it impossible to accommodate them all in your palace or in your city. I would therefore propose that our king should come to your city, not in state, but in a private manner; and that you send to the outskirts of your city your own elephants, horses, and conveyances, to bring him and only a few of his followers to your palace." "Many thanks, wise Sivalu, for this advice. I could not possibly make accommodation in my city for the followers of as great a king as your master is. I should be very glad if he did not come in state; and trust you will use your influence to persuade him to come in a private manner; for I should be ruined if he came in state." The jackal then gravely said, "I will do my best in the matter," and then returned to his own village, after the royal astrologer had fixed an auspicious day for the wedding.

On his return the jackal busied himself with making preparations for the great ceremony. As the weaver was clad in tatters, he told him to go to the washermen of the village and borrow from them a suit of clothes. As for himself, he went to the king of his race, and told him that on a certain day he would like one thousand jackals to accompany him to a certain place. He went to the king of crows, and begged that his corvine majesty would be pleased to allow one thousand of his black subjects to accompany him on a certain day to a certain place. He preferred a similar petition to the king of paddy-birds.

At last the great day arrived. The weaver arrayed himself in the clothes which he had borrowed from the village washer-men. The jackal made his appearance, accompanied by a train of a thousand jackals, a thousand crows, and a thousand paddy-birds. The nuptial procession started on their journey, and towards sundown arrived within two miles of the king's palace. There the jackal told his friends, the thousand jackals, to set up a loud howl; at his bidding the thousand crows cawed their loudest, while the hoarse screeching of the thousand paddy-birds furnished a suitable accompaniment. The effect may be imagined. They all together made a noise the like of which had never been heard since the world began. While this unearthly noise was going on, the jackal himself hastened to the palace, and asked the king whether he thought he would be able to accommodate the wedding-party, which was about two miles distant, and whose noise was at that moment sounding in his ears. The king said, "Impossible, Sivalu; from the sound of the procession I infer there must be at least one hundred thousand souls. How is it possible to accommodate so many guests? Please, so arrange that the bridegroom only will come to my house." "Very well," said the jackal, "I told you at the beginning that you would not be able to accommodate all the attendants of my august master. I'll do as you wish. My master will alone come in undress. Send a horse for the purpose." The jackal, accompanied by a horse and groom, came to the place where his friend the weaver was, thanked the thousand jackals, the thousand crows and the thousand paddy-birds, for their valuable services, and told them all to go away, while he himself, and the weaver on horseback, wended their way to the king's palace. The bridal party, waiting in the palace, were greatly disappointed at the personal appearance of the weaver; but the jackal told them that his master had purposely put on a mean dress, as his would-be father-in-law declared himself unable to accommodate the bridegroom and his attendants coming in state. The royal priests now began the interesting ceremony, and the nuptial knot was tied for ever. The bridegroom seldom opened his lips, agreeably to the instructions of the jackal, which was afraid lest his speech should betray him. At night when he was lying in bed he began to count the beams and rafters of the room, and said audibly, "This beam will make a first-rate loom, that other a capital beam, and that yonder an excellent sley." The princess, his bride, was not a little astonished. She began to think in her mind, "Is the man, to whom they have tied me, a king or a weaver? I am afraid he is the latter; otherwise why should he be talking of weaver's loom, beam, and sley? Ah, me! Is this what the fates kept in store for me?" In the morning the princess related to the queen-mother the weaver's soliloquy. The king and queen, not a little surprised at this recital, took the jackal to talk about it. The ready-witted jackal at once said, "Your Majesty need not be surprised at my august master's soliloquy. His palace is surrounded by a population of seven hundred families of the best weavers in the world, to whom he has given rent-free lands, and whose welfare he continually seeks. It must have been in one of his philanthropic moods that he uttered the soliloquy which has taken your Majesty by surprise." The jackal, however, now felt that it was high time for himself and the weaver to decamp with the princess, since the proverbial simplicity of his friend of the loom might any moment involve him in danger. The jackal therefore represented to the king, that weighty affairs of state would not permit his august master to spend another day in the palace; that he should start for his kingdom that very day with his bride; and his master was resolved to travel incognito on foot, only the princess, now the queen, should leave the city in a *palki*. After a great deal of yea and nay, the king and queen at last consented to the proposal. The party came to the outskirts of the weaver's village; the *palki* bearers were sent away; and the princess, who asked where her husband's palace was, was made to walk on foot. The weaver's hut was soon reached, and the jackal, addressing the princess, said, "This, madam, is your husband's palace." The princess began to beat her forehead with the palms of her hands in sheer despair. "Ah, me! Is this the husband whom *Prajapati*[①] intended for me? Death would have been a thousand times better."

As there was nothing for it, the princess soon got reconciled to her fate. She, however, determined to make her husband rich, especially as she knew the secret of becoming rich. One day she told her husband to get for her a pice-worth of flour. She put a little water in the flour, and smeared her body with the paste. When the paste dried on her body, she began wiping the paste with her fingers; and as the paste fell in small balls from her body, it got turned into gold. She repeated this

---

① The god who presides over marriages.

process every day for some time, and thus got an immense quantity of gold. She soon became mistress of more gold than is to be found in the coffers of any king. With this gold she employed a whole army of masons, carpenters and architects, who in no time built one of the finest palaces in the world. Seven hundred families of weavers were sought for and settled round about the palace. After this she wrote a letter to her father to say that she was sorry he had not favoured her with a visit since the day of her marriage, and that she would be delighted if he now came to see her and her husband. The king agreed to come, and a day was fixed. The princess made great preparations against the day of her father's arrival. Hospitals were established in several parts of the town for diseased, sick, and infirm animals. The beasts in thousands were made to chew betel-leaves on the wayside. The streets were covered with Cashmere shawls for her father and his attendants to walk on. There was no end of the display of wealth and grandeur. The king and queen arrived in state, and were infinitely delighted at the apparently boundless riches of their son-in-law. The jackal now appeared on the scene, and saluting the king and queen, said—"Did I not tell you?"

Here my story endeth,
The Natiya-thorn withereth, &c.

CHAPTER X
THE BOY WITH THE MOON ON HIS FOREHEAD

There was a certain king who had six queens, none of whom bore children. Physicians, holy sages, mendicants, were consulted, countless drugs were had recourse to, but all to no purpose. The king was disconsolate. His ministers told him to marry a seventh wife, and he was accordingly on the lookout.

In the royal city there lived a poor old woman who used to pick up cow-dung from the fields, make it into cakes, dry them in the sun, and sell them in the market for fuel. This was her only means of subsistence. This old woman had a daughter exquisitely beautiful. Her beauty excited the admiration of every one that saw her; and it was solely in consequence of her surpassing beauty that three young ladies, far above her in rank and station, contracted friendship with her. Those three young ladies were the daughter of the king's minister, the daughter of a wealthy merchant, and the daughter of the royal priest. These three young ladies, together with the daughter of the poor old woman, were one day bathing in a tank not far from the palace. As they were performing their ablutions, each dwelt on her own good qualities. "Look here, sister," said the minister's daughter, addressing the merchant's daughter, "the man that marries me will be a happy man, for he will not have to buy clothes for me. The cloth which I once put on never gets soiled, never gets old, never tears." The merchant's daughter said, "And my husband too will be a happy man, for the fuel which I use in cooking never gets turned into ashes. The same fuel serves from day to day, from year to year." "And my husband will also become a happy man," said the daughter of the royal chaplain, "for the rice which I cook one day never gets finished, and when we have all eaten, the same quantity which was first cooked remains always in the pot." The daughter of the poor old woman said in her turn, "And the man that marries me will also be happy, for I shall give birth to twin children, a son and a daughter. The daughter will be divinely fair, and the son will have the moon on his forehead and stars on the palms of his hands."

The above conversation was overheard by the king, who, as he was on the lookout for a seventh queen, used to skulk about in places where women met together. The king thus thought in his mind—"I don't care a straw for the girl whose clothes never tear and never get old; neither do I care for the other girl whose fuel is never consumed; nor for the third girl whose rice never fails in the pot. But the fourth girl is quite charming! She will give birth to twin children, a son and a daughter; the daughter will be divinely fair, and the son will have the moon on his forehead and stars on the palms of his hands. That is the girl I want. I'll make her my wife."

On making inquiries on the same day, the king found that the fourth girl was the daughter of a poor old woman who picked up cow-dug from the fields; but though there was thus an infinite disparity in rank, he determined to marry her. On the very same day he sent for the poor old woman. She, poor thing, was quite frightened when she saw a messenger of the king standing at the door of her hut. She thought that the king had sent for her to punish her, because, perhaps, she had some day unwittingly picked up the dung of the king's cattle. She went to the palace, and was admitted into the king's private chamber. The king asked her whether she had a very fair daughter, and whether that daughter was the friend of his own minister's and priest's daughters. When the woman answered, in the affirmative, he said to her, "I will marry your daughter, and make her my queen." The woman hardly believed her own ears—the thing was so strange. He however, solemnly declared to her that he had made up his mind, and was determined to marry her daughter. It was soon known in the capital that the king was going to marry the daughter of the old woman who picked up cow-dung in the fields. When the six queens heard the news, they would not believe it, till the king himself told them that the news was true. They thought that the king had somehow got mad. They reasoned with him thus—"What folly, what madness, to marry a girl who is not fit to be our maid-servant! And you expect us to treat her as our equal—a girl whose mother goes about picking up cow-dung in the fields! Surely, my lord, you are beside yourself!" The king's purpose, however, remained unshaken. The royal astrologer was called, and an auspicious day was fixed for the celebration of the king's marriage. On the appointed day the royal priest tied the marital knot, and the daughter of the poor old picker-up of cow-dung in the fields became the seventh and best beloved queen.

Sometime after the celebration of the marriage, the king went for six months to another part of his dominions. Before setting out he called to him the seventh queen, and said to her, "I am going away to another part of my dominions for six months. Before the expiration of that period I expect you to be confined. But I should like to be present with you at the time, as your enemies may do mischief. Take this golden bell and hang it in your room. When the pains of childbirth come upon you, ring this bell, and I will be with you in a moment in whatever part of my dominions I may be at the time. Remember, you are to ring the bell only when you feel the pains of childbirth." After saying this, the king started on his journey. The six queens, who had overheard the king, went on the next day to the apartments of the seventh queen, and said, "What a nice bell of gold you have got, sister! Where did you get it, and why have you hung it up?" The seventh queen, in her simplicity, said, "The king has given it to me, and if I were to ring it, the king would immediately come to me wherever he might be at the time." "Impossible!" said the six queens, "you must have misunderstood the king. Who can believe that this bell can be heard at the distance of hundreds of miles? Besides, if it could be heard, how would the king be able to travel a great distance in the twinkling of an eye? This must be a hoax. If you ring the bell, you will find that what the king said was pure nonsense." The six queens then told her to make a trial. At first she was unwilling, remembering what the king had told her; but at last she was prevailed upon to ring the bell. The king was at the moment half-way to the capital of his other dominions, but at the ringing of the bell he stopped short in his journey, turned back, and in no time stood in the queen's apartments. Finding the queen going about in her rooms, he asked why she had rung the bell though her hour had not come. She, without informing the king of the entreaty of the six queens, replied that she rang the bell only to see whether what he had said was true. The king was somewhat indignant, told her distinctly not to ring the bell again till the moment of the coming upon her of the pains of childbirth, and then went away. After the lapse of some weeks the six queens again begged of the seventh queen to make a second trial of the bell. They said to her, "The first time when you rang the bell the king was only at a short distance from you, it was therefore easy for him to hear the bell and to come to you; but now he has long ago settled in his other capital, let us see if he will now hear the bell and come to you." She resisted for a long time, but was at last prevailed upon by them to ring the bell. When the sound of the bell reached the king he was in court dispensing justice, but when he heard the sound of the bell (and no one else heard it) he closed the court and in no time stood in the queen's apartments. Finding that the queen was not about to be confined, he asked her why she had again rung the bell before her hour. She, without saying anything of the importunities of the six queens, replied that she merely made a second trial of the bell. The king became very angry, and said to her, "Now listen, since you have called me twice for nothing, let it be known to you that when the throes of childbirth do really come upon you, and you ring the bell ever so lustily, I will not come to you. You must be left to your fate." The king then went away.

At last the day of the seventh queen's deliverance arrived. On first feeling the pains she rang the golden bell. She waited, but the king did not make his appearance. She rang again with all her might, still the king did not make his appearance. The king certainly did hear the sound of the bell, but he did not come as he was displeased with the queen. When the six queens saw that the king did not come, they went to the seventh queen and told her that it was not customary with the ladies of the palace to be confined in the king's apartments; she must go to a hut near the stables. They then sent for the midwife of the palace, and heavily bribed her to make away with the infant the moment it should be born into the world. The seventh queen gave birth to a son who had the moon on his forehead and stars on the palms of his hands, and also to an uncommonly beautiful girl. The midwife had come provided with a couple of newly born pups. She put the pups before the mother, saying—"You have given birth to these," and took away the twin-children in an earthen vessel. The queen was quite insensible at the time, and did not notice the twins at the time they were carried away. The king, though he was angry with the seventh queen, yet remembering that she was destined to give birth to the heir of his throne, changed his mind, and came to see her the next morning. The pups were produced before the king as the offspring of the queen. The king's anger and vexation knew no bounds. He ordered that the seventh queen should be expelled from the palace, that she should be clothed in leather, and that she should be employed in the market-place to drive away crows and to keep off dogs. Though scarcely able to move she was driven away from the palace, stripped of her fine robes, clothed in leather, and set to drive away the crows of the market-place.

The midwife, when she put the twins in the earthen vessel, bethought herself of the best way to destroy them. She did not think it proper to throw them into a tank, lest they should be discovered the next day. Neither did she think of burying them in the ground, lest they should be dug up by a jackal and exposed to the gaze of people. The best way to make an end of them, she thought, would be to burn them, and reduce them to ashes, that no trace might be left of them. But how could she, at that dead hour of night, burn them without some other person helping her? A happy thought struck her. There was a potter on the outskirts of the city, who used during the day to mould vessels of clay on his wheel, and burn them during the latter part of the night. The midwife thought that the best plan would be to put the vessel with the twins along with the unburnt clay vessels which the potter had arranged in order and gone to sleep expecting to get up late at night and set them on fire: in this way, she thought, the twins would be reduced to ashes. She, accordingly, put the vessel with the twins along with the unburnt clay vessels of the potter, and went away.

Somehow or other, that night the potter and his wife overslept themselves. It was near the break of day when the potter's wife, awaking out of sleep, roused her husband, and said, "Oh, my good man, we have overslept ourselves; it is now near morning and I much fear it is now too late to set the pots on fire." Hastily unbolting the door of her cottage, she rushed out to the place where the pots were ranged in rows. She could scarcely believe her eyes when she saw that all the pots had been baked and were looking bright red, though neither she nor her husband had applied any fire to them. Wondering at her good luck, and not knowing what to make of it, she ran to her husband and said, "Just come and see!" The potter came, saw, and wondered. The pots had never before been so well baked. Who could have done this? This could have proceeded only from some god or goddess. Fumbling about the pots, he accidentally upturned one in which, lo and behold, were seen huddled up together two newly born infants of unearthly beauty. The potter said to his wife, "My dear, you must pretend to have given birth to these beautiful children." Accordingly all arrangements were made, and in due time it was given out that the twins had been born to her. And such lovely twins they were! On the same day many women of the neighbourhood came to see the potter's wife and the twins to which she had given birth, and to offer their congratulations on this unexpected good fortune. As for the potter's wife, she could not be too proud of her pretended children, and said to her admiring friends, "I had hardly hoped to have children at all. But now that the gods have given me these twins, may they receive the blessings of you all, and live forever!"

The twins grew and were strengthened. The brother and sister, when they played about in the fields and lanes, were the admiration of everyone who saw them; and all wondered at the uncommonly good luck of the potter in being blessed with such angelic children. They were about twelve years old when the potter, their reputed father, became dangerously ill. It was evident to all that his sickness would end in death. The potter, perceiving his last end approaching, said to his wife, "My dear, I am going the way of all the earth; but I am leaving to you enough to live upon; live on and take care of these children." The woman said to her husband, "I am not going to survive you. Like all good and faithful wives, I am determined to die along with you. You and I will burn together on the same funeral pyre. As for the children, they are old enough to take care of themselves, and you are leaving them enough money." Her friends tried to dissuade her from her purpose, but in vain. The potter died; and as his remains were being burnt, his wife, now a widow, threw herself on the pyre, and burnt herself to death.

The boy with the moon on his forehead—by the way, he always

kept his head covered with a turban lest the halo should attract notice—and his sister, now broke up the potter's establishment, sold the wheel and the pots and pans, and went to the bazaar in the king's city. The moment they entered, the bazaar was lit up on a sudden. The shopkeepers of the bazaar were greatly surprised. They thought some divine beings must have entered the place. They looked upon the beautiful boy and his sister with wonder. They begged of them to stay in the bazaar. They built a house for them. When they used to ramble about, they were always followed at a distance by the woman clothed in leather, who was appointed by the king to drive away the crows of the bazaar. By some unaccountable impulse she used also to hang about the house in which they lived. The boy in a short time bought a horse and went a-hunting in the neighbouring forests. One day while he was hunting, the king was also hunting in the same forest, and seeing a brother huntsman the king drew near to him. The king was struck with the beauty of the lad and a yearning for him the moment he saw him. As a deer went past, the youth slot an arrow, and the reaction of the force necessary to shoot the arrow made the turban of his head fall off, on which a bright light, like that of the moon, was seen shining on his forehead. The king saw, and immediately thought of the son with the moon on his forehead and stars on the palms of his hands who was to have been born of his seventh queen. The youth on letting fly the arrow galloped off, in spite of the earnest entreaty of the king to wait and speak to him. The king went home a sadder man than he came out of it. He became very moody and melancholy. The six queens asked him why he was looking so sad. He told them that he had seen in the woods a lad with the moon on his forehead, which reminded him of the son who was to be born of the seventh queen. The six queens tried to comfort him in the best way they could; but they wondered who the youth could be. Was it possible that the twins were living? Did not the midwife say that she had burnt both the son and the daughter to ashes? Who, then, could this lad be? The midwife was sent for by the six queens and questioned. She swore that she had seen the twins burnt. As for the lad whom the king had met with, she would soon find out who he was. On making inquiries, the midwife soon found out that two strangers were living in the bazaar in a house which the shopkeepers had built for them. She entered the house and saw the girl only, as the lad had again gone out a-shooting. She pretended to be their aunt, who had gone away to another part of the country shortly after their birth; she had been searching after them for a long time, and was now glad to find them in the king's city near the palace. She greatly admired the beauty of the girl, and said to her, "My dear child, you are so beautiful, you require the *kataki*[①] flower properly to set off

---

[①] *Colotropis gigantea.*

your beauty. You should tell your brother to plant a row of that flower in this courtyard." "What flower is that, auntie? I never saw it." "How could you have seen it, my child? It is not found here; it grows on the other side of the ocean, guarded by seven hundred Rakshasas." "How, then," said the girl, "will my brother get it?" "He may try to get it, if you speak to him," replied the woman. The woman made this proposal in the hope that the boy with the moon on his forehead would perish in the attempt to get the flower.

When the youth with the moon on his forehead returned from hunting, his sister told him of the visit paid to her by their aunt, and requested him, if possible, to get for her the *kataki* flower. He was skeptical about the existence of any aunt of theirs in the world, but he was resolved that, to please his beloved sister, he would get the flower on which she had set her heart. Next morning, accordingly, he started on his journey, after bidding his sister not to stir out of the house till his return. He rode on his fleet steed, which was of the *pakshiraj*[①] tribe, and soon reached the outskirts of what seemed to him dense forests of interminable length. He descried some Rakshasas prowling about. He went to some distance, shot with his arrows some deer and rhinoceroses in the neighbouring thickets, and, approaching the place where the Rakshasas were prowling

---

① *Aurum fornicctum.*

about, called out, "O auntie dear, O auntie dear, your nephew is here."A huge Rakshasi came towards him and said, "O, you are the youth with the moon on your forehead and stars on the palms of your hands. We were all expecting you, but as you have called me aunt, I will not eat you up. What is it you want? Have you brought any eatables for me?" The youth gave her the deer and rhinoceroses which he had killed. Her mouth watered at the sight of the dead animals, and she began eating them. After swallowing down all the carcasses, she said, "Well, what do you want?" The youth said, "I want some *kataki* flowers for my sister." She then told him that it would be difficult for him to get the flower, as it was guarded by seven hundred Rakshasas; however, he might make the attempt, but in the first instance he must go to his uncle on the north side of that forest. While the youth was going to his uncle of the north, on the way he killed some deer and rhinoceroses, and seeing a gigantic Rakshasa at some distance, cried out, "Uncle dear, uncle dear, your nephew is here. Auntie has sent me to you." The Rakshasa came near and said, "You are the youth with the moon on your forehead and stars on the palms of your hands; I would have swallowed you outright, had you not called me uncle, and had you not said that your aunt had sent you to me. Now, what is it you want?" The savoury deer and rhinoceroses were then presented to him; he ate them all, and then listened to the petition of the youth. The youth wanted the *kataki* flower, The Rakshasa said, "You want the *kataki* flower! Very well, try and get it if you can. After passing through this forest, you will come to an impenetrable forest of *kachiri*[①]. You will say to that forest, 'O mother *kachiri*! Please make way for me, or else I die.' On that the forest will open up a passage for you. You will next come to the ocean. You will say to the ocean, 'O mother ocean! Please make way for me, or else I lie,' and the ocean will make way for you. After crossing the ocean, you enter the gardens where the *kataki* blooms. Cood-bye, do as I have told you." The youth thanked his Rakshasi-uncle, and went on his way. After he had passed through the forest, he saw before him an impenetrable forest of *kachiri*. It was so close and thick, and withal so bristling with thorns that not a mouse could go through it. Remembering the advice of his uncle he stood before the forest with folded hands, and said, "O mother *kachiri*! Please make way for me, or else I die." On a sudden a clean path was opened up in the forest, and the youth gladly passed through it. The ocean now lay before him. He said to the ocean, "O mother ocean! Make way for me, or else I die." Forthwith the waters of the ocean stood up on two sides like two walls, leaving an open passage between them, and the youth passed, through dry-shod.

---

① Literally the *king of birds*, a fabulous species of horse remarkable for their swiftness.

Now, right before him were the gardens of the *kataki* flower. He entered the inclosure, and found himself in a spacious palace which seemed to be unoccupied. On going from apartment to apartment he found a young lady of more than earthly beauty sleeping on a bedstead of gold. He went near, and noticed two little sticks, one of gold and the other of silver, lying in the bedstead. The silver stick lay near the feet of the sleeping beauty, and the golden one near the head. He took up the sticks in his hands, and as he was examining them, the golden stick accidentally fell upon the feet of the lady. In a moment the lady woke and sat up, and said to the youth, "Stranger, how have you come to this dismal place? I know who you are, and I know your history. You are the youth with the moon on your forehead and stars on the palms of your hands. Flee, flee from this place! This is the residence of seven hundred Rakshasas who guard the gardens of the *kataki* flower. They have all gone a-hunting; they will return by sundown; and if they find you here you will be eaten up. One Rakshasi brought me from the earth where my father is king. She loves me very dearly, and will not let me go away. By means of these gold and silver sticks she kills me when she goes away in the morning, and by means of those sticks she revives me when she returns in the evening. Flee, flee, hence, or you die!" The youth told the young lady how his sister wished very much to have the *kataki* flower, how he passed through the forest of *kacniri*, and how he crossed the ocean. He said also that he was determined not to go alone, he must take the young lady along with him. The remaining part of the day they spent together in rambling about the gardens. As the time was drawing near when the Rakshasas should return, the youth buried himself amid an enormous heap of *kataki* flower which lay in an adjoining apartment, after killing the young lady by touching her head with the golden stick. Just after sunset the youth heard the sound as of a mighty tempest: it was the return of the seven hundred Rakshasas into the gardens. One of them entered the apartment of the young lady, revived her, and said, "I smell a human being, I smell a human being." The young lady replied, "How can a human being come to this place? I am the only human being here." The Rakshasi then stretched herself on the floor, and told the young lady to shampoo her legs. As she was going on shampooing, she let fall a tear-drop on the Rakshasi's leg. "Why are you weeping, my dear child?" asked the raw-eater, "Why are you weeping? Is anything troubling you?" "No, mamma," answered the young lady, "nothing is troubling me. What can trouble me, when you have made me so comfortable? I was only thinking what will become of me when you die." "When I die, child?" said the Rakshasi, "shall I die? Yes, of course all creatures die; but the death of a Rakshasa or Rakshasi will never happen. You know, child, that deep tank in the middle part of these gardens. Well, at the bottom of that tank there is a wooden box, in which there are a male and a female bee. It is ordained by fate that if a human being who has the moon on his forehead and stars on the palms of his hands were to come here and dive into that tank, and get hold of the same wooden box, and crush to death the male and female bees without letting a drop of their blood fall to the ground, then we should die. But the accomplishment of this decree of fate is, I think, impossible. For, in the first place, there can be no such human being who will have the moon on his forehead and stars on the palms of his hands; and, in the second place, if there be such a man, he will find it impossible to come to this place, guarded as it is by seven hundred of us, encompassed by a deep ocean, and barricaded by an impervious forest of *kachiri*—not to speak of the outposts and sentinels that are stationed on the other side of the forest. And then, even if he succeeds in coming here, he will perhaps not know the secret of the wooden box; and even if he knows of the secret of the wooden box, he may not succeed in killing the bees without letting a drop of their blood fall on the ground. And woe be to him if a drop does fall on the ground, for in that case he will be torn up into seven hundred pieces by us. You see then, child, that we are almost immortal—not actually, but virtually so. You may, therefore, dismiss your fears."

On the next morning the Rakshasi got up, killed the young lady by means of the sticks, and went away in search of food along with other Rakshasas and Rakshasis. The lad, who had the moon on his forehead and stars on the palms of his hands came out of the heap of flowers and revived the young lady. The young lady recited to the young man the whole of the conversation she had had with the Rakshasi. It was a perfect revelation to him. He, however, lost no time in beginning to act. He shut the heavy gates of the gardens. He dived into the tank and brought up the wooden box. He opened the wooden box, and caught hold of the male and female bees as they were about to escape. He crushed them on the palms of his hands, besmearing his body with every drop of their blood. The moment this was done, loud cries and groans were heard around about the inclosure of the gardens. Agreeably to the decree of fate all the Rakshasas approached the gardens and fell down dead. The youth with the moon on his forehead took as many *kataki* flowers as he could, together with their seeds, and left the palace, around which were lying in mountain heaps the carcases of the mighty dead, in company with the young and beautiful lady. The waters of the ocean retreated before the youth as before, and the forest of *kachiri* also opened up a passage through it; and the happy couple reached the house in the bazaar, where they were welcomed by the sister of the youth who had the moon on his forehead.

On the following morning the youth, as usual, went to hunt. The king was also there. A deer passed by, and the youth shot an arrow. As he shot, the turban as usual fell off his head, and a bright light issued from it. The king saw and wondered. He told the youth to stop, as he wished to contract friendship with him. The youth told him to come to his house, and gave him his address. The king went to the house of the youth in the middle of the day. Pushpavati—for that was the name of the young lady that had been brought from beyond the ocean—told the king—for she knew the whole history—how his seventh queen had been persuaded by the other six queens to ring the bell twice before her time, how she was delivered of a beautiful boy and girl, how pups were substituted in their room, how the twins were saved in a miraculous manner in the house of the potter, how they were well treated in the bazaar, and how the youth with the moon on his forehead rescued her from the clutches of the Rakshasas. The king, mightily incensed with the six queens, had them, on the following day, buried alive in the ground. The seventh queen was then brought from the market-place and reinstated in her position; and the youth with the moon on his forehead, and the lovely Pushpavati and their sister, lived happily together.

Here my story endeth,
The Natiya-thorn withereth, &c.

CHAPTER XI
THE GHOST WHO WAS AFRAID OF BEING BAGGED

Once on a time there lived a barber who had a wife. They did not live happily together, as the wife always complained that she had not enough to eat. Many were the curtain lectures which were inflicted upon the poor barber. The wife used often to say to her mate, "If you had not the means to support a wife, why did you marry me? People who have not means ought not to indulge in the luxury of a wife. When I was in my father's house I had plenty to eat, but it seems that I have come to your house to fast. Widows only fast; I have become a widow in your life-time." She was not content with mere words; she got very angry one day and struck her husband with the broomstick of the house. Stung with shame and abhorring himself on account of his wife's reproach and beating, he left his house, with the implements of his craft, and vowed never to return and see his wife's face again till he had become rich. He went from village to village, and towards nightfall came to the outskirts of a forest. He laid himself down at the foot of a tree, and spent many a sad hour in bemoaning his hard lot.

It so chanced that the tree, at the foot of which the barber was lying down, was dwelt in by a ghost. The ghost seeing a human being at the foot of the tree naturally thought of destroying him. With this intention the ghost alighted from the tree, and, with outspread arms and a gaping mouth, stood like a tall palmyra tree before the barber, and said—"Now, barber, I am going to destroy you. Who will protect you?" The barber, though quaking in every limb through fear, and his hair standing erect, did not lose his presence of mind, but, with that promptitude and shrewdness which are characteristic of his fraternity, replied, "O spirit, you will destroy me! Wait a bit and I'll show you how many ghosts I have captured this very night and put into my bag; and right glad am I to find you here, as I shall have one more ghost in my bag." So saying the barber produced from his bag a small looking-glass, which he always carried about with him along with his razors, his whet-stone, his strop and other utensils, to enable his customers to see whether their beards had been well shaved or not. He stood up, placed the looking-glass right against the face of the ghost, and said, "Here you see one ghost which I have seized and bagged; Ian going to put you also m the bag to keep this ghost company." The ghost, seeing his own face in the looking-glass, was convinced of the truth of what the barber had said, and was filled with fear. He said to the barber, "O, sir barber, I'll do whatever you bid me, only do not put me into your bag. I'll give you whatever you want." The barber said, "You ghosts are a faithless set, there is no trusting you. You will promise, and not give what you promise." "O, sir," replied the ghost, "be merciful to me; I'll bring to you whatever you order; and if I do not bring it, then put me into your bag." "Very well," said the barber, "bring me just now one thousand gold mohurs; and by tomorrow night you must raise a granary in my house, and fill it with paddy. Go and get the gold mohurs immediately; and if you fail to do my bidding you will certainly be put into my bag." The ghost gladly consented to the conditions. He went away, and in the course of a short time returned with a bag containing a thousand gold mohurs. The barber was delighted beyond measure at the sight of the gold mohurs. He then told the ghost to see to it that by the following night a granary was erected in his house and filled with paddy.

It was during the small hours of the morning that the barber, loaded with the heavy treasure, knocked at the door of his house. His wife, who reproached herself for having in a fit of rage struck her husband with a broomstick, got out of bed and unbolted the door. Her surprise was great when she saw her husband pour out of the bag a glittering heap of gold mohurs.

The next night the poor devil, through fear of being bagged, raised a large granary in the barber's house, and spent the live-long night in carrying on his back large packages of paddy till the granary was filled up to the brim. The uncle of this terrified ghost, seeing his worthy nephew carrying on his back loads of paddy, asked what the matter was. The ghost related what had happened. The uncle-ghost then said, "You fool, you think the barber can bag you! The barber is a cunning fellow; he has cheated you, like a simpleton as you are." "You doubt," said the nephew-ghost, "the power of the barber! Come and see." The uncle-ghost then went to the barber's house, and peeped into it through a window. The barber, perceiving from the blast of wind which the arrival of the ghost had produced that a ghost was at the window, placed full before it the self-same looking-glass, saying, "Come now, I'll put you also into the bag." The uncle-ghost, seeing his own face in the looking-glass, got quite frightened, and promised that very night to raise another granary and to fill it, not this time with paddy, but with rice. So in two nights the barber became a rich man, and lived happily with his wife, begetting sons and daughters.

Here my story endeth.
The Natiya-thorn withereth, &c.

CHAPTER XII
THE FIELD OF BONES

Once on a time there lived a king who had a son. The young prince had three friends, the son of the prime minister, the son of the prefect of the police, and the son of the richest merchant of the city. These four friends had great love for one another. Once on a time they bethought themselves of seeing distant lands. They accordingly set out one day, each one riding on a horse. They rode on and on, till about noon they care to the outskirts of what seemed to be a dense forest. There they rested a while tying to the trees their horses, which began to browse. When they had refreshed themselves, they again mounted their horses and resumed their journey. At sunset they saw in the depths of the forest a temple, near which they dismounted, wishing to lodge there that night. Inside the temple there was a *sannyasi*[①], apparently absorbed in meditation, as he did not notice the four friends. When darkness covered the forest, a light was seen inside the temple. The four

---

① Religious devote.

friends resolved to pass the night on the balcony of the temple; and as the forest was infested with many wild beasts, they deemed it safe that each of them should watch one *prahara*[①] of the night, while the rest should sleep. It fell to the lot of the merchant's son to watch during the first *prahara*, that is to say, from six in the evening to nine o'clock at night. Towards the end of his watch the merchant's son saw a wonderful sight. The hermit took up a bone with his hand and repeated over it some words which the merchant's son distinctly heard. The moment the words were uttered, a clattering sound was heard in the precincts of the temple, and the merchant's son saw many bones moving from different parts of the forest. The bones collected themselves inside the temple, at the foot of the hermit, and lay there in a heap. As soon as this took place, the watch of the merchant's son came to an end, and, rousing the son of the prefect of the police, he laid himself down to sleep.

The prefect's son, when he began his watch, saw the hermit sitting cross-legged wrapped in meditation, near a heap of bones, the history of which he, of course, did not know. For a long time nothing happened. The dead stillness of the night was broken only by the howl of the hyaena and the wolf, and the growl of the tiger. When his time was nearly up he saw a wonderful sight. The

---

① Eighth part of twenty-four hours, that is, three hours.

hermit looked at the heap of bones lying before him, and uttered some words which the prefect's son distinctly heard. No sooner had the words been uttered than a noise was heard among the bones, "and behold a shaking, and the bones came together, bone to its bone"; and the bones which were erewhile lying together in a heap now took the form of a skeleton. Struck with wonder, the prefect's son would have watched longer, but his time was over. He therefore laid himself down to sleep, after rousing the minister's son, to whom, however, he told nothing of what he had seen, as the merchant's son had not told him anything of what he had seen.

The minister's son got up, rubbed his eyes, and began watching. It was the dead hour of midnight, when ghosts, hobgoblins, and spirits of every name and description, go roaming over the wide world, and when all creation, both animate and inanimate, is in deep repose. Even the howl of the wolf and the hyaena and the growl of the tiger had ceased. The minister's son looked towards the temple, and saw the hermit sitting wrapt up in meditation; and near him lying something which seemed to be the skeleton of some animal. He looked towards the dense forest and the darkness all around, and his hair stood on end through terror. In this state of fear and trembling he spent nearly three hours, when an uncommon sight in the temple attracted his notice. The hermit, looking at the skeleton before him, uttered some words which the minister's son distinctly heard. As soon as the words were uttered, "lo, the sinews and the flesh came up upon the bones, and the skin covered them above;" but there was no breath in the skeleton. Astonished at the sight, the minister's son would have sat up longer, but his time was up. He therefore laid himself down to sleep, after having roused the king's son, to whom, however, he said nothing of what he had seen and heard.

The king's son, when he began his watch, saw the hermit sitting, completely absorbed in devotion, near a figure which looked like some animal, but he was not a little surprised to see the animal lying apparently lifeless, without showing any of the symptoms of life. The prince spent his hours agreeably enough, especially as he had had a long sleep, and as he felt none of that depression which the dead hour of midnight sheds on the spirits; and he amused himself with marking how the shades of darkness were becoming thinner and paler every moment. But just as he noticed a red streak in the east, he heard a sound from inside the temple. He turned his eyes towards the hermit. The hermit, looking towards the inanimate figure of the animal lying before him, uttered some words which the prince distinctly heard. The moment the words were spoken, "breath came into the animal; it lived, it stood up upon its feet;"

and quickly rushed out of the temple into the forest. That moment the crows cawed: the watch of the prince came to an end; his three companions were roused; and after a short time they mounted their horses, and resumed their journey, each one thinking of the strange sight seen in the temple.

They rode on and on through the dense and interminable forest, and hardly spoke to one another, till about mid-day they halted under a tree near a pool for refreshment. After they had refreshed themselves with eating some fruits of the forest and drinking water from the pool, the prince said to his three companions, "Friends, did you not see something in the temple of the devotee? I'll tell you what I saw, but first let me hear what you all saw. Let the merchant's son first tell us what he saw as he had the first watch; and the others will follow in order."

Merchant's son.—"I'll tell you what I saw. I saw the hermit take up a bone in his hand, and repeat some words which I well remember. The moment those words were uttered, a clattering sound was heard in the precincts of the temple, and I saw many bones running into the temple from different directions. The bones collected themselves together inside the temple at the feet of the hermit, and lay there in a heap. I would have gladly remained longer to see the end, but my time was up, and I had to rouse my friend, the son of the prefect of the police."

Prefect's son.—"Friends, this is what I saw. The hermit looked at the heap of bones lying before him, and uttered some words which I well remember. No sooner had the words been uttered than I heard a noise among the bones, and, strange to say, the bones jumped up, each bone joined itself to its fellow, and the heap became a perfect skeleton. A t that moment my watch came to an end, and I had to rouse my respected friend the minister's son."

Minister's son.—"Well, when I began my watch I saw the said skeleton lying near the hermit. After three mortal hours, during which I was in great fear, I saw the hermit lift his eyes towards the skeleton and utter some words which I well remember. As soon as the words were uttered the skeleton was covered with flesh and hair, but it did not show any symptom of life, as it lay motionless. Just then my watch ended, and I had to rouse my royal friend the prince."

King's son.—"Friends, from what you yourselves saw, you can guess what I saw. I saw the hermit turn towards the skeleton covered with skin and hair, and repeat some words which I well remember. The moment the words were uttered, the skeleton stood up on its feet, and it looked a fine and lusty deer, and while I was admiring its beauty, it skipped out of the temple, and ran into the forest. That moment the crows cawed."

The four friends, after hearing one another's story, congratulated themselves on the possession of supernatural power, and they did not doubt but that if they pronounced the words which they had heard the hermit utter, the utterance would be followed by the same results. But they resolved to verify their power by an actual experiment. Near the foot of the tree they found a bone lying on the ground, and they accordingly resolved to experiment upon it. The merchant's son took up the bone, and repeated over it the formula he had heard from the hermit. Wonderful to relate, a hundred bones immediately came rushing from different directions, and lay in a heap at the foot of the tree. The son of the prefect of the police then looking upon the heap of bones, repeated the formula which he had heard from the hermit, and forthwith there was a shaking among the bones; the several bones joined themselves together, and formed themselves into a skeleton, and it was the skeleton of a quadruped. The minister's son then drew near the skeleton, and, looking intently upon it, pronounced over it the formula which he had heard from the hermit. The skeleton immediately was covered with flesh, skin, and hair, and, horrible to relate, the animal proved itself to be a royal tiger of the largest size. The four friends were filled with consternation. If the King's son were, by the repetition of the formula he had heard from the hermit, to make the beast alive, it might prove fatal to them all. The three friends, therefore, tried to dissuade the prince from giving life to the tiger. But the prince would not comply with the request. He naturally said, "The *mantras*[1] which you have learned have been proved true and efficacious. But how shall I know that the *mantra* which I have learned is equally efficacious? I must have my *mantra* verified. Nor is it certain that we shall lose our lives by the experiment. Here is this high tree. You can climb into its topmost branches, and I shall also follow you thither after pronouncing the *mantra*." In vain did the three friends dwell upon the extreme danger attending the experiment: the prince remained inexorable. The minister's son, the prefect's son, and the merchant's son, climbed up into the topmost branches of the tree, while the king's son went up to the middle of the tree. From there, looking intently upon the lifeless tiger, he pronounced the words which he had learned from the hermit, and quickly ran up the tree. In the twinkling of an eye the tiger stood upright, gave out a terrible growl, with a tremendous spring killed all the four horses which were browsing at a little distance, and, dragging one of them, rushed towards the densest part of the forest. The four friends

---

[1] Charm or incantation.

ensconced on the branches of the tree were almost petrified with fear at the sight of the terrible tiger; but the danger was now over. The tiger went off at a great distance from them, and from its growl they judged that it must be at least two miles distant from them. After a little they came down from the tree; and as they now had no horses on which to ride, they walked on foot through the forest, till, coming to its end, they reached the shore of the sea. They sat on the sea shore hoping to see some ship sailing by. They had not sat long, when fortunately they descried a vessel in the offing. They waved their handkerchiefs, and made all sorts of signs to attract the notice of the people on board the ship. The captain and the crew noticed the men on the shore. They came towards the shore, took the men upon board, but added that as they were short of provisions they could not have them a long time on board, but would put them ashore at the first port they came to. After four or five days' voyage, they saw not far from the shore high buildings and turrets, and supposing the place to be a large city, the four friends landed there.

The four friends, immediately after landing, walked along a long avenue of stately trees, at the end of which was a bazaar. There were hundreds of shops in the bazaar, but not a single human being in them. There were sweetmeat shops in which there were heaps of confectioneries ranged in regular rows, but no human beings to sell them. There was the blacksmith's shop, there was the anvil, there were the bellows and the other tools of the smithy, but there was no smith there. There were stalls in which there were heaps of faded and dried vegetables, but no men or women to sell them. The streets were all deserted, no human beings, no cattle were to be seen there. There were carts, but no bullocks; there were carriages, but no horses. The doors and windows of the houses of the city on both sides of the streets were all open, but no human being was visible in them. It seemed to be a deserted city. It seemed to be a city of the dead—and all the dead taken out and buried. The four friends were astonished—they were frightened at the sight. As they went on, they approached a magnificent pile of buildings, which seemed to be the palace of a king. They went to the gate and to the porter's lodge. They saw shields, swords, spears and other weapons suspended in the lodge, but no porters. They entered the premises, but saw no guards, no human beings. They went to the stables, saw the troughs, grain, and grass lying about in profusion, but no horses. They went inside the palace, passed the long corridors—still no human being was visible. They went through six long courts— still no human being. They entered the seventh court, and there and then, for the first time, did they see living human beings. They saw coming towards them four princesses of matchless beauty. Each of these four princesses caught hold of the arm of each of the four friends; and each princess called each man whom she had caught hold of her husband. The princesses said that they had been long waiting for the four friends, and expressed great joy at their arrival. The princesses took the four friends into the innermost apartments and gave them a sumptuous feast. There were no servants attending them, the princesses themselves bringing in the provisions and setting them before the four friends. At the outset the four princesses told the four friends that no questions were to be asked about the depopulation of the city. After this, each princess went into her private apartment along with her newly-found husband. Shortly after the prince and princess had retired into their private apartment, the princess began to shed tears. On the prince inquiring into the cause, the princess said, "O prince! I pity you very much. You seem, by your bearing, to be the son of a king, and you have, no doubt, the heart of a king's son; I will therefore tell you my whole story, and the story of my three companions who look like princesses. I am the daughter of a king, whose palace this is, and those three creatures, who are dressed like princesses, and who have called your three friends their husbands, are Rakshasis. They came to this city some time ago, they ate up my father, the king, my mother, the queen, my brothers, my sisters, of whom I had a large number. They ate up the king's ministers and servant. They ate up gradually all the people of the city, all my father's horses and elephants, and all the cattle of the city. You must have noticed, as you came to the palace, that there are no human beings, no cattle, no living thing in this city. They have all been eaten up by those three Rakshasis. They have spared me alone —and that, I suppose, only for a time. When the Rakshasis saw you and your friends from a distance, they were very glad, as they mean to eat you all up after a short time."

King's son.—"But if this is the case, how do I know that you are not a Rakshasi yourself? Perhaps you mean to swallow me up by throwing me off my guard."

Princess.—"I'll mention one fact which proves that those three creatures are Rakshasis, while I am not. Rakshasis, you know, eat food a hundred times larger in quantity than men or women. What the Rakshasis eat at table along with us is not sufficient to appease their hunger. They therefore go out at night to distant lands in search of men or cattle, as there are none in this city. If you ask your friends to watch and see whether their wives remain all night in their beds, they will find they go out and stay away a good part of the night whereas you will find me the whole night with you. But please see that the Rakshasis do not get the slightest inkling of all this; for if they hear of it, they will kill me in the first instance, and afterwards swallow you all up."

The next day the king's son called together the minister's son, the prefect's son, and the merchant's son, and held a consultation, enjoining the strictest secrecy on all. He told them what he had heard from the princess, and requested them to lie awake in their beds to watch whether their pretended princesses went out at night or not. One presumptive argument in favour of the assertion of the princess was that all the pretended princesses were fast asleep during the whole of the day in consequence of their nightly wanderings, whereas the female friend of the king's son did not sleep at all during the day. The three friends accordingly lay in their beds at night pretending to be asleep and manifesting all the symptoms of deep sleep. Each one observed that his female friend at a certain hour, thinking her mate to be in deep sleep, left the room, stayed away the whole night, and returned to her bed only at dawn. During the following day each female friend slept out nearly the whole day, and woke up only in the afternoon. For two nights and days the three friends observed this. The king's son also remained awake at night pretending to be asleep, but the princess was not observed for a single moment to leave the room, nor was she observed to sleep in the day. From these circumstances the friends of the king's son began to suspect that their partners were really Rakshasis as the princess said they were.

By way of confirmation the princess also told the king's son, that the Rakshasis, after eating the flesh of men and animals, threw the bones towards the north of the city, where there was an immense collection of them. The king's son and his three friends went one day towards that part of the city, and sure enough they saw there immense heaps of the bones of men and animals piled up into hills. From this they became more and more convinced that the three women were Rakshasis in deed and truth.

The question now was how to run away from these devourers of men and animals? There was one circumstance greatly in favour of the four friends, and that was, that the three Rakshasis slept during nearly the whole day; they had therefore the greater part of the day for the maturing of their plans. The princess advised them to go towards the sea-shore, and watch if any ships sailed that way. The four friends accordingly used to go to the sea-shore looking for ships. They were always accompanied by the princess, who took the precaution of carrying with her in a bundle her most valuable jewels, pearls and precious stones. It happened one day that they saw a ship passing at a great distance from the shore. They made signs which attracted the notice of the captain and crew.

The ship came towards the land, and the four friends and princess were, after much entreaty, taken up. The princess exhorted the crew to row with all their might, for which she promised them a handsome reward; for she knew that the Rakshasis would awake in the afternoon, and immediately come after the ship; and they would assuredly catch hold of the vessel and destroy all the crew and passengers if it stood short of eighty miles from land, for the Rakshasis had the power of distending their bodies to the length of ten *Yojanas*[①]. The four friends and the princess cheered on the crew, and the oarsmen rowed with all their might, and the ship, favoured by the wind, shot over the deep like lightning. It was near sun-down when a terrible yell was heard on the shore. The Rakshasis had wakened from their sleep, and not finding either the four friends or the princess, naturally thought they had got hold of a ship and were escaping. They therefore ran along the shore with lightning rapidity, and seeing the ship afar off they distended their bodies. But fortunately the vessel was more than eighty miles off land, though only a trifle more: indeed, the ship was so dangerously near that the heads of the Rakshasis with their widely distended jaws almost touched its stern. The words which the Rakshasis uttered in the hearing of the crew and passengers were—"O sister,

---

① A *yojana* is nearly eight miles.

so you are going to eat them all yourself alone." The minister's son, the prefect's son, and the merchant's son, had all along a suspicion that the pretended princess, the prince's partner, might after all also be a Rakshasi; that suspicion was now confirmed by what they heard the three Rakshasis say. Those words, however, produced no effect in the mind of the king's son, as from his intimate acquaintance with the princess he could not possibly take her to be a Rakshasi.

The captain told the four friends and princess that as he was bound for distant regions in search of gold mines, he could not take them along with him; he, therefore, proposed that on the next day he should put them ashore near some port, especially as they were now safe from the clutches of the Rakshasis. On the following day no port was visible for a long time; towards the evening, however, they came near a port where the four friends and the princess were landed. After walking some distance, the princess, who had never been accustomed to take long walks, complained of fatigue and hunger; they all therefore sat under a tree, and the king's son sent the merchant's son to buy some sweetmeats in the bazaar which they heard was not far off. The merchant's son did not return, as he was fully persuaded in his mind that the king's son's partner was as real a Rakshasi as the three others from whose clutches he had escaped. Seeing the delay of the merchant's son, the king's son sent the prefect's son after him; but neither did he return, he being also convinced that the pretended princess was a Rakshasi. The minister's son was next sent; but he also joined the other two. The king's son, then, himself went to the shop of the sweetmeat seller where he met his three friends, who made him remain with them by main force earnestly declaring that the woman was no princess but a real Rakshasi like the other three. Thus the princess was deserted by the four friends who returned to their own country, full of the adventures they had met with.

In the meantime the princess walked to the bazaar and found shelter for a few days in the house of a poor woman, after which she set out for the city of the four friends, the name and whereabouts of which city she had learnt from the king's son. On arriving at the city, she sold some of her costly ornaments, pearls and precious stones, and hired a stately house for her residence with a suitable establishment. She caused herself to be proclaimed as a heaven-born dice-player, and challenged all the players in the city to play, the conditions of the game being that if she lost it she would give the winner a *lakh*[①] of rupees, and if she won it she should get a *lakh* from him who lost the game. She also got authority from the king of the country to imprison in her own house anyone who could not pay

---

① Ten thousand pounds sterling.

her the stipulated sum of money. The merchant's son, the prefect's son, and the minister's son, who all looked upon themselves as miraculous players, played with the princess, paid her many *lakhs*, but being unable to pay her all the sums they owed her, were imprisoned in her house. At last the king's son offered to play with her. The princess purposely allowed him to win the first game, which emboldened him to play many times, in all of which he was the loser; and being unable to pay the many *lakhs* owing her, the prince was about to be dragged into the dungeon, when the princess told him who she was. The merchant's son, the prefect's son, and the minister's son, were brought out of their cells; and the joy of the four friends knew no bounds. The king and the queen received their daughter-in-law with open arms and with demonstrations of great festivity.

Everyone in the palace was glad except the princess. She could not forget that her parents, her brothers and sisters had been devoured by the Rakshasis, and that their bones, along with the bones of her father's subjects, stood in mountain heaps on the north side of the capital. The prince had told her that he and his three friends had the power of giving life to bones. They could then reconstruct the frames of her parents and other relatives; but the difficulty lay in this—how to kill the three Rakshasis. Could not the hermit, who taught them to give life, not teach also how to take away life? In all likelihood he could. Reasoning in this manner, the four friends and the princess went to the temple of the hermit in the forest, prayed to him to give them the secret of destroying life from a distance by a charm. The hermit became propitious, and granted the boon. A deer was passing by at the moment. The hermit took a handful of water, repeated over it some words which the king's son distinctly heard, and threw it upon the deer. The deer died in a moment. He repeated other words over the deal animal, the deer jumped up and ran away into the forest.

Armed with this killing charm, the king's son, together with the princess and the three friends, went to his father-in-law's capital. As they approached the city of death, the three Rakshasis ran furiously towards them with open jaws. The king's son spilled charmed water upon them, and they died in an instant. They all then went to the heaps of bones. The merchant's son brought together the proper bones of the bodies, the prefect's son constructed them into skeletons, the minister's son clothed them with sinews, flesh, and skin, and the king's son gave them life. The princess was entranced at the sight of the reanimation of her parents and other relatives, and her eyes were filled with tears of joy. After a few days which they spent in great festivity, they left the revivified city, went to their own country, and lived many years in great happiness.

Here my story endeth,
The Natiya-thorn withereth, &c.

CHAPTER XIII
THE BALD WIFE

A certain man had two wives, the younger of whom he loved more than the elder. The younger wife had two tufts of hair on her head, and the elder only one. The man went to a distant town for merchandise, so the two wives lived together in the house. But they hated each other: the younger one, who was her husband's favourite, ill-treated the other. She made her do all the menial work in the house; rebuked her all day and night; and did not give her enough to eat. One day the younger wife said to the elder, "Come and take away all the lice from the hair of my head." While the elder wife was searching among the younger one's hair for the vermin, one lock of hair by chance gave away; on which the younger one, mightily incensed, tore off the single tuft that was on the head of the elder wife, and drove her away from the house. The elder wife, now become completely bald, determined to go into the forest, and there either die of starvation or be devoured by some wild beast. On her way she passed by a cotton plant. She stopped near it, made for herself a broom with some sticks which lay about, and swept clean the ground round about the plant. The plant was much pleased, and gave her a blessing. She wended on her way, and now saw a plantain tree. She swept the ground round about the plantain tree, which, being pleased with her, gave her a blessing. As she went on she saw the shed of a Brahmani bull. As the shed was very dirty, she swept the place clean, on which the bull, being much pleased, blessed her. She next saw a *tulasi* plant, bowed herself down before it, and cleaned the place round about, on which the plant gave her a blessing. As she was going on in her journey she saw a hut made of branches of trees and leaves, and near it a man sitting cross-legged apparently absorbed in meditation. She stood for a moment behind the venerable *muni*. "Whoever you may be," he said, "come before me; do not stand behind me; if you do, I will reduce you to ashes." The woman, trembling with fear, stood before the *muni*. "What is your petition?" asked the *muni*. "Father *Muni*," answered the woman, "thou knowest how miserable I am, since thou art all-knowing. My husband does not love me, and his other wife, having torn off the only tuft of hair on my head, has driven me away from the house. Have pity upon me, Father *Muni*!" The *muni*, continuing sitting, said, "Go into the tank which you see yonder. Plunge into the water only once, and then come to me again." The woman went to the tank, washed in it, and plunged into the water only once, according to the bidding of the *muni*. When she got out of the water, what a change was seen in her! Her head was full of jet black hair, which was so long that it touched her heels;

her complexion had become perfectly fair; and she looked young and beautiful. Filled with joy and gratitude, she went to the *muni*, and bowed herself to the ground. The *muni* said to her, "Rise, woman. Go inside the hut, and you will find a number of wicker baskets, and bring out any you like." The woman went in to the hut, and selected a modest-looking basket. The *muni* said, "Open the basket." She opened it, and found it filled with ingots of gold, pearls and all sorts of precious stones. The *muni* said, "Woman, take that basket with you. It will never get empty. When you take away the present contents, their room will be supplied by another set, and that by another, and that by another, and the basket will never become empty. Daughter, go in peace." The woman bowed herself down to the ground in profound but silent gratitude, and went away.

As she was returning homewards with the basket in her hand, she passed by the *tulasi* plant whose bottom she had swept. The *tulasi* plant said to her, "Go in peace, child! Thy husband will love thee warmly." She next came to the shed of the Brahmani bull, who gave her two shell ornaments which were twined round its horns, saying, "Daughter, take these shells, put them on your wrists, and whenever you shake either of them you will get whatever ornaments you wish to obtain." She then came to the plantain tree, which gave her one of its broad leaves, saying, "Take, child, this leaf; and when you move it you will get not only all sorts of delicious plantains, but all kinds of agreeable food." She came last of all to the cotton plant, which gave her one of its own branches, saying, "Daughter, take this branch; and when you shake it you will get not only all sorts of cotton clothes, but also of silk and purple. Shake it now in my presence." She shook the branch, and a fabric of the finest glossy silk fell on her lap. She put on that silk cloth, and wended on her way with the shells on her wrists, and the basket and the branch and the leaf in her hands.

The younger wife was standing at the door of her house, when she saw a beautiful woman approach her. She could scarcely believe her eyes. What a change! The old, bald hag turned into the very Queen of Beauty herself! The elder wife, now grown rich and beautiful, treated the younger wife with kindness. She gave her fine clothes, costly ornaments, and the richest viands. But all to no purpose. The younger wife envied the beauty and hair of her associate. Having heard that she got it all from Father *Muni* in the forest, she determined to go there. Accordingly she started on her journey. She saw the cotton plant, but did nothing to it; she passed by the plantain tree, the shed of the Brahmani bull, and the *tulasi* plant, without taking any notice of them. She approached the *muni*. The *muni* told her to bathe in the tank, and plunge only once into the water. She gave one plunge, at which she got a glorious head of hair and a beautifully fair complexion. She thought a second plunge would make her still more beautiful. Accordingly she plunged into the water again, and came out as bald and ugly as before.

She came to the *muni* and wept. The sage drove her away, saying, "Be of you disobedient woman. You will get no boon from me." She went back to her house mad with grief. The lord of the two women returned from his travels and was struck with the long locks and beauty of his first wife. He loved her dearly; and when he saw her secret and untold resources and her incredible wealth he almost adored her. They lived together happily for many years, an had for their maid-servant the younger woman, who had been formerly his best beloved.

Here my story endeth,
The Natiya-thorn withereth;
"Why, O Natiya-thorn, dost wither?"
"Why does thy cow on me browse?"
"Why, O cow, dost thou browse?"
"Why does thy neat-herd not tend me?"
"Why, O neatherd, dost not tend the cow?"
"Why does thy daughter-in-law not give me rice?"
"Why, O daughter-in-law, dost not give rice?"
"Why does my child cry?
"Why, O child, dost thou cry?"
"Why does the ant bite me?"
"Why, O ant, dost thou bite?"
Koot! Koot! Koot!